Riding the Stang is the first novel from writer Dawn Robertson. Based on historical fact and set in the Upper Eden Valley, it tells the story of a notorious incident which happened before the First World War.

Other books by the author, who works in collaboration with her photographer husband Peter Koronka, include *The Plains of Heaven, Secrets and Legends of Old Westmorland* and *A Country Doctor.*

First published 2000

by Hayloft Publishing,
Great Skerrygill, South Stainmore,
Kirkby Stephen, Cumbria, CA17 4EU.

Tel. 017683 42300 or Fax. 017683 41568
e-mail: icetalk@icetalk.co.uk
website: www.hayloft.org.uk

© 2000 Dawn Robertson

ISBN 0 9523282 2 4

A catalogue record for this book is available
from the British Library

Cover Photograph by Peter Koronka
Design & Production by Hayloft Publishing

Printed & bound by Lintons Printers, Co. Durham.

THIS PROJECT IS BEING PART-FINANCED BY
THE EUROPEAN COMMUNITY

European Regional Development Fund

For Peter

So many people have helped with the research for this book that it is impossible to thank all of them individually. Some of those who helped, like Henry Dixon and William Atkinson, remembered the actual events but are sadly no longer alive.

People who helped with ideas or research include Adam Koronka, Sheila Wilkinson, Betty Koronka, Mike Birtles and Alan Shaw in Australia. Oliver's help with the lengthy task of transcribing court reports was invaluable. Finally thanks go to my husband, Peter Koronka, for his patience and support throughout.

Riding the Stang

Dawn Robertson

A Hayloft Publication

1
The Slip Inn - October 1903

An old horse, head down and ears back against the October drizzle, pulled a cart of Tanhill coal slowly along the road. The carter, Isaac Wilson, had the same hunched look as the horse, his cap pulled down hard on his head. The cold damp air had crept into his bones on the long trudge down from the mines at Tanhill and the Slip Inn was a welcome sight.

As the horse pulled up near the metal ring in the wall where it knew it would be tied, a trap was swaying and rattling along the track, its wheels creaking and complaining over the stony road. Isaac waited as the trap drew up. The driver leaned over and asked: "Is this the right road for the Vicarage?"

Isaac rubbed his damp chin as he gave the driver a long look, as if to try and read his whole past history and future intent. "Ay..." he paused, trying to extract some more juice of information from the situation and casting a glance at the occupants of the trap, before going on: "You turn just up yonder, near t'old Chapel there."

The driver nodded his thanks and Isaac touched his cap at the people in the carriage, a spark of curiosity lightening his depressed look. Six miles of rough, lonely, tracks down from Tanhill, there and back every day in all weathers, left plenty of reason to be curious about the unusual. He stood and watched as the strangers' trap turned down towards Swinstonewath.

The horse blew through its nose to remind Isaac where they were. He climbed down, from his hard wooden seat, a little cramped, his arthritic knees creaking as he touched the ground as if they'd forgotten quite how heavy his body was. He looped the reins through the ring by the door, reached in the cart for a nose bag, blackened with coal dust and half-filled with oats. The horse's ears pricked with anticipation, a small pleasure in a long day. They still had another four miles in the mizzly wet to get to Brough and then back to Mouthlock where Isaac lived in a cottage beneath the chapel with his wife Alice.

Although everyone called the pub The Slip Inn, it had once been the Black Horse, and the old sign hung unmoving, dripping in the dampness. The paint had long since peeled from the image of the horse but Isaac remembered it when it was new and the horse's coat seemed to shine. He had always admired it as a thing of beauty. A work of art. Now the picture had peeled and the weather bleached wood showed through. Isaac felt similarly worn, faded and, if his skin had been paint, it would be flaking and peeling to the wood beneath after almost forty years as a carter.

The horse fed, Isaac went into The Slip Inn. A peat fire smouldered and glowed in the hearth, three faces turned with expectation to see who entered, a cloud of smoke wafted up as the door banged shut. Mrs. Ivy Pounder the landlady pulled herself to her feet. She wore a long pinafore over her broad front, probably four yards of floral print material had been used in the homemade garment. She had three pinafores. One for the afternoons and evenings when she was inn keeping, one plain huge sacklike garment for morning when she farmed and one with flowers and frills for Sundays, Christmas and other special days.

"How are you Isaac? The usual?" she asked as she swayed her way like a ship between the islands of chairs and tables to the bar.

"Ay, alright" said Isaac in answer to both questions.

Mrs. Pounder was in her middle age but was one of those women who would always be there, solid and strong. Her broad, rather red face, did not show many lines. She had a genuine interest in life which gave her energy to carry on against any adversity. She went to pull Isaac his usual pint of thin brown ale.

As Isaac approached the fire, the young man sitting staring at the smoke curling upwards and sucking on a clay pipe, turned

9

and enquired: "Is t'well Isaac?" William Hill was 18-years-old and lived next door to The Slip Inn but was as much in the pub as in his father's kitchen. "Come up by t'fire and warm thee sel."

"It's drying ah needs, and that fire's not got enough about it. Stir it up a bit William" said Isaac as he scraped his chair nearer the fire.

William took the pipe from his mouth and poked the fire, lifting a turf to let the air under. He had lived all his life on Stainmore and worked during the day for his father who was a cattle dealer, or as a farm labourer for any farmer who needed an extra hand. He'd been walling that day up at Barras Farm until he'd trapped his finger under a slab of limestone, scraping the skin and crushing the flesh. With throbbing finger and depressing wetness he'd made his way home early for an afternoon's drinking and smoking.

"Has t'been for coals today?" William asked after another long moment staring at the peat and wondering if the tiny flame he'd encouraged would grow any bigger.

"Ay" said Isaac, "I'll fetch thee some coals in, to get that going. Where's t'shovel?"

Ivy Pounder, sailing back through the tables, brought Isaac's pint and placed it on the table. She reached into the large black hearth for the shovel and gave it to Isaac who went out again for some of the wet black coal. As he closed the door another big cloud of smoke welled out of the chimney and hovered. With nowhere to go it gradually dispersed, soaking into the white wash to deepen the brown of the stains. The walls and blackened beams told the story of many an escape of smoke, many nights of smokey clay pipes puffing and an atmosphere thick with unspoken words. Isaac returned and shovelled a bit of the coal onto the fire and sat back in his chair in anticipation of a blazing warmth.

The third face which had lifted and brightened momentarily when Isaac first came in belonged to Jane Johnstone, the serving maid. Isaac was not the hoped for figure and she had gone back to her work. She was busy with some embroidery, but was not at peace with sewing. She could barely see in the dim light and poked and pulled at the stuff in a resentful way. It bored her, but it was better to do something than to sit forever waiting. If she had sat day dreaming at the window Mrs. Pounder would have found her some tankards to polish or shelves to wipe down. Jane had a bloom about her which for a moment had shone as Isaac entered but was now lost again in her pent up frustration which would have found better use with a hammer than a needle.

She had just turned nineteen and she was in love, but the man she loved had eyes only for someone else. She burned with jealousy. Her life as a barmaid and housekeeper at the Slip Inn had begun to open up before her as one blank day after another. She longed for excitement, for a life of her own, maybe even for her own home, but all seemed far away and impossible.

Jane was a strong girl, dark-haired and blue-eyed. She was pretty with the freshness of youth and health but she was troubled by the responsibilities of adulthood. She could not return home to Dowgill because her parents were getting older and they relied on her wages. There were too many mouths to feed and her only escape from a life of service was getting married. Her brother Thomas was now seventeen and was working on the farm and one day would inherit it but there was no place for her.

She looked back on the innocent days of her childhood and realised how blissful these had been and what fun she had had. Her father and his brothers were excellent fiddle players and, in the spring, before the hay was gathered, the loft of the barn was used for dances, organised at the drop of a hat, or the visit of a few neighbours who felt the tapping in their feet as the grass began to grow. Once started, the fiddle music would drift across the fields and attract more dancers, or those simply curious to see the fun. Some nights the floor would bounce and creak with a

11

hurtling throng of bodies, in their Sunday clogs, reeling and thumping, while the fiddle music seemed to race faster and faster.

She loved the fiddle nights, her father would find energy that had been lost to him all day in the fields. Her uncles, red in the face and wet with sweat would beam at the power of the music and the elation of the dancers. She came alive with the music, forgetting hard work and cares. Her dancing was joy, she shrugged off her plain day-time self and was beautiful in her ability to dance. She was unconscious of self in the movement, as if she were part of the music. A few of the men watched her with predatory interest. They knew she became careless with the elixir of the dance. One had stolen her heart - Joseph Stephenson a plate-layer on the railway.

Jane thought of him now and the pleasure of the moments they had stolen while cooling off from the dance. She felt sure he would marry her but, when she told him a child was on the way, he had raised objections. He said he was too young and they did not have a house and he did not want to be ground down by the same poverty as his parents. Jane knew Joe also had another excuse which he never told her. He was in love with the Station Master's daughter.

The baby was born and taken in by her parents as one of their own. Young Joe was two-years-old now and she hardly saw him. He did not realise she was his mother. Her parents had sent her out to work and her wages went to support the child. For the thousandth time she thought if only Joe would see how good their life could be, even if they were poor. If he didn't she would be forced to consider marrying someone else. She knew Joe liked her and maybe one day he would think again, maybe one day he would realise she was the wife for him. She pricked her finger and looked up at Mrs. Pounder who was talking to old Isaac about the price of beer at Tanhill pub.

Even though she was so much older Jane envied Mrs. Pounder. She knew how to enjoy life without worrying. She seemed content with her lot and had patience that would last forever. Mrs. Pounder liked company and liked to hear what everyone had to say. Nothing seemed to worry her or upset her, except her own company and she used to say there was nothing worse than that.

The Slip Inn was also famous for its dances and this was its blessing as far as Jane was concerned, because Joe would never miss a dance. Upstairs there was a special dance floor, 45' by 15'. When it wasn't used for dancing it was turned into three bedrooms with special numbered plank walls which fitted together. At least once a month the planks would be dismantled and stacked and the furniture cleared to make way for one of the local bands to play and the dancers to dance.

The pub was popular too and Mrs. Pounder's character, her interest in everything, her enjoying a good laugh and a good tale and the fact that she never censured, drew in the customers. She encouraged people to put aside their cares or to tell her their worries. Her customers in the pub were almost all men. Mrs. Pounder became something of a second wife to them, an understanding ear to complaints and worries which she would quietly pass back to the women folk when next she saw them. Not many women went into a pub, though they always came to the dance nights.

The conversation about the price of beer had wound to a close. Mrs. Pounder was thinking of other subjects to raise to keep Isaac entertained. She leaned forward, large elbows on even larger knees spread beneath the apron and asked: "Has t'heard Isaac, the new vicar's due to arrive any day now?"

"Ay" said Isaac. They all considered for a time, Isaac supping at the thin ale, Jane stabbing her needlework and William sucking his pipe. Suddenly a flame leapt up from the coal.

Isaac mused "Fire's caught now. A bit of warmth. Mebbe's Jane could get me a sup more? I'd buy thee a pint William but tha'd nivver sup it."

William smiled at the old joke Isaac kept for anyone younger than himself. Jane dropped her sewing and went, unspeaking, to pull him another pint.

"Ah wonder" said Mrs Pounder, thinking aloud, "What he'll be like this new vicar. They say he comes frae Ambleside, and he's no family bar his wife. They'll not match Revd. Winton, nay, he'll be sadly missed. His sister Maria's gone back to Appleby they say, and both his lads away with their beuks at college. That poor woman. Ah know how she feels, living half her life bringing up her brother's children and never marrying. Maria Winton, she was a religious woman an' she nivver did enjoy hersel. She was just stuck with her brother's life and now she's got none."

"I may well end that way" Jane sulked.

"Ah'll hev thee, if it's a husband tha's wantin." croaked Isaac, with a beery glint in his eye.

"Away with you Isaac, ah've got me eye on a man, as you know. But I have to wait." said Jane.

Silence fell a while and they all withdrew to their own thoughts. The fire flickered brighter and Isaac stretched out his legs and the steam began to curl up from his sodden clothes giving the air a stronger flavour, with something of horse, leather and wood about it. After a while it seemed to percolate into his nostrils and remind him of his cart of coals and the four damp miles to Brough before he could finish his day's work and get himself back to Mouthlock for his supper.

"Ah'd best be off afore it's too late. Here's a copper for t'beer. Thoo mentioned t'vicar well a carriage stopped and asked me t'way t'vicarage just as I landed here."

"Ay, well, mebbe he's here at last. That'll give us sommat to talk aboot. We'll see yer tomorrow night Isaac," said Mrs. Pounder, "William ye'd best get home or yer father'll wonder what's up, an' ah'll mebbe get t'tea tonight Jane, if tha's busy with that table cloth."

Isaac and his steaming trousers clumped out, the door banging and the chimney belched out another eye-stinging cloud of smoke. Jane coughed and thought sadly how another day had gone by without seeing Joe. As Isaac set off along the track down to Brough the evening closed around him, drawing in early and clinging with wet mistiness.

2
The Unknown Carriage

The trap bumped and rattled down the ever rougher track. The horse slowed and picked its way more carefully, squeezing over the narrow bridge at Mousegill Beck and up the steep hill between Swinstonewath and Gillses. In the growing dusk the details of the houses were hard to discern but it seemed curtains moved at windows. A man scraping a yard straightened himself and leaned on his shovel to watch the trap pass. There were six gates to open and at the end of a day's journey they made the way ever more tedious. The driver was cursing under his breath.

Finally the Vicarage came in sight. It was built perhaps eighty years before when the previous humble dwelling, called "Knowah" had become too small and, according to the vicar of the day, too incapable of improvement. His pride established the need and his pocket the funds to build a house of status, square and imposing with tall windows and a proper garden. A cut above the rough farmhouses. The house asked for respect. It was built with ideas brought from vicarages further afield and had an air of being a stranger, a newcomer, on the fellside.

A light shone from one of the windows as darkness crept quietly down with the drizzle. As the trap pulled into the yard the door opened and a woman's figure was framed in the light. She came forward to help the vicar and his wife. The Revd. John George Law stepped down, stretching his tall and burly body with a sense of relief not merely physical.

"Good evening, Mrs. Cowper. It is a pleasure to meet you," said the vicar, holding out his large hand to shake hers.

"Good evening Revd. Law . I hope your journey was not too weary. It's a nasty night. Come on in. I got Mr. Cowper to help me light the fires and I've made you your supper," Mrs. Cowper talked quickly but calmly. She was a middle-aged, friendly woman, with an air of quiet motherliness and capability.

"Oh thank you, Mrs. Cowper. That is kind of you. My wife is exceedingly tired by the travelling. I didn't expect you would trouble with supper for us, but that is very kind. Are you coming my dear?"

"It's Rupert. I'm trying to fasten the leash so that he doesn't run away home, or get lost. Can you help, please?"

John leaned back into the carriage and it seemed difficult to imagine him being able to fold his huge limbs into such a tiny space. He re-emerged with an excited red setter, bouncing with pent up energy.

"Sit, Rupert, Sit. Mrs. Cowper could you hold him a moment? Oh, I'm sorry he's dirtied your pinafore. He's so spoilt and he's been cooped up too long."

"Not to worry Revd. It's only mud." said Mrs. Cowper, her eyes waiting to meet those of Mrs. Law.

"Ellen, dear, do hurry up. You complained enough of wanting to be out of the carriage before. We're all getting damp waiting for you."

Ellen Law stepped carefully onto the carriage step, holding her skirts up with an air of displeasure at everything. She took the dog's lead from Mrs. Cowper, who brushed her pinafore with her hand, trying to remove the mud. She watched Mrs. Law and wondered what to say to her.

"You'll have to walk Rupert, John. I'm really too tired for anything but bed. I expect they'll be damp. Oh, Mrs. Cowper is it? How nice to meet you," she said, almost as an afterthought.

"Good evening Mrs. Law. It's a pleasure to meet you," said Mrs. Cowper smiling at the vicar's wife.

"I'm so tired by that rattling carriage and these dreadful roads. I think I have one of my headaches coming on. Do you get headaches Mrs. Cowper?"

"No, not so often. But come on inside and make yourselves

comfortable. The driver will no doubt see to the baggage. The kettle's boiling and I can soon have some supper on the table."

"Oh, that's kind, though I don't have an appetite. John are you taking Rupert? Please don't go too far or he'll get very wet and you know the damp doesn't agree with him."

"Yes, yes. I shan't be long. I'll just walk down to the church and back. There's enough light left. Come on, Rupert, here boy. Come on !"

Mrs. Law and Mrs. Cowper disappeared inside the house, as the driver continued to unload the boxes and bags into the porch. Inside the gloom of the hallway it was hard to discern any features. Ellen stood and felt the chill of a long neglected house. It crept up her nostrils. It seemed to be clinging to her hair. She overcame the feeling of revulsion and the strong wave of homesickness which filled her.

Mrs. Cowper put her hand on her arm and felt Ellen shivering: "Are you alright Mrs. Law?"

"Yes, I think so. It's just been a long day. It was hard for me to leave Ambleside. I've always lived there and my late father ran a very successful business in the town. It was hard for me to leave my mother to come so far away to such a..." here words seemed to fail Ellen.

Mrs. Cowper said: "Yes I understand it will all be different for you. But you're just tired by the journey. I'm sure everything will be alright tomorrow. Come on into the sitting room and I'll fetch you a cup of tea."

The sitting room was the first door along the hall and was a large room, facing west. The two large windows were black and reflective with no curtains, like the pupils of eyes. What depth of darkness is out there with no cheery street lights, just blackness on and on, thought Ellen.

The fire was burning cheerily but everything else in the room was dismal. Ellen ran her hand along the mantlepiece smudging her cream coloured glove with dust. Everywhere was dusty and in the corners of the ceiling were old spider webs, heavy with dust.

A solitary tortoiseshell fluttered, woken from its hibernation by the warmth of the fire. It fluttered drunkenly towards the light of the oil lamp and kept vainly struggling against the glass towards the light.

Ellen looked at the floor – stone flags. She had never imagined a floor being made of anything else but wood. How could she clean these? The floor was like a yard. Her mother would never be able to visit. How long would it take her to turn this place into a proper house? There wasn't even any wallpaper, just white-wash on the walls, and large dark patches where she suspected water had been getting in. It was impossible. She felt tears welling in her eyes. And John, he hadn't even come in with her to see the house, as usual he was off outside on some jaunt.

She heard Mrs. Cowper returning with the tea and wiped her eyes and choked back the tears, walking quickly to the other side of the room.

"Oh Mrs. Cowper, how kind. I think that really will make me feel better" said Ellen.

"That's alright dear" said Mrs. Cowper. She thought she could hear the trace of tears in Mrs. Law's voice.

"Look" she continued, "I'll just pop out and offer the driver a cup of tea because he must be tired coming all that way and he's still unloading the boxes".

"Yes, Mrs. Cowper, how kind." said Ellen.

Glad of an excuse to avoid the embarrassment of watching the vicar's wife hold back her tears, Mrs. Cowper went out. "Can I get you a bite of supper too, when you've finished? You'll be stopping here till morning?"

"Ay, that would be grand. Ah'll be half an hour mind. The hoss needs wiping down and feeding" said the driver with an attitude of resigned patience that would take years to acquire.

"Just come in the kitchen door. It's round yonder, and I'll set you something up," said Mrs. Cowper smiling. The driver smiled back in a way that expressed understanding of their relative posi-

19

tions in the order of things and turned to heave another trunk from the carriage.

As John strode down the lane, the dog pulled at the lead, almost choking itself in its excitement to dash off to explore. Both man and dog breathed in the damp air, full of the smell of wet grass and fallen leaves. John Law was a big, broad man. He was the sort of man whose bulk meant his jacket sleeves were never quite long enough.

He looked a country man though his clothes were smarter than the average farmer's. His hair was dark and thick, with the first hint of grey at his temples. He was clean shaven and had a dark complexion as if he spent many hours outside. He looked younger than his 36 years. His features were regular and unremarkable. What people remembered most about his face were his intelligent and expressive green-grey eyes.

He looked a good man - the sort who could be tender and kind to animals or children. His great love was botany and, though it was nearing dark, he scanned the sides of the lane for plants. It was a habit. The names would spring to his mind, as familiar as the names of places on a map.

The dog strained and rasped at the lead, scenting real or imaginary rabbits. He had never learned patience, not even obedience, and was bounding with pent up excitement. John strode alongside him his steps twice as long as the average. He bent his head to the fine rain which gathered and dripped off his hat.

As he reached the wall of the small church yard he looked up and, for a moment, thought he saw the figure of a girl, slight and small, hurrying away down the track between the trees. A drip of rain found its way from his hat and ran cold down his neck and inside his stiff shirt collar. He hunched himself against the pervading dampness and made for the church door.

The dark outline of the church, squat and solid, with its simple bell tower stood out against the last light in the western sky over the Lake District he had so recently left. The church reminded him of a barn. It was much the same size and very plain but he loved this simplicity. It seemed real and true after the hypocrisy he had seen in places with bigger churches. He wanted this uncomplicated way of life in which he felt he could be nearer to God, with nature for company and simple farmers for a congregation. The Dales folk he was sure would be more honest and sincere than the "society" people of Ambleside whose faith seemed so complex.

He tied Rupert's lead to the heavy ring of the door handle in the porch and lifted the latch. The heavy door opened easily on massive hinges. Inside the gloom was nearing darkness. John left the door open and let his eyes adjust until he could discern the pews and the whiteness of the walls. He fumbled on the table by the door for a candle, knocked a book onto the floor and then found a small candlestick.

He lit the candle and picked up the book - an old and much thumbed bible. He straightened the corner of the pages where they had crumpled when they fell and noticed that the damp air had permanently waved the edges of the book. A clinging fungal smell of damp plaster, and mouldering cloth filled his nose.

"I'll have to try and get some heat into the church, or let the doors open to blow away the worst of this damp" he thought as he picked up the candlestick and made his way to the altar.

He knelt and prayed on the hard stone step, the candle flickering beside him. He mumbled, his words like those of a dreamer, impossible to quite grasp his meaning, though Ellen seemed to be one of the names. Then he became silent and knelt, head bowed, deep in thought, for a few moments more before standing and leaving, snuffing out the candle and closing the door.

He stood for a time outside the church, despite the damp and chill air, looking and listening to the sounds of the evening. He decided to let Rupert loose from his lead and off went the dog sniffing everywhere, tail wagging and then he stopped and looked down the lane. John looked too and soon heard someone making their way along the road. He decided to wait to greet whoever it was, as to turn and walk away might seem ill-mannered.

A figure moved in the shadows under the dripping trees and slowly came towards John. The man was wearing a heavy coat and cap and seemed to be mumbling to himself. He did not see John until Rupert gave a bark and went up to the stranger wagging his tail.

"Good evening," said John.

"There's not much good about it, with this rain. Who are you?" asked the man who was not as old as his walk had made him seem.

"I'm the new vicar of Stainmore, Revd. John Law. And who are you?"

"Me name's Harold Boldron and I live up yonder at Seats Farm. I'm a signal man on the railway"

"Oh yes. Have you just finished work?"

"No, I finished earlier but I'm just coming along to put me hens to bed. I've a hen house in yon field there near t'church. You can never tell but there could be a fox about."

"Yes, that's true. Do you have many foxes up here?" asked John.

"Ay, a few. But we gets Brough hunt to come up and t'game-keeper for Lord Hothfield, he deals with them like, so we're not as bothered as some places. But I wouldn't like to lose any of me hens. I hope your dog doesn't chase hens, like," said Harold.

John had been looking closely at the man as he spoke. His coat was missing a button and his shirt looked crumpled. He guessed the man was a bachelor. He had a beard which looked as if it contained remains of several meals. His eyes had a wily, distrusting, look as if he was not going to be taken in by any fox or vicar, for that matter.

"Well, I'd best be getting on. I've an early start tomorrow at the box. Good night to you Revd." and he turned and walked on.

"Good night, Mr. Boldron. I hope to see you in church," John called after him before carrying on up the track towards the Vicarage. He realised his feet were soaked by the wet grass and Rupert kept giving himself a hopeful shake to get rid of the rain. He could just discern the hen house in the gathering darkness and heard the hens cluck quietly as the wooden door was fastened. Simple things, good things, thought John, this feels like home.

"Come on Rupert, we need some supper to warm us through, prayers alone won't help," The dog was eager to leave, eager to go anywhere and smell the scents in the wet grass. "Do you think we'll be happy here then?" he mused to the dog. "Do you think the mountain air will clear Ellen's headaches? It seems a good place for you - plenty of rabbits. I wish it hadn't been raining, it's not much of a first impression for Ellen. Maybe the sun will shine tomorrow and we'll go a walking to meet some more of our congregation. That's the best idea and maybe Ellen will come too."

3
Prayers at homecoming

As he bounded along, as enthusiastic as the dog, John mused to himself, revived by stretching his legs even in the rain and by the visit to his new church. He was soon back at the Vicarage where Mr. Davis, the driver, was just closing the stable door.

"You'll be coming in for some supper, Mr. Davis?"

"Ay, sir, the woman asked me into the kitchen,"

"You must be drenched, have you some dry clothes?"

"Oh, I'm not particular like. Ah'll soon dry out in front of t'fire. Good night sir."

"Good night Mr. Davis and thank you for all your help."

The driver trudged off thinking it would be a fine thing to have spare clothes but some supper and a glass of beer would help.

John went in and found Ellen and Mrs. Cowper in the sitting room where supper had been laid on a small table in front of the fire.

"Everything alright dear? I've stretched my legs and Rupert isn't too wet. I'll put him in the kitchen."

"Yes, alright, John. Perhaps you could get him something to eat too, or Mrs. Cowper might, later on," said Ellen, smiling to Mrs. Cowper who stood rubbing her hands as if nervous or cold.

Ellen was sitting as close as she dared to the fire, thinking of her complexion. She was blonde, frail looking and rather thin. Her face was colourless rather than pale and her large blue eyes might have been attractive if they had not appeared so restless and unhappy. Her hair was fine and straight. She pinned it up but never quite seemed to be able to catch all the strands. She was aware that there was always a stray piece sticking out somewhere and felt it made her look slightly ridiculous, so she constantly put her hands to her head to check her hair. Her hands were never still, her whole body in fact was in permanent motion. She would stand up and walk restlessly around or go to look out of the blank windows as if she had heard a noise.

She would go and sit again and then notice a piece of cinder on the floor which irritated unless she moved again to tidy it up. Her conversation had the same uneasiness; she chattered to Mrs. Cowper, sometimes following a thread of logic but as often as not just adding comments together like stitches with no pattern. Often she did not wait for a reply.

Mrs. Cowper listened quietly, nodding and agreeing here and there without contradiction. She took in the information and resorted it into some pattern of sense, and had already gathered the impression that all was not well with Ellen Law.

Mrs. Cowper was a farmer's wife, from Borren House, the nearest house, just the other side of the Church. She was not used to being treated as a servant, though she would volunteer to help anybody in trouble. She had been asked by the vicar from Brough, Revd. Lyde, who had been filling in until the appointment of a new vicar, if she would clean up the house and meet the new arrivals. She had done her best to make the large and somewhat draughty vicarage welcoming.

Not all the Law's furniture had arrived from Ambleside, the remainder was due by rail in the next few days, so it was difficult to make the bare and echoing rooms feel homely. She wondered how Mrs. Law would manage with the housekeeping and looked at her dainty white fingers and the flash of a wedding ring. She did not seem used to such work, but Mrs. Cowper knew that the living of the parish was only £100 and could not support the extravagance of a maid.

Ellen interrupted her thoughts, asking: "I understand that Borrenthwaite Hall is the largest house near here and that Dr. and Mrs. Alston-Dewbanke live there. Do they entertain a lot? We used to visit Dr. Brown a good deal in Ambleside. His wife is a pretty woman, though her taste was a little gaudy. Do you think deep wine red curtains would suit this room?"

"Yes, Mrs. Law, they might well do," said Mrs. Cowper clasping her hands together and rubbing them as if she were cold.

"I think John said that a playwright lives at Augill Castle? That sounds exciting. Is he married?"

"Yes, well, there used to be a writer, an American I think, but the castle's up for sale and they say a London doctor's interested in it. The American was a Mr. Kester, I only saw him once, he was never really here."

"Oh a doctor. It will be interesting to meet him and his wife when they come. If he's a London doctor perhaps he might be able.... In Ambleside my mother always came visiting with me, even after I was married. She knows everyone and is so good with people. She introduced me to John you know. He was on a walking holiday in the Lakes. He comes from Manchester really you know. But anyway, she invited him to tea and we wrote to each other for quite some time. We were married in Ambleside you know."

"Oh?....Would you care for some more tea Mrs. Law? I shall have to be going soon. Mr. Cowper will have finished milking and I'll have to get him some supper and then there's the children to get to bed."

"Do you have to go so soon? We were just getting acquainted. Did you say you had made up a bed? I'm sure it will be damp. The house feels very cold. Damp is so bad for the health. I believe it causes many illnesses, rheumatism especially. Mrs. Peters at Bassenthwaite House had terrible rheumatism. She blamed the Lake District. Her house was damp and she never could get rid of a fusty smell in her drawing room. It smells a bit fusty here too."

"Well it's bound to really. It's been three months since Revd. Winton died and the house has just stood empty. I'm sure it will dry out soon and you'll have it nice in no time," said Mrs. Cowper.

"Yes, I'm sure I will...where did you say you lived? It's close by isn't it? Just in case I should need you for anything."

"Yes, just past the Church, Borren House. You can call if you'd like, though I don't have much time, except on Sundays."

"That would be nice. Yes, and maybe, you might, you could perhaps come up and help me get the house organised when the rest of the furniture comes. John is no good, he's only interested in his plants and his books and he doesn't really care what the house is like. You could help me choose where to put everything."

"Yes, I might be able to help. I have the children and I have to help Mr. Cowper on the farm, mainly with the dairy side..."

"But you might spare me some time. I really need a maid, but John says we can't afford one. I've never really been a housekeeper on my own. Mother lived with us in Ambleside. She was so good with colours."

"I really must be going Mrs. Law. I'm sorry. It has been nice to meet you. Ah, here's your husband coming for his supper. Good night."

"Good night Mrs. Cowper. I'll come to see you."

Ellen watched as Mrs. Cowper pulled an old grey cape, that looked very much like a blanket, over her shoulders and hurried out into the darkness.

"John, the tea will be almost cold. Will it be alright? I don't want to go into the kitchen tonight. I expect I'll get started tomorrow when my headache's better. She's nice isn't she? She's going to come and help me sort things out."

"Yes she is, but I didn't think you'd need help here. We're on our own now my dear and we can be ourselves," said John as he sat down and began to eat as if he meant to clear every plate. He poured himself some cold tea.

Ellen was pacing around the room, glancing at her husband every now and again. "She'll just help while we get settled in you know, then it will be as you say. Do you think mother's bookcase should go in here? Or do you want it in your study? It is a bit large for this room, and old-fashioned. Perhaps you'd

27

have it in your study. Where are your books by the way?"

"The books should be here in a day or two on the train. I don't really mind where the bookcase goes. You'd better decide," said John as he reached for another slice of bread and jam.

Silence fell and they drifted apart into their separate worlds. It was an effort for them to meet in a common place. He slid comfortably into his thoughts, appreciation of the food and the warmth of the fire.

Ellen perched on the arm of a chair uneasily. She missed the ticking of her mother's clock measuring the moments. It was better than this silence which hung so heavily in the air. She liked chatter. John's chewing began to get on her nerves but he seemed unaware. He reached for a slice of Mrs. Cowper's currant pastry.

Ellen went to the window where her own reflection met her in the dark glass. She tried to measure the opening with her arms but could not reach a precise conclusion. She returned to the fire and said: "I think I'll go to bed. My headache's coming back and I'm so tired."

"Yes dear. I'll be up shortly," said John absent mindedly. "Oh, I'm sorry, wait a moment Ellen. This will be our first night in our new home. Our home." He stood up and Ellen noticed all the crumbs dropping to the floor. "I just wanted to say that in the church, I prayed for a while. Do you remember when we met?"

"Yes, my mother had a tea party...."

"That's right. Your mother. Well, when I left your house that day I prayed I might see you again. That I might talk to you on your own. I felt somehow very sad and I wanted to help you, even rescue you. I feel now at last I've been able to do that, and I prayed for our happiness tonight. We can just think of each other here, without the distractions of society. We can be close and I hope we can be happy." He put his hands on her shoulders and she had nowhere else to look but into his eyes.

"You don't need to worry about anything any more and I'm sure your health will improve with the mountain air. Dear Ellen,

I prayed that we might be truly happy in our marriage, as God intended."

Ellen stood, hands clasped tightly before her. Her eyes wandered from his face and she couldn't help wondering if the red hearth rug would match the curtains.

"Ellen, you know what I'm saying?" he asked gently.

"Yes, John I know."

"We've been married quite some time now and, I've wanted to say this to you so many times, but I felt, in your mother's house, it was difficult. We ought to...I feel this change of scenery will help you. I love you Ellen, I want to take care of you, and with God's blessing we can be man and wife and we can have a family" He took Ellen's clasped hands and kissed her tight pressed lips. He put his arms around her.

"Yes John I understand and I love you too, but please, not just yet. Let me settle in a little, let me organise the house, please?"

He did not reply, but just continued to hold her, feeling the warmth of her body through her dress.

"John please, I want to go to bed. You've dropped crumbs all over the floor, John, please."

"Yes, alright, Ellen. I can wait until you feel happy. I only want you to be happy," he tried to sound convincing but felt removed again to a familiar despondency. Ellen took a candle and hurried away as if she were frightened.

John returned to the fire and sat mulling over the conversation, as if chewing a cud which would not be swallowed. If only I were more experienced in these matters, he thought, I've spent too much time with books, studying flowers and roaming mountains, yet every Sunday I stand in the pulpit and read my sermon. I try to help others to live their lives,

I teach little children about God. I watch them grow, I marry the young men and women and baptise their babies; I bury the dead. I comfort people stricken by grief, and yet I cannot consummate my own marriage. It is not a marriage. Ellen isn't strong I know. I married her and I thought she would be mine but she isn't. I am to her like another piece of furniture to be put in the right place in her life. Her mother. I've finally got her away from her mother. Dear God, forgive me for my thoughts.

Things must improve here; we'll be alone. Ellen will relax. She'll perhaps even take an interest in poetry as she used to do. Dearest Lord, please help us to love each other. I can turn to nobody else. The animals, the plants, they know without lessons; I don't want to hurt her. I am in the prime of my life and a man should experience these things. I almost wish I had strayed from the path, so that I knew. Perhaps, is that how it should be?

I start towards her sometimes with energy within me, but then a thousand thoughts flood my mind and she fills me with doubt. I cannot live like this, divided from her, loving her and hating her. My mind and body seem torn apart. I pray that this place will bring us together and that we might have children. Then the hypocrisy I have to wear would fall away. I would be your servant and a man, leading and guiding your people in wisdom. I am not fully experienced in life, how can I help others lead theirs? Guidance cannot come always from books, they have failed me in this. The simple life we can have here among honest people and the farming life, all that must surely help.

Dear Ellen, Dear God, let us be fulfiled. I realise I've been thinking again, things that have so often troubled my mind. They haunt me these thoughts. Tomorrow will be a fresh start. Tomorrow I will start something positive and let these troubles alone and hope that time will do its work. I will go to visit people and think about mending the church. He sat for a while longer, his big hands clasped between his knees, his shoulders hunched, staring at the embers of the fire.

4
The Breakfast

October's blustery winds left nothing at peace. The clouds raced and jostled, sometimes breaking momentarily to let the sun stab through, but more often than not shades of grey coloured the sky and browns washed the land. The leaves rattled and twisted and gave up their hold on summer, being blown along until at last they found a resting place. The Vicarage appeared still asleep, setting a grim face to the weather.

A face appeared suddenly white in the black of a window and then the door opened. Rupert came bounding out in great red setter excitement, without his lead and John came after him. They both looked as if they had been too long hemmed in by walls and were ready to explore.

Man and dog set off up the track, sending a bunch of sheep into a panic. The flock ran away across the field and then, as if of one mind, stopped and turned to consider the pair. The wind blew some crows across the sky, flapping like pieces of rag. Rupert tail up and nose down set off down the field and John strode after him. He stopped to look at a plant for a moment carefully picking a piece of the foliage for identification later. Then off again heading down towards the river and the trees. A roe deer started on the brink of the gill and bounced carelessly off into the bracken sodden by the night's rain, with Rupert barking and running with wild enthusiasm after the deer.

All this pleased John, lifting the weight of the previous evening's thoughts from his mind, unwrinkling his brow. It wasn't the best time of year for botanical specimen hunting, but he saw a great deal which promised well for the spring and summer. It was a piece of wilderness down by the river, too steep and rocky for farming and tangled with trees, bushes and plants with here and there a promising looking boggy patch.

The blustering cold wind meant nothing in the excitement of discovering new places, possible habitats for rare plants. He knew there must be plenty of wild creatures too, but Rupert's clumsy interest, crashing along in the undergrowth, would scare any bird or animal. John sat on a rock by the river which was full with autumn rain and brown with peat. He knew he ought to be thinking of visiting his congregation but that could wait until later.

Ellen awoke with a start. She felt nervous and looking round the bare room wasn't reassured. She noticed in the daylight, how stained the plaster was, especially round the west facing window where the wind had driven the rain in. Slowly she got out of bed and went to look out, shivering at the draughts as the panes rattled in the wind. She looked out at the tossing trees and wished the world would be still and quiet and things would not change so quickly. Pulling on her housecoat and slippers she went to find John.

"John, are you there?" She went into his room. His bed was rumpled, his clothes gone. She felt the bed. It was cold. Hurrying downstairs she nearly slipped, catching her foot in her gown on the uncarpeted and unfamiliar stairs. Her nervousness verging on panic.

All the rooms were empty, even Rupert had gone. She went and sat by the fire, now long cold. "How could he go out, like that? He didn't wake me, nor bring me any tea, nothing. He's left me all alone, even taken Rupert, my dog. I don't know where anything is. I wonder where Mrs. Cowper lives? Mother will have to come. Where could he be? I wonder what time it is?" She felt helpless, unable to move.

The door banged and she jumped. "John, John, is that you?"

"Of course, who were you expecting?" John and Rupert came

32

in, wind blown, muddy and wet. Rupert flopped down as if exhausted. John's eyes sparkled and his cheeks shone.

"Ellen it's lovely. Better than I ever imagined. We've been down to the river. Rupert chased a roe deer, and we saw a green woodpecker. It's beautiful, beautiful and there's a perfect place for summer picnics, with a waterfall. I've found all sorts of specimens, even two that I've never seen before. Where are my books?"

"You said they'd be here on the train."

"Oh, of course, that's a shame. I'll have to put them in water or press them until the books arrive. I wonder...haven't you lit the fire?"

"John, I don't know where anything is."

"You've found some tea and breakfast though? Rupert and I are starving."

"No, I...."

"You've not even found the kitchen?" he laughed and she looked as if she would cry.

"Come on, come on, let's go and get breakfast together. I don't mind helping, but you know," he teased, "a vicar's wife must feed her husband - feed the body and the mind feeds itself." He took her hand. "Come on, cheer up, this is our house, we can do just as we please. Look you sort out some food, porridge and tea will do me fine, and bread if you've got some. I'll get the fire going and you'll soon feel much better."

Ellen said nothing but began to search in boxes and cupboards. She found some milk and bread left by Mrs. Cowper and the association of these items with that warm, motherly, person suddenly cheered her a little and she smiled at John as he whistled and laid the kindling in the grate. He always seems so happy she thought. So robust and capable, he is a good man. The fire lit, John stood up and seeing the ghost of her smile came and slipped his arm round her waist carefully placing a kiss on her cheek.

"I'm sure we'll be happy here. We'll soon have the place sorted out. I can almost see our children round the table here, would-

33

n't it be perfect?"

Catching his mood she smiled her agreement and he bent to kiss her properly. The wind suddenly rattled its bony fingers on the window and she twisted around.

"It's nothing just the wind."

"I thought there was someone banging on the window. Someone watching us. It gave me a fright."

She turned away from him and, her hands shaking, started cutting slices of bread, thick lumpy slices that would be impossible to butter. Anyway, she thought, I forgot to bring butter.

"What else do we need for our first feast together?" asked John, cheerful again after the momentary loss.

"Well, sugar for the tea but I'm afraid I forgot to bring butter. Blackcurrant jam will have to do."

John went looking for sugar in the pantry and returned a moment later. "Look what I've found. Mrs. Cowper brought us some of her home-made butter and cheese. I'm hungry enough for lunch. You'd better hurry up or breakfast won't be enough!" he laughed.

He asked: "Shall we have hens and a cow? We do have some fields with the Vicarage, you know, and it would help make ends meet. Can you milk a cow? What do you think?'

"I'm frightened of cows, you know that. And I really don't care much for hens either. They make such a mess in the garden. Can't we just get things from Mrs. Cowper?"

"Well I suppose for the time being, but when we get properly sorted out I think it would be a good thing. Maybe we should have a few sheep too. We'd fit in more with the farmers, have a better understanding."

"Oh John, no, I don't want to be a like a farmer's wife, all rough hands and coarse, with all that dirt and children. My mother would be so upset, you know I'm not like that, I like poems and tea parties, and oh John, don't make me keep a cow, you'll want a pig next. We've got a position in society, we have to keep that."

"Don't be silly Ellen. All those times we've talked about 'society' and what a falsity it all is. You liked Mrs. Cowper. She's not coarse and rough and she's a farmer's wife. You're just imagining and getting all upset. Look the kettle's boiling now, let's have some tea. Just think of the Nativity - the shepherds and Kings all came to Jesus. You should forget about 'society' now. Ambleside society was mostly snobbery and nonsense, you told me so yourself often. Aren't we all God's children? The farmer's wife, the vicar's wife, all of us. I don't want to make any great divide, I want us to be happy together and to get to know and care for all the people here. Keeping a pig is a good idea - we could have bacon for breakfast and not just porridge."

Ellen looked glum. She asked: "What will you do today? Will you help me unpack?"

"Oh, let's leave that for a day or two, wouldn't you like to come with me and visit our new neighbours? I think I'll go to Borrenthwaite Hall and call on all the farms along the way. Then perhaps I'll call in at the school too."

Ellen sipped her tea and he knew she was considering her excuses. Would it be too windy? Was she too busy? Had she got a headache? He hoped she would simply say "yes" and they could walk out together arm in arm.

"I will go visiting," she said, "but just down to see Mrs. Cowper, and then I think I'd better write to mother to let her know we've arrived safely and perhaps unpack a few things."

"Alright, my dear" John said knowing that arguing would get nowhere.

Silence fell between them as it so often did and both felt disappointment as if a longed for meeting had yet again been postponed. The windows rattled and the wind sucked at the chimney, occasionally belching back a cough of smoke.

Rupert sensing scraps might be ready came over to the table with a look of "What about me?"

"Oh what a state, my poor puppy, how will we get all that mud off? Did you have to get him in such a mess John? My poor

35

thing, we'll find a brush and clean you up when you're dry" she looked reproachfully at John and felt that everything was his fault.

He was unaware of the look as he tried to butter a triangular chunk of bread. His mind had wandered back to the plants he'd found - perhaps that was hart's tongue fern? He wasn't absolutely sure. Perhaps the school might have some botanical books, he would have to visit anyway to discuss scripture lessons. He didn't hear the door close as Ellen left the room.

She went upstairs to dress and decided that, as soon as John had gone out visiting, she would go down to see Mrs. Cowper. She would wear her blue tailor-made suit which she thought was quite suitable and the hat with the daisy trim. She could not bear the thought of a day alone in this empty house.

At Borren House Ellen soon realised her visit was not expected and everything was difficult. She was shown through to the cold front room, kept for best, and Mrs. Cowper and her youngest daughter sat with her and they talked a little. Much of the time the little girl was the centre of the conversation and when Mrs. Cowper realised that her day's chores were to be disrupted she went to fetch her knitting basket so that she should not sit idle all morning.

Finally Mrs. Cowper said she would have to get lunch as her husband would be home soon. She invited Ellen to share their meal which Ellen gladly accepted. After lunch Mrs. Cowper said she would have to get on as it was washing day and the clothes needed putting out on the line now the day seemed brighter and then she would have the ironing.

Although the conversation had not flowed easily, Ellen felt she at least had someone who might understand and listen to her. The two women were unlikely friends - the one so entangled in work and the other so removed from the practicalities of life.

Ellen realised she had stayed as long as she could at Borren House and began to feel embarrassed so she thanked Mrs. Cowper and promised to see her again soon and set off for the

Vicarage. As she left the farm yard she passed the church and decided to call in to have a look at the building but a brief glance was enough for her to realise it was much like the Vicarage and needed repairs and heating.

She arrived home in the early afternoon and set about writing to her mother, trying her best to sound cheerful yet sure that some of her despair would slip into the envelope with the letter.

She was almost finished when there was a knock at the door. For a moment she wondered what to do and then, rather frightened, went to the door where a boy stood holding an envelope out.

She opened it in front of the boy and he noticed how her hands were almost as white as the paper. He waited in case there might be a penny tip or a message to take back. Ellen read: "To The Revd. Law. Dear Sir, Your furniture arrived by the 2.30pm train and has been unloaded at the station. I would be grateful for your instructions as to delivery. Yours faithfully, Mr. James Dennison, Station Master."

Ellen looked at the boy and said: "Our furniture has arrived."

"Ay," said the boy.

"I wonder what I should do? Revd. Law is away from home visiting."

"Well you might be able to borrow a cart," said the boy, trying to be helpful as Mrs. Law looked so worried.

"Yes, that's a good idea. I'll go down and see Mrs. Cowper and ask if her husband's got a cart," said Ellen. She turned and left the boy standing on the step as she got her cloak and her hat. "Wait" she called, as she remembered Rupert and went to the kitchen to get him. "Come on Rupert. Come on, we have to get the furniture."

"Shall I give a message to the Station Master, Mrs?" asked the boy as she came back to the door.

"Yes, thank you, could you tell him the farmers are helping," and she closed the door and set off briskly down to Borren House, leaving the hopeful boy disappointed.

5
The Visit

Jane was cleaning round the front of the Slip Inn. She had swept the floor, cleaned the downstairs windows and had just knelt to polish the step when she heard someone coming down the road. She straightened to see who was coming and saw Maggie Towers, the maid from Oxenthwaite House, coming along with a basket over her arm. Maggie was of a similar age to Jane and in a similar situation so they helped each other out when they could and always stopped for a chat to liven the time between the chores.

Maggie's job was a step up from Jane's because there was no farm work to be done, just the inside work, though that was hard enough. Maggie worked for the Hendersons who came from near Manchester. Mr. Henderson was a business man wealthy enough to spend most of his time in the country where he spent the days in season shooting and the evenings entertaining. He and his wife had two unmarried daughters. Jane put down her polish and brush and waited for Maggie to come up.

"Hello there, how are you?" asked Jane

"Oh, not so bad, though they've had me polishing silver this morning and if there's one thing I can't abide it's polishing endless forks and spoons," replied Maggie with a smile. She had red hair and a good dose of freckles across her nose which made her look younger than her 20 years.

"Have you heard? The new vicar and his wife are here and they say they're a handsome couple," said Maggie.

"No, though old Isaac said he'd seen some strangers last night when he stopped, but you know Isaac he didn't have much to say," said Jane.

"Oh, well, they've come at last. And Mrs. Cowper had told

Mrs. Thompson, and she came down this morning to see Miss Henderson. Apparently they've no children, but they've got a big red dog."

"Fancy that. It'll be a pet no doubt, not like our Jip." said Jane.

"Well yes, and Mrs. Cowper said Mrs. Law suffers terrible headaches and she'd asked her to go up and help."

"And what's the vicar like then?"

"Well Mrs. Cowper ses he's nobbut a young chap, but very big and strong looking, even handsome," she giggled.

"That makes a change after old Mr. Winton. Maybe his sermons will be a bit more exciting." said Jane.

"I don't suppose that I'll understand them even if they are. I never could understand anything of that. I know they're clever an all that, but I can't follow them. Chapel's different. I prefer that meself, but Mrs. Henderson ses I've got to go to church at least once of a Sunday, so I alus go, an to Chapel as well. Will you be going tomorrow for the christening?" asked Maggie

"You mean the gamekeeper's son?"

"Yes" said Maggie.

"Well I just might with there being a new vicar and everything. It might be interesting and maybe even Joe might be there. Are you off up to the station again?"

"Yes, I'm just popping up to post some letters and collect a parcel from Manchester for Mrs. Henderson."

"Could you ask Mr. Dennison if there's a parcel for us? I was expecting some new material for a dress. See if they know any more about the new vicar up there too." said Jane, "See you later"

"Yes, bye now. Don't polish that step too much or they'll all slip over as they go in."

"No, they slip over when they come out usually," laughed Jane.

When John left the Vicarage he decided to head east, further along the track across the fields. He had studied the map and, as he came to the brow of a hill a small hidden valley opened out before him. To the left was a line of Scots Pines, planted in a moment of hope some 100 years ago and now leaning at the angle the prevalent westerly winds had forced them to take. To the right on top of the hill he could see what must be Seats Farm and decided not to call on Mr. Boldron, the man who kept hens.

He strode down the hill and could see Borrenthwaite Hall in the distance with woods of tall trees, copper beech, oaks and sycamores, to either side. On the side of the hill opposite Borrenthwaite a train was steaming its way up to the top of Stainmore with heavy chugs of smoke as it struggled up the incline to one of the highest stations in the country at Stainmore Summit.

Everything made him feel happy even though the weather was dull and the clouds heavy. This was his parish and he felt a warmth in his heart for it. It was strange how familiar it all seemed as if he had seen this place in his dreams. He put aside the cares of the past for it was hard for him to be pessimistic. It was contrary to his nature which was full of an almost boyish eagerness for new experiences, whether these be finding a rare flower or enjoying a good meal.

Down in the bottom of the hill was a house, painted white, with ash trees planted round to protect the buildings from the worst of the weather. That must be Skerrygill, John thought to himself, and there's smoke going up so I'll call in there.

As he came to the gate a collie dog came bounding across the cobbled yard, barking ferociously. The door opened and a woman shouted: "Come here, Meg. Here!" The dog, gave the vicar a second look and another bark as if to say, next time you won't be so lucky and then went, tail between its legs to the woman who chained it near the door.

John opened the gate and said: "Good morning. I'm the new vicar, Revd. John Law. I'm just having a walk round to meet some of the residents. Now who are you?"

"Hello. I'm Nancy Douthwaite."

"Well, and have you lived here long?"

"Ay, since I was born." She stood on the step which meant she remained eye to eye with the vicar. She was not a big woman but she looked as if she would stand no nonsense from man nor beast. Nancy thought she ought to invite him in, but she had been plucking a hen and there were feathers everywhere and she was in her working clothes - a long plain dress, her work clogs and a plain white pinafore, stained with various farm and kitchen substances.

So she stood her ground and waited for him to do the talking as she eyed him up and down.

"Do you live here on your own?"

"No, there's father and mother here too, but mother's not too well, so I do most of the work," she said.

"Do you go to church?"

"Ay, sometimes, and sometimes chapel, depends," she said.

"Well I hope you'll come along when you can. I'd be very glad to see you. Now, I'm off up to the next farm, Rampson isn't it?"

"Ay, the Andersons, but they're not in today. They're away at the market in Kirkby and Mrs. Anderson has gone to see her sister." said Nancy.

"Oh well, another time, perhaps. I'll make my way over to Borrenthwaite Hall then. Nice to meet you Miss Douthwaite. Goodbye."

She said goodbye and stood and watched as he picked his way back across the cobbled yard to the gate. As he passed the dog it gave a sudden bark, waiting for the moment at which it thought it might have maximum impact, but the vicar did not jump.

Neither did he notice a pair of eyes twinkling in the byre opposite, the body they belonged to blending in with the shadows of the building. Fred Douthwaite, Nancy's father had been cleaning out cows when he heard the footsteps and saw the vicar cross the

41

yard. He did not come out but stood quietly beside his cows trying to hear the conversation between his daughter and the vicar.

As the vicar walked away up the lane, Fred came out and called across the yard: "What sek a fella is he?" Nancy said: "He's just a vicar. He seemed alright, just what you'd expect."

Fred Douthwaite was a small man, just over five foot tall, and wore clogs which clattered as he crossed the yard to quiz his daughter further. He also wore a suit, with waistcoat and collar less shirt, his trousers tied by bailer twine. The suit looked as if it had been worn since he was a young man and, as its better days passed, the jobs it was worn for became more menial until now it was only suitable for mucking out cows.

As well as Skerrygill, Fred had the land at Gillses Farm, and walked the half mile or so along past the Vicarage and church to feed and water his beasts at Gillses. He loved nothing better than to talk, though not with people like the vicar because he'd have nothing in common with him but, every day on his walk along to Gillses he met up with Tommy Nixon from Upmanhow and they'd spend half an hour, smoking their pipes and talking about whatever there was to talk about.

Tommy Nixon would be walking along to check his sheep and the arrangement, though never formalised had become a solid habit over the years. They always met near the church and their gossiping was so well known that people called the pair "The Daily Mail". Fred was hoping that Tommy hadn't met the vicar yet as the details he had gleaned from the briefest glimpse of the vicar's face and a long look at his back would provide conversation for a good half hour's talk.

Unaware of the interest he had left behind him, John walked on towards Rampson and then down towards the river where there was a tiny cottage with arched windows, like Stainmore's answer to the grand gate houses of stately homes. John strode over the bridge and up the hill under the copper beech trees and then out into a field which opened up before Borrenthwaite Hall.

His knock on the door was answered by a maid who bobbed a

42

curtsy and blushed. He said: "Are Dr. and Mrs. Alston-Dewbanke at home?"

"Yes, sir" whispered the maid.

"I wonder if you could tell them that I was passing this way and, if it were convenient, would like to meet them. My name is Revd. John Law."

"Yes, sir. Come in for a moment, sir" and she hurried away down a passage beside the stairs leaving him in the hall to look at the paintings and the numerous relics of past hunts, from stags heads to fox tails. He could hear voices and someone with a young voice singing rather tunelessly from one of the upstairs rooms.

The maid reappeared and said: "Dr. Alston-Dewbanke can see you in a minute or two, just come through here." She showed him into a drawing room stuffed with so much furniture he could hardly make his way to a seat. It looked as if the family had kept everything for the last two centuries and were gradually running out of room. After a while the door opened and in came Dr. Alston-Dewbanke, a red-faced, grey haired man with a large moustache. It was easy to see he enjoyed good food and strong spirits.

"Good morning, Revd. Law. It's good to see you," said the doctor with an absent-minded air, as he reached out his hand to shake that of the vicar.

"Good morning, Dr. Alston-Dewbanke. I'm pleased to meet you" said Revd. Law .

"Now I've asked for a cup of tea to be brought in, or would you prefer something stronger?" asked the doctor.

"Thank you, Dr. Alston-Dewbanke, tea will be fine. Actually I don't drink at all," said the vicar.

"How about amateur dramatics? Are you interested in that?"

"Well no, actually, I can't say I am" said John Law.

"Well, you must be keen on hunting. There's nothing else left to amuse a man in a place like this, unless you like women, but I understand you are a married man?" the doctor laughed like a

43

gun shot, his moustache shaking on his face like a small furry animal with a life of its own.

"Yes, that's correct," said the vicar feeling rather uncomfortable with this man who reminded him of the gentry in Ambleside he had been so keen to leave behind.

The doctor stood with his back to the vicar and gazed out of the window, hands behind his back.

He seemed to have forgotten that Revd. Law was there and started humming to himself, the same tune which John had heard being sung as he came into the house.

"That's a pleasant tune," said the vicar, trying to make conversation.

"Ah, yes. It is. That's a song my daughter Camilla is learning. She's singing in the school concert. Star role. Takes after her mother you know. They both like amateur dramatics." said the doctor turning round as the door opened and the blushing maid came in with a tray of tea and scones.

"Thank you, Annie, we'll manage to pour," said the doctor and the maid practiced another curtsy and left.

"Do you just have the one child?" asked the vicar.

"No, we have a boy too, Gerald. He spends all his time with these new fangled machines. First it was pedal cycles and now he's after one of these motorbikes. He'll kill himself one of these days. But Sis, that's what we call Camilla, Sis is a good child. She's just twelve, now she'll make someone a good wife one day. Do you have children Revd.?"

"No, I'm afraid we don't though we would like a family but Mrs. Law is not very strong you know..."

The doctor looked critical, as if he did not believe in the idea of anyone being in anything but the best of health. He had not practiced as a doctor since he married Miss Dewbanke who was the sole heiress to the Borrenthwaite estate, though he did look after his own family and was an excellent veterinary surgeon having a lot more interest in the ailments of horses, cattle and sheep than in those of people.

"So, what does make you tick, Revd. Law? You must have some interests outside the church?" asked the doctor.

"Well yes, botany, actually. I'm very keen on natural history and, of course, reading,"

"Botany, well, well, " said the doctor as if this was quite a revelation and gave the vicar a long look from under eyebrows which met in the middle. He was thinking that this vicar wouldn't be much good if he wasn't interested in the theatre or hunting or drinking.

He smiled and continued: "Well I'm sure you'll fit in very nicely. It's an easy parish really, you just have to stick to the old routine and all will be well. I expect they'll want you to help at the school too with scripture lessons and the like."

"Yes, I'm sure. I'm planning to call in at the school later today," said the vicar as he took a scone.

"There are one or two people you'd better meet, you know. There's James and Susan Breeks, at Helbeck Hall. He had a distinguished career in India and she's the daughter of the governor of Madras. They were married in Madras Cathedral you know. Good sorts. We haven't got anyone at Augill Castle at the moment. It's up for sale. You'll have met Revd. Canon Lyde from Brough. Now he's a good man to have on your side and then there's the Hendersons at Oxenthwaite House, though we don't have much to do with them. Business people you know but very well to do."

"Oh yes, I've met Revd. William Lyde and he does seem very nice and I've heard of the Hendersons because I'm to do a christening tomorrow for their gamekeeper's baby." said John, finishing his tea as quickly as he could.

"Well, it's been very nice to meet you," said the doctor with a polite smile. "I've got a mare due to foal and I was just going round to see how she was doing when you came."

"Oh, I'm sorry to inconvenience you. Can you give my regards to your wife, and to your son and daughter. I do hope you'll be able to attend the services when you can," said John, glad that this duty was almost over.

As he left the house and walked across the lawn he felt someone was watching him and turning, he saw a child at an upstairs window, with blonde curls and a pale green dress. It must be Camilla he thought, the girl who was singing. She raised her hand to wave and he touched his hat in return and then walked away feeling her eyes on his broad back until he was through the next field.

The clouds were muscling together and the sky was darker. Some of the further fells were lost in mist and underfoot the going was muddy and wet from the rain the night before. But he was undaunted by the lack of success of his two visits so far. They had not been disasters but neither had he found lambs to follow God's shepherd. Still it was early days yet and he was sure things would improve. He was always happy outside and as he strode along the sun pushed briefly through the sky before disappearing again behind the thickening clouds.

He called in at several more farmhouses on his way back to the Vicarage and at each was greeted with a similar response, as if people were not quite expecting him to visit them and were not prepared and so felt ill at ease. It began to rain and in the end he did not visit the school.

By the time John arrived home it was raining hard. He was thinking Ellen would be happier after a day getting used to her new home. What met his eyes as he came towards the house was a scene of chaos with piles of furniture everywhere getting soaked in the rain, two carts and men slipping and sliding in the wet trying to man-handle the furniture indoors. Ellen's face was streaming wet, whether with tears or rain he could not tell.

She was standing, bedraggled and helpless, watching the men heaving, shoving and, mindful of the vicar's wife, cursing under their breath, as they lifted heavy Victorian pieces of furniture out of the cart. John hurried to help as the men struggled with a large wardrobe. As he took hold of a corner the mirrored door which had been fastened, somehow worked its way loose and fell open, smashing the mirror to a thousands slivers of glass which fell, mixed with raindrops to the muddy ground.

"Hold the front door open for us," shouted John to his wife, " and get inside, out of this rain. There's nothing you can do out here."

The following day the weather broke and a fine autumn sunshine warmed the hills. Everything seemed to steam a little but it was hard to say whether it was the first sign of frosts to come or of dampness beginning to dry. John welcomed the sunshine as the start of better things and, despite the muddle of sodden furniture, whistled a tune as he prepared for his first christening at Stainmore Church.

Ellen said she had a chill after standing in the rain so long and was staying in bed so he had taken her a tray of tea and buttered bread, given her a quick brush of a kiss and promised to help her start sorting things out after the christening.

He had not had time to prepare a sermon but had managed to find one from his days as curate which he had been pleased with. It was one he had taken quite some time to write and followed the general theme of seeing the work of God in every blade of grass, in every new born child and in all of nature. It seemed appropriate for the service to come and for his feelings towards his new parish.

John arrived at the church early so he could prepare for the service. He left the door open to allow the air in and went to kneel before the altar on the cold stone steps. As he prayed half his mind was aware of the legs of the table which poked out beneath the white cloth which covered the altar. He laid out the bibles and prayer books, tidied the threadbare kneelers, prepared the candles and the font. He then went to the back of the church where a simple curtain on a rail served as a vestry.

People began to arrive and he greeted each in turn. Mr. Dennison, the Station Master, arrived and introduced himself as one of the church wardens and took over the duty of handing out hymn books. Mr. Henderson's gamekeeper, Robert Davidson and his wife, Eleanor, in their Sunday best, came in with their baby son wrapped in his christening gown. Revd. Law spoke to them in the corner of the church away from the door and then everyone took their places for the service to begin. People spoke in hushed whispers which gradually grew quieter until silence fell as the vicar walked to the front of the church.

The church was three-quarters full of people, some associated with the family and others curious to see the new vicar. The harmonium was not working so Revd. Law had to lead the singing of hymns in his strongest voice followed by the low mumble of the congregation with an occasional clear voice helping to lead the singers through the fog of the tunes.

The baby was christened James Ambrose Davidson and did not cry as the vicar spotted water onto its tiny head. Revd. Law felt the moment as significant as he held the baby in his arms and for an instant did not want to hand the baby back to the waiting arms of its mother.

After another hymn the vicar went to read his sermon. The service had so far felt like a performance on stage in front of an unsympathetic audience and he hoped his words would warm the congregation and break the chill which seemed to have settled in the church.

Jane Johnstone and Maggie Towers, sat side by side, and watched the vicar occasionally taking side-long glances at others in the church. Jane was wearing her newest bonnet, trimmed with violets and primroses, and had primrose coloured gloves to match. Joe was not here to appreciate them so she had lost interest in the event. She played with her gloves and fiddled with her prayer book. Maggie sat, hands folded, and seemed to have gone to sleep, though her eyes were open.

The sunshine slanted in through the windows and seemed

almost solid in the thickness of the silence within the church, only the voice of the vicar reading his sermon droned. His words were long and buzzed around people's heads like flies, easily swotted away. Jane thought she might go to Chapel in the evening in case Joe went there and she thought of the Methodist minister's sermons. When he spoke his words were barbed and stung into your head so that they were hard to forget.

After the service John spoke to Mr. Dennison the church warden and told him that he was going to write to Lord Hothfield to ask if the church could be repaired. He also asked Mr. Dennison if he knew of anyone who would be able to get the old harmonium going again. Mr. Dennison said: "Harold Boldron from Seats is probably your man. He's good at mending clocks and watches and I'm sure he'll work out how to get the harmonium playing again."

"Do you mean the man who keeps hens?"

"Yes, that's him. I'll tell you what I'll see him tomorrow and ask him for you," said Mr. Dennison as he opened the heavy church door.

The vicar was alone. Instantly he remembered the strange feeling he had had while holding the baby. It had been a feeling of foreboding, almost a premonition and now, with the church empty he walked towards the altar and knew what the moment had meant. It was a feeling of loss, a realisation that he would never have a child of his own. He felt a great welling of self pity and was about to kneel to pray when the door opened and the bright sunshine streamed in, throwing a long shadow of a woman across the flags of the church floor.

"I'm sorry to disturb you Revd. Law. I'm Mary Dennison."

"I'm pleased to meet you..." said John as he went up the aisle feeling slightly dazed by the emotion which had overcome him a moment before.

"I just, I was here at the Christening. I'm the Station Master's daughter," she said nervously.

"Oh yes, I was speaking to your father, Mr. Dennison. How

49

can I help you?" As he came closer to her she seemed to shrink and he to grow.

"I was just wondering. I would like to help and I have learned to play the piano. My father was saying you wanted the harmonium mended, well, I'm just offering, if it can be mended, I'll play it."

"Oh, how kind of you. That would be a great help, really that is very kind, for as you would hear I'm not the best of singers," he smiled down at her and she smiled back. She was only a girl he thought, perhaps seventeen or eighteen but she was the first person on Stainmore who had shown him kindness.

6

The Station Master's Daughter

The thread of fate twisted when Mary Dennison was born so, though at first glance she seemed an ordinary girl, her upbringing had promised her something more than the ordinary. She was slight, pretty and dark-haired. A closer look would reveal that she took great care over her clothes which were immaculate and rather more stylish than might be expected of a country girl. She liked large hats which made her tiny waist look even smaller emphasising her womanly shape. Her features were symmetrical, her eyes grey, her complexion pale.

Mary did not want what other girls expected. She did not want to marry and settle down to raise a family. She wanted to travel and to experience some of the things she had read about - Paris, Rome, New York, the names of places seemed exotic in themselves and her ambition was to visit as many of them as she could. She had read of women who went to university and she believed education was her only means of escape from the position in life to which she had been born.

Mary's father, James Dennison was a railway porter in Darlington when he met and married her mother Anne. He had ambitions to improve his position in life. He worked hard, was always immaculate in his railway uniform and he cultivated the manners and speech of the middle classes. He knew his Geordie accent would hold him back so he practiced talking like the first class passengers and the senior railway officials.

In 1871 James Dennison was moved to Barras Station to take over the position as head porter and, in the same year his first son, Charles, was born. At first the young couple found Stainmore rather lonely and quiet but they had free passes for train travel and were able to get back to see the family in

Darlington whenever James had time off.

Two years later Anne was pregnant again but from the moment she felt the first changes in her body she began to feel ill and soon came to believe the child must be sickly too. When the baby was eventually born, two months early, it was still born. Anne grieved for the baby girl she had lost and for more than a year she could not look at a baby without tears pricking her eyes. Her grief was a weight she carried with her and she continued to suffer from coughs which gripped her chest and developed into bouts of bronchitis.

Charles was a fine young boy and his happiness and interest in life helped his mother's grief to heal and she slowly regained her strength. In 1877 another baby boy was born after a long and difficult birth. The baby was christened at South Stainmore Church, where James Dennison was now a church warden. This second child was christened James after his father.

Four years later the station master at Barras retired and James was offered the position. All the years of service had paid off and James was delighted to take this step up the ladder. The job of Station Master meant more money, more responsibility and the family would move from their small cottage to the Station Master's house with its grand big rooms and its spectacular views over the Eden Valley. His sons were now both at school and James served on the school committee and had been elected to serve on the parish council.

Dressed in his Station Master's uniform, walking up and down the platform, James would remember how he had started work when he left school and how lowly he had been. He thought nothing could be better - he was proud of his position, happily married and had two bright young sons who would have a better start in life than he did. He was determined about that.

As the years passed Anne had become sure she would have no more children until one morning she felt a familiar sickness. She could hardly believe it and as the baby grew within her she sometimes felt joy that they would have another child and then she would feel dread that something was not right and memories of the baby she had lost would flood back. With James' better wages they were able to afford reasonable food and she was able to take things easy to avoid the illness which had plagued her early pregnancies. She began to feel that all would be well and was looking forward to seeing the baby which she felt sure was a girl to replace the one she had lost.

Anne went into labour late one stormy March night. James woke the signal man, Anthony Boldron, who lived in a cottage nearby, and asked him to go for the midwife, Edith Ingham, who lived next door to Isaac Wilson at Mouthlock Chapel. It seemed an age before the midwife arrived. James went from holding his wife's hand, to pacing the bedroom to running downstairs to see if the noise he thought he had heard was the midwife. At one point young James came in and stared at his mother, her hair down and her face taut with pain, until his father hurried him back to bed.

Finally Mrs. Ingham arrived and James felt better, as she asked him to make a cup of tea, fetch towels and bowls of water. Anne was relieved to see the midwife and her presence made the pain easier to bear. All through the night the labour continued and James paced backwards and forwards downstairs. It seemed to him the house was a ship that night, in the midst of a storm of wind and rain with the crew screaming in terror within as the ship was tossed helpless on the ocean.

Occasionally when the noise of the wind and rain on the windows abated, seeming to gather its breath for a stronger blast, he could hear the midwife's calm and encouraging voice as if she was guiding them through the perils of the mighty waves. He kept going to the window where he had drawn back the curtains but he could see nothing outside but blackness and then he could hear nothing but the cries of his wife.

Finally the dawn began to break. A greyness came over the land and he could just discern the trees tossed by the wind. He watched and prayed that all would be well. The house seemed

53

quieter. He stood and looked as the greyness began to gather colour and the dark clouds gathered shape. The wind no longer moaned and thumped against the house but seemed to have lost its strength. Calm was returning and he watched as some crows flew from the trees and set off into the wind, flapping in untidy pairs as they set off to search for food.

He did not know how long he had stood there before the door opened behind him and Mrs. Ingham came in smiling with a tightly wrapped bundle in her arms. "Mr. Dennison, you have a beautiful baby daughter" she said. He went up to her and gazed at the tiny miracle. "Will you hold her, Mr. Dennison, while I go and see to your wife?"

"Yes, of course. Is she alright?" he asked suddenly feeling a stab of concern.

"Well, she's lost a lot of blood and she's very weak. I hope she will pull through." said Mrs. Ingham. He noticed that she looked tired and her face was tight with worry. He took the child and sat down feeling suddenly overcome with weariness himself. He sat and gazed at the baby as the daylight increased. He held her tight to him and after a while both father and daughter fell asleep.

The baby was christened Mary Anne Dennison in July 1886. Her mother died two months later, aged 36. Her body was taken by train back to Darlington where she was buried. James felt his world had come to an end. The pride he had felt in his position, his family, his home seemed empty and worthless. Everything seemed meaningless without Anne by his side. Sometimes his memory played tricks on him and as he went through the door he expected to see her in the kitchen with flour on her hands as she baked and cheeks rosy with the heat of the oven.

The hardest thing was having to continue. But he could not just stop because he had to care for the boys and for the baby. His sister Isabelle came to live at the station house to help look after the children. James carried on with the outside events of his life, his work and his meetings but he no longer felt part of the community. He was isolated by his grief and from the time of his wife's death he withdrew inside himself. He felt like an actor on stage playing the part he used to live. He became more involved with the church and spent his spare time helping old Revd. Winton with whatever needed doing.

One evening, as James and his sister sat over the remnants of their tea, Isabelle said: "Do you know what happened today?"

"No" said her brother.

"Anthony Boldron came and asked me to a dance."

"What did you say?"

"I said he had two left feet and I wouldn't go" she laughed and her brother smiled. She continued: "But I was thinking, I can't stay here forever James, much as I love little Mary and the boys. They need a mother, someone who can be here all the time. I was thinking James, perhaps you ought to think of marrying again."

James looked at his sister and realised he was being selfish in his grief. He had not thought of her or of his baby daughter. "Yes, perhaps you're right, but I would find if difficult. Where would I start looking for a wife?"

"There'd be plenty of girls happy to be a Station Master's wife, you know. I could help you find someone suitable if you like. Someone who would look after you and the children."

The idea seemed strange to James at first, but he realised his sister was right. He had lost his wife but his children had lost their mother. The baby meant everything to him and he was determined she should have the best in life and not suffer as her mother had.

Fifteen months after Anne was buried, James was back at the same church in Darlington. He visited his wife's grave where he laid some flowers before going into the church to marry Betty Boustead the wife his sister had found him. She was a farmer's daughter, had been employed as a maid and was twenty years younger than James. She was plain and hard-working and happy to marry a man with a good, secure, income who would give her a home.

She was different to Anne in almost every way - where Anne had been small and dark-haired, Betty was strong of bone, broad and her hair was a light brown. Where Anne would have laughed, Betty sat silent. It was good that she was different thought James for it was easier for him to accept her. He felt she was not a companion like Anne, rather she was a good servant.

As the years went by a form of happiness returned to the station. James could not complain about Betty's house-keeping and she cared for the children as if they were her own. The boys were both away from home now and working but Mary was still at home. As she grew James saw his first wife's features in Mary and often, when they were alone, he would tell her about her mother. He encouraged her to read and write and to work hard at school. The pride he used to feel in his own position now fell to Mary and her achievements meant everything to him. She was naturally intelligent and wanting to please her father worked hard at school. When the other children went out to play or found an excuse not to work, Mary carried on with her reading and, though they might tease her she felt strong in the sense that her father was right.

Betty was sometimes jealous of her husband's pride in Mary. As the years passed they had five children of their own but somehow James did not seem to take the same pride in them as he did in Mary. Betty often felt lonely with none of her friends around her. She missed the shops and streets of Darlington.

She did not mix with the local farmer's wives and one of her only friends was Anthony Boldron, the signalman at Barras

Station, who would always stop and chat to her if he saw her. He would tell her about the first Mrs. Dennison and about the night that Mary was born when he had gone for the midwife and about how James Dennison had wept as they put the coffin onto the train to go to Darlington.

This made Betty feel kinder towards her husband and she would feel sorry for him. She missed her family and she began to think that James would be happier away from Stainmore. She would tell him that she thought he could never really be happy again in the house where his wife had died and how much better it would be to be back in Darlington among friends and family.

As the years went by James began to agree with Betty but said he would not move until Mary's education was finished or she was old enough to take care of herself. As the brightest pupil she was a jewel at Stainmore School and he felt this was better for her than to be moved to a big school in a town where the sparkle of her intelligence might be dulled.

Betty would bite back her jealousy as James bought new clothes for Mary. She kept her patience as far as she could. Sometimes she would ask Mary to do something and there would be a bitter argument with Mary always ending by saying: "You're not my mother, so you can't tell me what to do." Betty tried to keep the peace, knowing that Mary would soon be old enough to leave home and then she would finally have James to herself and they would return to Darlington, away from all the memories of Barras Station.

At the age of twelve, when many of her classmates left school, Mary decided that she would become a school mistress. There were few other options open to her and her father approved saying she would be able to keep studying and as a teacher could have an independent income. Her classmates went to be hired out as farm servants or to work at home. Though she had school friends, Mary had always kept a part of herself reserved and hidden from them, sensing that they would disapprove of her ambitions or mock her. When her friends left school to go to work she

57

was left with few friends her own age, though she sometimes chatted to Maggie Towers, the maid from Oxenthwaite who was often up at the station collecting parcels for the Hendersons.

She did not miss having friends as she found companionship in the books she read. However as she grew into a young woman she did not go unnoticed by the men and one in particular, Joseph Stephenson, called in to see her often. He was eighteen, a year older than herself, and working as a plate-layer on the railway. He lodged up at Bleathgill Farm and his family also came from the north east. Joe thought her as pretty as any girl he had seen and he admired her for her education. She was different from the other girls, somehow a bit above him, and that made the challenge of attracting her all the more appealing.

Whenever he could he would call in at the station and talk with her. Sometimes they would walk together and she would tell him about the books she was reading and her hopes for the future. She would lend him books and he would try to read them. He had very little time, and after he had finished work and eaten his evening meal, he just wanted to go to bed but he would stay up to read the books Mary had given him so he could be closer to her. His daydream was that one day they would be married and he would be a Station Master like her father and she would give up being a school teacher to be his wife.

Mary dreamed of the future too and sometimes she could picture marrying Joe but then she would remember something coarse he had said, or the roughness of his hands and she somehow could not make him fit the dream. If she had to picture the man she might marry he would be someone older, someone more genteel, someone kind and encouraging like her father, someone who wanted her to fulfil herself.

She felt her dead mother was watching over her and guiding her away from a marriage which would bring baby after baby and end in the drudgery of housework. Though she was drawn to Joe she also felt afraid of him, because she knew she did not want to follow him down the path he would lead her. When she listened to him talking she felt his words were like dry stones he was using to build a wall. She enjoyed listening to him but she could see the gaps between the stones where the wind whistled through.

7
The School Room - 1904

Mary Dennison was a bright pupil and almost from her first day at South Stainmore free grammar school had settled in and enjoyed her work. She was good at reading and writing, and flourished in all her studies. The other children were happier to be outside playing, but Mary always felt closer to her teacher and wanted to stay behind to help put the books away, to clean the slates or to talk. Her world revolved around school and days when she had to stay at home were dull.

The children were obliged to stay at school until they were twelve years old but, once past ten many of them were kept off at busy times of year such as hay time to help on the farms. The older they got the more they resented school and, though they were never disobedient in class, they were full of rebellion in the play ground and could not wait for the day when they could leave.

The education was basic, but better than their parents or grandparents had received, and all had grasped the fundamentals of reading, writing and arithmetic by the time they left, and occasionally one of the boys would go on to Appleby Grammar School for further education and the possibility of university. Almost without exception the girls had to content themselves with a primary education because, even though they could have gone on to Kirkby Stephen Girls Grammar, most farming people did not approve of a girl becoming too educated and, even for a boy, too much education was seen as a waste of time. Even if the parents thought an education was a good thing there were hard economic realities to face - a farm to run, other children to feed and no extra money to allow for luxuries like schooling.

When her friends left school to go to work, Mary's father was delighted when she suggested she could continue at school and work for her exams to become a school mistress. He felt she deserved more than just a life as a servant and, on his wages, he had enough to manage without needing her to earn much more than pin money. There would be several years of study and during this time Mary would be what the children called the "under-teacher" at South Stainmore School.

Joe was pleased too at the idea that his Mary was special and, though he had long left school, he tried to keep an interest in what she was doing. Sometimes, when he managed to get off work early, he would meet her at the school gate and carry her books home to the station. They would talk about how she was doing with her studies and he would tell her his dreams of one day going to work in a town where he might be able to get a better job and more pay.

Occasionally a slight doubt would cross Joe's mind when they talked. Sometimes Mary would talk about a book she had read which he had not heard of. Once she was talking about "David Copperfield" and he thought she meant someone who had come to the school and she laughed at him as she explained about a man called Dickens. He began to feel shy of her, where once he had felt completely at home in her company. As the months went by Joe still met her at the school gates when he could, or would walk up to the station on a Sunday to see if she was in, but he became more surly and hid inside himself his distrust and his doubts. Mary started to make excuses when he called and this made him even more determined to see her.

One rainy day, as she was walking home carrying her books and trying to keep them dry under an umbrella, she saw him waiting for her by a stone wall where two paths met. His clothes were soaked as if he had been standing out in the rain for some time and he looked upset.

"What's wrong Joe?" she asked.

"It's...I need to talk to you. I thought you and me were, you know, courting," he said looking down at his muddy clogs.

"Well, yes, we are friends but I'm not sure..."

"Well you keep avoiding me. I knew you were in on Sunday when I called, but your step-mother said you were out. Why wouldn't you see me?" he spat the words out as if they tasted bad and now raised his hurt and angry eyes to her face.

"Yes I was in. I'm sorry. But you see I was working. I've got exams soon and I have a lot of work" said Mary looking up at him and feeling sorry for him and for herself.

"What good's it going to do?"

"What do you mean?"

"I mean, what good's it going to do taking this exam?"

"I want to do it, you know that Joe. I thought you understood I want to be a school teacher"

He looked at her and she could almost feel his mind seething with words but he was trying not to spill any more of them out. She searched for words that might calm him, that might mend the situation but could not decide which would be best so she just stood, her umbrella dripping around her. Suddenly he reached forward, grabbed the books from her hand and threw them into the mud and puddles by the side of the path. "That's it then" he shouted as he strode off back towards Bleathgill. She knew he would regret his anger and that his anger came from the frustration of many unspoken words.

She bent and picked up her books, Carey's Gradus, the Pickwick Papers and an arithmetic book. Tears started to her eyes and she clutched the muddy books and set off for home, her thoughts in a tangle. She was not sure what to do - how could she make the peace with Joe? Did she want to make friends with him again? Was he right, was it a waste of time to carry on to become a teacher? She had no one she could confide in, only her father and she knew he didn't think much of Joe, so she knew what he would say.

As she hurried home, her head bent, tears blurring her eyes and the umbrella over her head she almost ran headlong into the vicar. She jumped with fright and looked up from his large muddy shoes, his black trousers, his long black coat until her eyes met his concerned face. He asked: "What's wrong? Are you alright?"

"Yes, I'm fine really, I'm.."

"Something's happened to you. Look, let me carry your books and see you home."

"Oh, thank you, but it's alright. I'm alright" but he had already taken the wet and muddy books and her umbrella which he held over her.

"Look" said the vicar, "Don't worry. You don't have to tell me what's wrong. I'll just see you up the road a little to make sure you get home alright."

"Thank you" she said and was almost choked by new emotion on top of the old. She cried partly with embarrassment at having been found in this state by the vicar who she hardly knew. He strode along beside her and said nothing. She hurried to keep up and when they reached the gate to the Station House, he asked: "Will you be alright now? You know you can always talk to me if you have any troubles. I'm always here to listen." He smiled and handed her the books and the umbrella. "I'll see you at Sunday's service, then. Goodbye."

"Yes, thank you. Goodbye" she said as he turned and set off back down the hill towards the Vicarage. The way he walks she thought, is so sure, as if nothing could stop him and he never had any doubts.

Revd. Law had been coming into school every week since he first moved to Stainmore to give lessons in scripture. Recently he had been at the school even more regularly because, with financial help from Lord Hothfield, he had organised the restoration of the church and had also had the school rooms, just behind the church, redecorated. But though they saw each other several times a week, they had never had a conversation, only the necessary politeness.

As church warden Mary's father never missed a service and Mrs. Dennison was regularly at church too. They had been down

63

to the Vicarage for tea once or twice after the services but Mary had been too shy to go and had made excuses that she had to stay at home to study. Mary went to church with her parents most Sundays and played the repaired harmonium as she had promised Revd. Law when she had first seen him, but she had barely said two words together to him since that first day.

The service the vicar mentioned as he left her at the Station House was a special celebration for the newly decorated and improved church which was now complete. Added to her worries about Joe was how she would be able to play the harmonium on Sunday and how she would be able to look at him if he spoke to her. She knew she would be so embarrassed and nervous to see the vicar again after what had happened that her hands would shake and she wouldn't be able to play.

Neither would she be able to make an excuse not to go. It had been years since the church had had so much as a lick of paint and now the plaster had been mended, the walls painted and the old cast iron stove cleaned out so that a fire could be lit to warm the building. A new curtain had been put up to improve the vestry and Mrs. Law and Mrs. Cowper had started to make embroidered seat covers for the hard wooden pews. The four paraffin lamps, two by the pews, one by the pulpit and one by the lectern, had been cleaned and restored so that they worked perfectly giving off a warm glow for evening services.

Everyone would be at the service, even those who didn't go regularly to church and Mary had heard that the local reporter from the Kirkby Stephen newspaper, Mr. Braithwaite, was coming too. Her concern at being found crying in the rain carrying a pile of muddy books by the vicar over took her worries about Joe but she could see no way out of going to the service, unless she pretended to be ill and that would only serve to prolong her distress. She would just have to go and pretend nothing had happened.

The next day at school Mary was surprised when a knock came at the class room door and Revd. Law came in. It was not scripture day and she had not expected to see him until Sunday.

"May I just have a word Miss Dennison?" he asked.

"Of course, Revd. Law" she turned to her class who were all staring as one at the vicar. "Just carry on with your letters now for a minute while I talk to the vicar. Annie, Laura, can you keep order?" she said to two of the older girls. "Yes, miss" the girls replied.

Mary went over to the door where the vicar was standing, holding his hat in his hands. He said: "Thank you, Miss Dennison. I won't disturb your class for long. I just wanted to say I hoped you were alright after yesterday ,"

"Yes, thank you Revd. Law," she said, feeling a blush rise in her cheeks.

"And also, Miss Dennison, I understand that you are studying for your school certificate. I've meant to say something before now, but have been so busy with the redecoration at the church, but yesterday's meeting reminded me. What I was going to say was, I would be very happy to help you in your studies and, if you pass the school certificate, which I'm sure you will, and you decided you wanted to go on to do the Local Senior examination, I would be very glad to help with any extra tuition you might need."

"That's very kind, thank you. I'm sure I will need extra tuition. I'll have to ask my father what he thinks. But thank you, for everything" she smiled wanting the conversation to end before her shyness overtook her. He smiled back and the embarrassment of their meeting the previous day seemed to melt away and was laid to rest.

On Sunday at the celebration service the Alston-Dewbankes took pride of place in the church. The family seemed to take up more room than anyone else in the church. Young Gerald obviously had a cold and kept sneezing in a theatrical way which made Camilla giggle until her mother looked sternly at her children. Behind them sat the Andersons from Rampson. Miss Douthwaite from Skerrygill sat next to her father who kept whispering to his friend Tommy Nixon as if he had not seen him for some time, though they had met only that morning, as every other day, to chat as they smoked their pipes.

Mrs. Pounder from the Slip Inn sat near the back with Jane beside her in her new hat trimmed with blue ribbons and pale yellow primroses. Jane's eyes kept sliding from the vicar as the service went on and found themselves caressing the back of Joseph Stephenson's neck. She thought how handsome he looked with his clean white collar and his strong shoulders under his Sunday jacket. She had placed herself so she could see him and, if he glanced round he would see her too, but he kept his eyes firmly on his hymn book or to the front of the church.

Mr. Braithwaite, the reporter, was conspicuous among the congregation with his tweed cape and deer stalker hat among all the plain jackets of the men and colourful dresses of the women. He seemed to be writing the service down word for word and occasionally looked up to glance around at the faces of those around him.

Miss Dennison's harmonium playing was perfect and she looked lovely in a navy blue dress and jacket, trimmed with white, and a large hat to match. Joe kept looking up from his hymn book to steal a glimpse of her and the words of his apology went round and round in his head. He would wait outside the church for her and say how sorry he was and he hoped she would smile up at him as she used to do and he would promise never again to be angry with her...

As the service drew to a close and the final hymn was sung, people were shuffling on their feet, thinking of what they would say or do after the service. Revd. Law went to the door and thanked everyone as they left. He invited the Alston-Dewbankes back to the vicarage for tea but they declined because of Gerald's cold. Mr. Braithwaite accepted and stood chatting to Mr. Nixon and one or two of the other farmers while he waited for the vicar.

Jane waited by the gate, hoping to have a chance to speak to Joe, and he in turn waited for Mary. As she came out of the church the vicar took her hand and thanked her for playing the harmonium so well and told her he had already spoken to her father who had happily agreed to the idea of extra tuition.

Mary felt the vicar had given her a special message, beyond what his words had said, and as she turned to leave she saw Joe waiting for her. She felt her heart sink. Jane was watching from the church gate and as Joe started talking earnestly to Mary, she also felt her heart sink and turned away, sad and angry, to walk home to another comfortless night at the Slip Inn.

8
Pennies under the Carpet - 1905

Mary Dennison passed her school certificate with excellent marks and in 1905, at the age of nineteen, began
to study for the Local Senior examination with Revd.
Law as her tutor.

The arrangement they had come to was that she would go to
the Vicarage three evenings a week after school where the vicar
helped her study for her final examination as a certified teacher.
Often Mrs. Law would come and sit with them in the study, for
she hated being alone more than anything, but she found the tuto-
rials boring. She wanted to interrupt the talk of history, geogra-
phy and grammar to ask Mary a question about her family, or
where she had her dresses made but, if she began to speak her
husband would give her a black look or worse, say something in
which she detected the bitter taste of sarcasm.

Ellen had not settled in to her life on Stainmore at all. Though
they had been in the Vicarage for two years now, she still felt it
was not home. Often she would try and rearrange the furniture,
or decided to change all the curtains around, to try and make the
place look better but her attempts usually ended in failure one
way or another and the burst of energy which had inspired her
would quickly drain away as she realised the blue velvet curtains
were an inch too short for the drawing room windows and would
have to go back in the bedroom.

She felt her only friend was Mrs. Cowper and, as often as she
felt politeness allowed she would go down to see her. Most days
she would spend her time walking with Rupert for she could not
bear to be left at home on her own and John was out most days.
Her only happy times had been the first Christmas when her
mother had come to stay and had helped her get the muddle of

furniture sorted out and then last year she had gone to Ambleside for a week to stay with her mother. She cried when she got on the train to come back to Stainmore. When she arrived home John was waiting to meet her at the station and they walked home together. After a few remarks about the weather and how was her mother, Ellen asked: "John do you think we could go back to live in Ambleside? I can't bear this place for much longer. I cried all the way in the train because all I want to do is go home. John, please, will you consider it?"

John looked at his wife and saw the streaks of tears on her cheeks and her reddened nose but, instead of softening his heart her grief angered him. He felt she had not tried. From the very first she had set her heart against Stainmore and, by inference, against himself. He said: "Ellen we cannot leave. This is my living and I care for the people here. I don't want to leave. Please don't mention this subject ever again." They fell into a silence which deepened with every step nearer to the Vicarage, and Ellen felt the gulf between them as a hollow, empty, hopeless place in her heart.

Sometimes she wondered if she would go mad. Most days she had headaches which sometimes forced her to stay in bed. On the days she felt well enough to go out she walked with Rupert for miles over the fellsides, hardly seeing anyone to speak to. Once she had gone to visit the Alston-Dewbankes but, she decided, they were peculiar. The day she called, as she stood at the door, she could hear music and someone singing at the top of their voice. When the maid opened the door she had a funny smile on her face and, when Ellen went in she could see the stout shape of Mrs. Alston-Dewbanke dancing round the kitchen table with a man who looked like one of the farm labourers.

Ellen had gone into the kitchen and stood nervously by the door. Mrs. Alston-Dewbanke sort of nodded as she passed in her crazy dance and her two children smiled at Ellen but kept on clapping to the music hall tune blaring from the gramophone. The man she now recognised was old Mr. Johnstone who played

69

the fiddle sometimes at dances. He winked at Ellen as he hurtled past.

After a few minutes Gerald and Camilla decided they would join in the dancing too and, with four people dancing round the kitchen table, Ellen felt they were being rude and with a smile left the room. The maid was waiting outside and said: "They often have a dance you know. They're a bit funny but they're alright really." Ellen just nodded and said: "Goodbye".

Ellen thought, I have no hope left. There is nobody here to talk to. Everyone is so busy with their own lives. The farmer's wives are always working, I can't go to the pub and talk to Mrs. Pounder, Mary Dennison would be fine but she is too busy studying and, now she had been to meet the Alston-Dewbankes properly it seemed they were too eccentric. If she had been able to talk to John that would not have been so bad, but he was never at home or he was working in his study. They had drifted further and further apart. The move to Stainmore had not brought them closer. They were chained together but every part of their minds, bodies and souls were separate.

The worst time of all was winter because then, when the blizzards blew, she could not go out. She was completely trapped in the house and in her own thoughts. Sometimes there seemed to be no way out but death and she would spend hours just sitting gazing out of a window, not seeing anything, her mind as blank as the whirling snowstorm. To an observer it would seem she was lost in deep thought but she would just sit there thinking nothing at all. Days would pass with this heavy depression gripping her so that it seemed too much effort even to climb the stairs to go to bed. The only thing she wanted was to return to Ambleside.

When Spring came Ellen felt better and when Mary started to visit for her studies, Ellen was momentarily happy for the crumbs of kindness which might pass between them when she arrived and then again in the moments when Mary was putting on her coat about to leave. The discussions in her husband's study on history, literature, philosophy and art, would rouse in

70

student and teacher an enthusiasm and lively conversation but Ellen felt excluded from the debate, though she often sat and listened. Her thoughts would drift back to Ambleside and the idyllic days before she had been married. Something about John's voice as he talked to Mary Dennison, or read her a passage from a book, reminded her of those days.

John enjoyed teaching as much as Mary enjoyed learning. For him it rekindled the days of his youth and his own studies. He picked up books he had not read for ten years and read them so that he could help Mary understand and the books reminded him of how he had been then, as a young man, but also the books themselves seemed to hold deeper meaning on second reading.

As well as the study evenings with Mary, there were scripture classes to take at the school, his sermon to write and he continued to visit homes all over the scattered parish so his days and weeks were full. He felt more alive than he had for many years and even the rift with Ellen could not depress him for long. As his days filled with activity, so Ellen's days became emptier. She was lonely and her only occupation was walking with Rupert, covering miles of lonely tracks.

One day in late May, as the vicar walked down to the school for his weekly scripture lesson, he was struck by how exhilaratingly beautiful everything was. The grass was getting longer in the fields, he could almost hear it growing and it was full of buttercups, soldier's buttons and ragged robin. The sun was shining and full of warmth and the birds were silent, busy feeding nestfuls of babies. Even the curlew and lapwings were too busy to bother as he hastened down to the school.

As he arrived at the gate he decided to ask Mary if they could leave the scripture lesson for tomorrow and take the children on a nature walk to collect botanical specimens. It was just too wonderful to be cooped up with restless children trying to remember their lessons. Mary agreed readily to the idea and the children were eager to be outside, so they spent a happy hour finding flowers and talking about botany on the road sides near the

71

school.

When they got back to school, Mary got the children to press the flowers and, when they were dry, they glued them to card and labelled each plant and made a display on the schoolroom wall.

Nature study became one of Mary's regular lessons and the display grew as the children found more and more plants. Once when one of the children brought in a plant she could not identify she asked Thomas Allinson, the gamekeeper's son from Tufton Lodge, if he would take the flower and a note up to the vicarage to ask Revd. Law if he could tell them what the plant was. Thomas happily agreed, knowing he could make the ten minute walk take at least half an hour. Clutching the flower with strict instructions not to damage it, he set off across the field for the Vicarage where the vicar was working in his garden.

Thomas waited while Revd. Law read the message. The vicar asked him to wait a moment and went into the house. He came out a few minutes later with a note for Miss Dennison and an apple for the boy. Just as Thomas was leaving the Vicarage, the vicar called him back. He picked a pink rose from his garden and gave it to the boy saying it was for Miss Dennison.

Thomas wandered back to school, stopping to look at a spider which had caught some sort of fly in its web strung between stalks of grass. He watched as the fly struggled and buzzed. After the first struggle the spider was just sitting on the edge of its web watching. Thomas wondered if he should try and help the fly to get out but all of a sudden it stopped buzzing and seemed to be dead. The sound of shouting made him look up and he realised it was play time so he forgot the spider and set off to run back to school. He dashed into the classroom with the pink flower and the note and then out to play.

Thomas' best friend Henry Nixon was waiting for him, sitting on a step in the playground, and Thomas went over to him. "Look what I've got" he boasted, showing Henry his apple. "You can have a bite if you like" he added, seeing Henry's look. So the boys sat and shared the apple while Thomas told him all about the vicar and the pink flower and the spider with the fly.

Later that evening, as a perfect spring day drew to a close, John decided to take a stroll down the field to the church before he turned in for the night. He had been preparing some arithmetic tests for Mary for the following evening and wanted to stretch his legs before going to bed. The sun was just nearing the tops of the Lake District fells as he walked down the field. The air was heavy with the scent of a thousand flowers and a curlew called mournfully from further up the hill. The sky was spectacular, a joyous red near the skyline, fading to orange and then yellow and finally a deep blue overhead. Clouds etched in brilliant gold stood out black on the red as the sun fell slowly towards the fells.

John felt full of awe. The scene, the scents and the sounds seemed to fill him with their beauty and he felt life was perfect. As he came close to the church the mood was suddenly broken as he heard someone hammering and laughing near the church. He hurried towards the building and could see two youths near the church.

"Hey, what are you doing you two?" he shouted

"Oh...it's the vicar" he heard one voice say. "Oh no.."

"What do you think you're doing there?" John asked angrily as he came up to the two. He could see now it was the signal-man's son young Jim Boldron and William Hill from the Slip Inn.

"Well, sir," said Jim, "We're putting up a sort of tent. We were going to sleep out because it's such a nice night, just for a lark, you know. We were mebbe going to see some spirits we thought." The pair looked at each other and laughed.

"But you can't fix your tent to the church. What are you doing hammering nails in? You both know the church has just been repaired at Lord Hothfield's expense. I shall have to see your fathers about this. Look what you've done. You've knocked all the pointing out." John felt himself getting more and more angry. The two lads just looked at him, half smiling with embarrassment and, he thought, insolence.

73

William said: "We weren't doing any harm. There's no need to get like that."

"Well clear all this up, right now. I'm waiting and I'm not going until you're out of my churchyard with all your canvas and ropes and nails. Go on, clear up and be off with you."

John stood and watched as the pair started to pack up their things. They muttered to each other and kept looking at the vicar who was beside himself with anger that they could start driving nails into the wall of his church.

"Right then. Is that it? Be off with you and don't ever let me catch you in here again" said John.

"You shouldn't talk to people like that you know, vicar or no vicar" said Jim as he walked out of the gate.

"He wants his eye blacking that's what he wants. They're all the same them vicars. All high and mighty and thinking they're better than the rest of us," said William to his friend in a voice loud enough for the vicar to hear as they went off down the road. John stood and watched them head off down the lane towards the Slip Inn.

He felt a rage far beyond the wrongs of the situation. Logically he knew they were just a couple of lads and it was a prank which had done little damage to the church. But he was seething with a rage at ignorance, vandalism and insolence. He looked at the sky which not long before had given him such joy. The sun was gone but the blood red stain still spread across the sky and the clouds, no longer etched in gold were black and heavy with threat.

9

Dancing at the Slip - Autumn 1905

The summer of 1905 slid past, day blending into day, and John saw no more of William Hill and Jim Boldron. They no longer came to church and, in the end he decided not to go to speak with their parents. The weather was excellent and the farmers gathered in the hay in record time. Mary Dennison's studies were going well and sometimes they even talked of her going on to university - a thing almost unheard of at the time.

The only shadow cast on the vicar's life was his concern for his wife. She hardly came to church, saw no one except Mrs. Cowper and spent most of her time out walking with Rupert or mooning around the house. After the initial short-lived enthusiasm to make the Vicarage as she wanted it, she seemed to have lost interest in everything. She had grown thinner and paler and sometimes, when he came in he could hear her talking to herself, even arguing with herself. She stopped as soon as she saw her husband and hurried to busy herself with arranging cushions on the sofa, or plates in the kitchen. Though sometimes he tried to talk to her she had become lost in a world of her own and was further and further from his reach.

October brought excitement to the whole district as the King was to drive through Brough and over Stainmore. He was visiting Brougham Hall and was going over to Raby Castle in a car. Public plans for banners in the streets and flags were made and private plans occupied every household, as to what should be worn for the great day and all the children were granted a day off school. John asked Ellen if she would like to see the King and she looked at him as if he had asked if she would like to go to Mars. For a while she refused and said she would not know what to wear and there would be so many people but John said: "How will it look if I am there but not you? You are the vicar's wife, you have to accompany me for the day. Come on Ellen, you'll enjoy the day, and I'm sure you'll find something to wear in your wardrobe."

On the morning of the King's visit, the lanes and paths were busy with people in happy, holiday, mood making their way down to Brough. Everyone was dressed in their Sunday clothes and laughed and shouted to each other. John and Ellen walked together, arm in arm, but Ellen kept her head down looking at her feet as she walked, whereas the vicar was looking around at everyone. He marched along making Ellen breathless in her tight dress and high-heeled shoes as she tried to keep up. She wore a brown coat over a tweed skirt and she knew her hat was not right. It was the wrong colour brown and the feathers still looked squashed and ruffled despite her efforts to straighten them.

When they got to Brough the village was already a mass of people and colour with Union Jacks flying from every window and banners across the street. Stalls had been set up to sell drinks, biscuits and souvenirs. As they neared the clock tower Ellen saw Mrs. Cowper and made her way over to see her. John looked round and, across the street, saw Mary waving. She looked lovely, as she stood between her brother and her father, both dressed in smart dark suits.

Without thinking John made his way across the street to be with them and, just as he got to the other side, he heard a great cheer ring out from further down the road. He could not go back to his wife and cross the street in front of the King's car. He stood behind Mary who was waving a flag and jumping up so she could get a better view. He looked over her head and across the street where he could see the pale face of Ellen looking steadily at him from a sea of colourful and animated faces, hers alone was blank, and staring at him. He felt embarrassed and to hide his feelings, looked for the King's car which came slowly along the road, the Monarch waving his hand and smiling to both sides, but all the time John felt Ellen's stare.

Once the car, and the official vehicles following had passed, the crowd dissolved onto the street. John looked down at Mary and said: "Well, so much for the King. I'd better go and find Ellen. I think she's a little upset by all the crowds."

"Yes" said Mary smiling up at him with the infectious gaiety of the occasion shining in her eyes, "Yes, she did look a little lost. I'll see you tomorrow afternoon as usual. Goodbye."

In that moment all three people, John, Ellen and Mary, knew something had shifted. The angles of the triangle had moved and something which had been changing so gradually was recognised in an instant as different. None of them understood the significance of the realisation but each felt a certainty, as if some historic step had been taken as the King's car drove slowly past them.

The moment did not go unnoticed by Joe who was standing with William Hill and Jim Boldron under the clock tower. They all watched as the vicar hurried across the road and all saw his embarrassment and the hasty farewell. None of them said anything but Joe felt his suspicions about Mary and her education were confirmed. She had been leading him on with all this talk of learning and being busy with her studies whenever he called. She was, well the only word he could call it was flirting, and the vicar, well he was leading her on. He was taking Mary away from him.

Joe had hoped to talk with Mary again today. He hoped they might walk home together and, if things had gone well, he was going to ask her to go to the Christmas dance with him at the Slip Inn. There was no point in that now. He felt angry and jealous. William and Jim wanted to go round the pubs and, with nothing else to do, he followed them into the Castle Hotel. He did not notice Jane sitting with her parents and playing with the little boy who was their son. Jane's eyes filled with tears as she watched him go into the pub. She was wearing a new dress she had made specially for the occasion. It was lovely to have a day off, to see the King and her little boy, but she had hoped Joe might have said something to her. She decided she would stay in Brough and try to see him later, even if he was drunk, she could walk home with him.

By the time the three had been the rounds of the pubs, finishing at the Golden Fleece, Joe had forgotten his sorrows and was pleased to see Jane standing talking to Maggie over the road. He called to her and she came over and he said: "Jane, Jane, I'm sorry for everything. Really I'm sorry. Will you walk home with me?" His voice was not sober and he swayed slightly on his feet as he stood before her. "Of course, don't be sorry, Joe. Come on, I'll walk home with you."

As they walked the four miles home, Joe told her everything. He told her how he loved Mary above anyone else and how the vicar was taking her away. Jane said: "But that can't be right, Joe, he's married and he's a vicar. Look you've had too much to drink, you're talking nonsense."

"But I saw them Jane. I'm telling you. When the King came all three of them were standing looking at each other, him, Mary and Ellen, it was the oddest thing. I'm telling you Jane. I've not said anything to anyone else, not even William and Jim because they'd just laugh at me. I know I've drunk too much, but I know what I saw."

"Alright Joe, alright. Don't get so upset." said Jane as they walked through the gathering darkness. They were now more than half way home and were just coming to Argill Bridge when Joe took her arm. "Look Jane I know I've treated you badly and you don't deserve it. I promise you I'll try to get Mary out of my thoughts forever. Already I don't trust her anymore. I don't believe what she says. Jane come with me, let's take a short cut back through the wood here. Come on Jane."

Jane looked at him and could not help loving him whatever he said. She just wanted to hold him in her arms to feel his strong limbs but she feared another baby. "Joe, I can't. We've already got Joe and you've not even looked at him. He was there today and I hoped you'd come over. Joe, he's so like you, you'd love him. I do love you Joe. I want to marry you but my parents can't look after another baby for me and I don't want them too. You must understand Joe. Please."

Joe looked at her and felt how bad he had become. Jane was pretty, she was strong and she would make a good wife, yet he could only think of Mary and kept having to stop himself using the wrong name. As he stood and looked at her they heard voices approaching in the darkness. It was William, Jim and Maggie, with a group of others making their way back, laughing and joking. Joe and Jane just stood looking at each other until the group were around them and then they were caught up in the foolery and joking. The gang made their way up the hill to the Slip Inn for another drink before the day's holiday was over.

Jane did not see Joe again for several weeks but she knew she would see him at the Christmas dance. She could not wait. She had told Maggie what Joe had said. Again and again they had gone over the conversation and Maggie said she was sure Jane was right and that Joe did love her after all. Jane felt that above all she must not chase him. She must be patient above all else and he would come to her. She knew that the affair with Mary was nearly over and Joe would come round and she would be waiting.

Each day of November dragged past with Mrs. Pounder seemingly unaware of Jane's excitement. Yet it was funny but you could never surprise Mrs. Pounder. She always seemed to have thought what you were going to say before you said it. She just went on from day to day as if nothing would change and, if things did change, so much the better.

On the morning of the dance Jane was up as usual at six o'clock and started her work in the dairy. It was a bitterly cold December morning and it would have to be churning day. Once the churning was finished she would have to help get everything ready for the dance. Her father and brother would be playing fiddle and an accordion player was coming up from Kirkby Stephen. Some of Brough Brass Band usually turned up too and joined in and Jane could not wait.

She had separated the blue milk for the cheese and set it in a large brown basin beside the kitchen fire to warm to the right temperature. She was churning the butter, her arm aching with the effort. The cream was sometimes awkward and would not turn. It was always slow when it was cold and slower when you were in a hurry.

Her mind had quickly drifted away from the job and she was wondering where Joe might be today. He was a plate-layer on the railway and could be working anywhere between the Summit and Belah Viaduct. He worked with a team of men, including his father, who had left farming as a young man for the better wages of the railway when it was being built back in the 1860s.

Joe's father had some stories to tell and he liked nothing better than to be asked about working for Gilkes Wilson, the foreman in charge, when they built the Belah Viaduct. He always ended by reciting the poem that one of the men had composed to honour the physical effort and the engineering skill, the achievement in metal and stone that allowed trains to cross the Belah Gill. The poem went:

> *To future ages these lines will tell,*
> *Who built this structure o'er the dell;*
> *Gilkes Wilson with these eighty men;*
> *Raised Belah's viaduct o'er the glen.*

Joe's father was a great lover of stories, poems, songs, anything that involved words. He composed some himself, but shrugged them off, never even wrote them down because "I'm not an edicated man" he would say. Jane hoped that one day Joe would be like his father. Jane thought of him nearly all the time. She measured and weighed the time until she could see him again. She dreamed of the day they would marry and live in the cottages built beneath the chapel at Mouthlock.

She had her eye on old Mr. Peacock's cottage but Mr. Peacock, the coal miner, just hung on, walking to the pits up near Tanhill every day. His wife had died years ago, but Mr. Peacock went on, surviving on bread and tea. His cottage would surely be the first and they'd put their names down for it. They just had to wait. Jane stopped churning for a while and opened the barrel to have a look. "Still nowhere near" she sighed. She went through to check the milk wasn't getting too warm for cheese making, it had to be just right before adding the rennet. Mrs. Pounder was in the back kitchen peeling potatoes and humming one of her favourite dance tunes.

Jane went to have a look out of the door, a habit she had got into in case Joe should be coming. The habit had extended so that she would go and look out even when there was no chance of his being anywhere near. Finally the butter was made, the cheese renneted and William Hill from next door came in to help take down the planks so the dance floor would be ready. Once everything was ready Jane went to wash and change. She lay on her bed for a while gathering her energy for the dance to come.

Downstairs in the pub the men began to gather. Old Isaac had finished his coal delivery early and had got himself firmly seated near the fire. He wasn't going to dance but he was looking forward to drinking, talking and watching the young ones enjoy themselves. William Hill came in and sat with him, then Jim Boldron, Jane's brother Thomas Johnstone, Christopher Fothergill from High Ewbank, James Smith from Light Trees and John and Richard Boustead, all lads of a similar age and finally Joe came in. He joined the group round the fire, all drinking beer and waiting for the music to start. They had to have a few pints first to warm themselves for the dance. Jane was behind the bar and kept smiling at Joe. When she brought him his beer, he held her briefly round the waist and whispered in her ear: "You're the bonniest girl here, Jane. We'll dance tonight won't we?" She laughed and said: "I'm the only girl here so far

81

Joe, unless you count Mrs. Pounder!"

Joe turned to Isaac and asked: "Tell us one of your stories Isaac. Come on, one from the old days when you were a lad. Get him a pint Jane, that'll get him talking."

"Well, fer a pint, now what can ah tell about for a pint?" he looked around his audience of young men, waiting for them all to look his way. "Shall I tell thee about Luke Fair, or Brough Hill? Or what them navvies got up to when they built yon railway? Or what about Riding the Stang? I bet none of thee know about that then?"

The lads all looked at each other, winking, ready for a good laugh at Isaac and his story, and they urged him to tell them about Riding the Stang.

"Well, now, when I was nowt but a lad, they hed a thing called Riding the Stang. The last time it happened was in Kirkby Stephen and it was a fella called Taylor. Now Riding the Stang ye see was a sort of punishment. It was done when men beat their wives, though oftener for women beating their husbands." Isaac looked around for the laughter and to make sure no one's attention had wandered.

"Now I was saying about this fella Taylor, now he hed committed adultery they said. He hed overstepped modesty with this married woman and everyone knew about it. Well, ye see if it was a one off thing, ye know, mebbe's no one would have done anything, but when everyone knew about it then something hed to be done. Well they'd hev a meeting and such like and they'd appoint a night when there was no moon for Riding the Stang.

"One of them would like pretend to be the one who had committed the sin, and he was always called Bobby Dodge. Now Bobby would climb onto a pole, what they called the stang. But a pole's rather a slippery thing so sometimes they used to use a ladder, a plank or even a hand-barrow and all the men from Kirkby would carry the stang from door to door around the town.

"I remember, I was just a boy, but I can remember them all laughing an' shouting. An' there was always this woman with them. They called her Roaring Tabby because she was half-witted and she'd be right there shouting an' laughing with the crowd. She was a funny old body was Roaring Tabby. I was a bit feared of her. She was all rags and tatters and she had these large pockets hanging down at each side, filled with odds and ends, and her clothes were all tied round the middle with a bit of string. She had a home-made rabbit skin hat, home-made stockings and clogs and I nivver much liked meeting her, specially when I was on me own.

"Any road, the rider of the stang stopped at every door and explained to people why he was appearing with his followers. There was some sort of a rhyme he would say. I seem to think it was mebbe obscene but I can't remember the words. I didn't understand them then but they would all holler and laugh when Bobby said the rhyme. People would give them money to go to the pub later."

Isaac stopped to drink from the pint which Jane had put in front of him, wiping the beery froth from his mouth onto his sleeve. Under his bushy eyebrows his eyes twinkled. He had a look which said the story was not finished but he was waiting for them to encourage him. Joe was the first to speak. "What happened then Isaac? Did they go to the culprit's house or what?"

"Well, aye, they did. Now me father told me, because I don't remember this bit. There was a big crowd thoo knows and I was just laal and couldn't see everything. Well, me father said, when they got to Taylor's house his wife wasn't pleased, even though her husband had been at fault. Now some say she threw boiling water at them but me father told me she emptied the chamber pot on them. When they got to the woman's house, which was down in the Market Square, her husband came out with a flail and he was after beating them. And that was it. The Stang was Ridden and they'd all go off to the pub to talk about what they'd done and what had happened.

"They'd mebbe talk about other Stang nights. It wasn't just for married people thoo knows. I once heard tell of a young joiner

83

who thrashed his sweetheart and they rid the stang for him."

"We'll drink to that Isaac," said Joe. "Now that was a good story. Mebbe we should do a bit more Riding the Stang. Or mebbe we should just go and get dancing, I can hear the fiddler warming up, come on lads."

The room had filled while Isaac told his tale. The girls and women had gone straight upstairs and Thomas Johnstone's father had gone up and was warming up to play. Joe went over to Jane and said: "Can you get Isaac another pint and then shall we go and dance?" Jane's eyes shone and for the first time she felt an equal understanding between herself and Joe. He spoke to her as if she mattered to him. The floorboards above began to creak and then the stamping of feet began as the music wound its spell around the dancers. Jane hurried to get the beer and then she and Joe walked upstairs arm in arm, ready to dance the night away.

10
The School Photograph - 1906

One cold morning in late January the wind began to blow from the east. The hard hills were frozen, mud was turned to rock and the sky had a yellowish colour. Everything was quiet in anticipation of the storm blowing in from the North Sea, across Yorkshire and up over the Pennines. The cold crept through the Vicarage, seeming to force its way through the walls and up through the floor. Ellen found it hard to get out of bed and, when she did, she was so cold her hands were permanently blue. The first snow flakes fell quietly and innocently to the ground and settled on the stiff grass. The wind began to gather strength and, within an hour everything was a roaring whiteness.

The windows were soon plastered in snow, dimming the light so that Ellen had to light lamps downstairs. Even in this blizzard John was out. He was never at home. The fire had not been lit and Ellen could not face going out to be blinded by needles of snow to get wood and coal. She could not face eating. Instead she sat staring at the door, so deep in sorrow that she could no longer find the energy to cry. Rupert lay by her feet. Occasionally he would get up and rest his nose on her knee and she felt the dog was the only being who understood anything of how she felt. She felt imprisoned by John, by the blizzard, by the Vicarage, by Stainmore itself. She hated every part of it.

She did not know how many hours had passed before John came back. He stumbled in and struggled to get the door shut in the face of the blizzard. He was covered from head to foot in snow, his face reddened by the cold. After he had taken off his coat, gloves, hat and scarf he came into the living room expecting a fire, a smiling wife and a cup of tea.

Ellen just stared at him, as she had been staring at the door. She was as white as the snow and her blonde hair was all uncombed and straggled round her face. She did not move. For a moment John thought she was dead for there was not even a glimmer of emotion in her face, not a shiver of recognition in her body.

"Are you alright, Ellen? What's happened? Ellen?"

Ellen looked at him as if she wondered who he was and spoke as if in a trance: "I'm a prisoner and I'm cold. No one has fed me and there's no fire."

"What do you mean a prisoner? Ellen what's matter with you? Why are you sitting here like this?" John took her hands. "Ellen you are frozen. I've been out in a blizzard but you are frozen. Look I think you'd better go back to bed and I'll get the fire going, make you some tea and fill the bed warmer. Perhaps you've caught a chill."

He helped her to get up and led her up the stairs. As she walked she began to shake convulsively. "Look I'm going to have to get a doctor, Ellen. You're not well. I'll go down and ask Mrs. Cowper if she can come up and look after you and then I'll walk down to Brough to see if young Dr. Bainbridge can come to see you."

"Oh no. I'm not ill. I'm just a prisoner. He can't get me out. I've already looked for the door and there isn't one. I know. I've been locked in for so long. I know now."

"Look don't worry. Let's just get you into bed and then we'll talk later. You must get warmed up first." As he tucked her into the bed she lay and the glazed look came back into her eyes as she stared at the ceiling. He waited for a moment or two but she just continued to stare with eyes that no longer recognised the familiar things around her.

When the wind finally eased everything was blanketed in white. Thick carpets and extravagant rolls of snow drifted across fields and behind walls. The frost continued so the snow stayed for almost a month and Ellen lay in bed staring at the white ceiling day after day. Young Dr. Bainbridge managed to struggle through the snow but, after examining Ellen, said he could find nothing physically wrong with her, though she was very thin. He prescribed some restorative medicine, recommended to him for cases such as this, by one of the Professors at Newcastle where hc had recently finished studying.

When the doctor had left, John suddenly felt lonely. He went to his study and took down Gibbons "The Decline and fall of the Roman Empire" and started reading. His eyes followed the words but he could not make sense of them. He thought of Ellen lying up there and he knew the doctor's restorative medicine would not work. He knew something had broken in her mind. He started to pray but found himself getting up and walking towards the door. Through the words of the prayer which ran round in his head he felt an overwhelming need to tell Mary what had happened.

When he reached the school he realised Mary was teaching and it was another half an hour until break time. He knocked at the door and went in. All the faces turned to look. Twenty eight pairs of curious eyes and inquisitive minds studied the vicar who usually only called on Fridays.

"Can I talk to you please, Miss Dennison? It's rather urgent." he asked.

"Yes, of course, yes," said Mary. She looked at the clock and said: "Children, I know it's a little early, but take your break now. We'll continue with the number work when you come back in. Off you go now. Put your coats on because it's cold. Henry you did bring your coat today didn't you?"

"Yes, miss"

"Off you go then and you big ones don't throw snowballs at the little ones, remember now. Hurry up Wilf, Rosie, Isabelle, off

87

you go now. I'll come and call you back in soon."

The children trooped out into the snowy yard leaving John and Mary standing in the empty room.

John came closer to her and said: "It's very difficult for me to talk about this, but I must tell someone. I think Ellen has lost her mind."

Mary looked up at John and saw his concern. She could feel him wrestling with his emotions and with embarrassment. "What's happened Revd. Law? What makes you think your wife has lost her mind?"

John sat down on one of the desks and began to tell her how Ellen had always been sensitive and how he had loved her for this very quality. Grasping for words he said: "I thought her sensitivity hid a deep understanding of things but, as time went on I found it was a shallow pool of worries about things I was not interested in. She has always had terrible headaches. We drifted apart and I thought, when we came to Stainmore, we would be able to start again. But she's lost in a world of her own and this winter she's become more and more odd. Now she just stares and says she's a prisoner. What she says partly makes sense but she rambles on about things that don't make sense. She looks at me as if she did not know who I was...I just don't know what to do." John's head was bent looking at the floor as he spoke.

Mary came to his side and, reaching out, touched his hand. He looked down at her small white hand resting on his and thought it was like a little wild bird. A strange feeling that he must not move in case he frightened it away came over him. She said: "I'm sorry, Revd. Law. I'm so sorry about your wife."

Outside in the yard the children were getting cold. Two of the bigger girls, Laura Lizzie Fothergill and Annie Allinson, were not interested in snowball fights or making slides but had been talking about why the vicar might have come at such an odd time. "It seems funny she should turn us out like that, when it's so cold," said Laura. "Yes, and I wonder what they're doing in there all this time?" said Annie, "Could you give me a leg up and

I could peep through the window? What do you think?" "Yes, go on, let's" said Laura, "But I want a look too."

As Revd. Law sat, looking at Miss Dennison's hand, and she stood beside him looking concerned, the white face and blue hat of Annie popped up at the window for a moment or two and then Laura's pink cheeks framed by her green hat bobbed up.

"What did you see then?" asked Annie. "Well I think he was holding her hand. It looked like it anyway," said Laura. "That's what I thought too," said Annie.

John felt full of grief about his wife's condition but, as she lay immobile, staring and muttering to herself, day dragging into day, he had to continue with his work. He could not concentrate under a continual burden of sadness and guilt, so pushed the feelings away and carried on. The congregation was never very large but he felt a duty to those who came. Miss Dennison had passed her final teacher's certificate examination with merit and was now a qualified school mistress. He had thought this would be the end of her studies but she had asked if he would help her study for the Oxford Local Senior exam and he had happily agreed.

Revd. Law was her tutor in scripture, English literature, political economy, English history and arithmetic. It was nearly twenty years since he had studied and he felt it essential to keep one step ahead of his pupil so, with his wife ill and with winter gripping the natural world, he was busy in his study reading and preparing classes for Mary. She still called at the Vicarage three nights a week but now the lessons had been extended and lasted from six o'clock to around half past eight.

The days of February brought no relent from winter and the only times John felt happy were those when he could look forward to Mary's company in the evening. Often on the days when he was not expecting her, young Thomas Allinson would bring a note at lunchtime or playtime asking if she could borrow a book and, as winter finally loosened its grip, the first spring flowers began to blossom and sometimes Thomas would bring a flower, folded into an envelope, for him to identify.

At first Thomas would wait by the door and after a moment or two the vicar would reappear with the requested book or a note with the name of the flower. As the spring wore on Thomas began to think that it took the vicar longer to write his notes and, once he was sure there must be several pages inside the envelope, it was so thick. He thought it was funny too the way they both smiled at him. It wasn't the season for apples so the vicar would give a penny and often he would have to carry a little bunch of flowers which the vicar picked from his garden to give to Miss Dennison. He said to Thomas: "These are specimens of various species of plants for Miss Dennison. She might ask you children to identify them."

Thomas took the pennies home to his mother but, after the first two or three she asked him what was going on and he heard her talking to his father about the pennies. Thomas asked his friend Henry what he should do and Henry said the best thing would be to hide them. So Thomas started hiding them under the carpet runner on the stairs. The blue and red patterned carpet was held down by brass rods but it was easy to slip a penny under and nobody noticed.

Then one day the old teacher, Mr. Brown, was taken ill and Miss Dennison had to get the older children to help her take classes. Revd. Law offered to help until a new teacher could be found and he was in school almost every day. With the quick perception of children the meeting of eyes, the whispers, were never missed but neither were they fully understood. Two weeks later in October 1906 a new head teacher was appointed, a German scholar called Herr Ritzema. In the same month Mary was appointed school mistress at South Stainmore School. The children took to Herr Ritzema immediately. He was almost deaf and he loved painting. The children laughed at his accent and his classes were bedlam, with everyone shouting to be heard, but Herr Ritzema did not seem to mind. In his spare time Herr Ritzema wandered the fellsides with his easel and paints. He painted the farms and buildings and, when he brought the pictures into school to show the children they were thrilled to recognise their homes. A few months after the arrival of Herr Ritzema the governors decided it would be a good idea to have a school photograph.

One mild April morning the photographer arrived and there was great excitement. All the children in their best clothes, and so curious to see all the equipment the stranger had brought with him. Boxes were unloaded from his trap and it seemed to take an age to get everything put together.

John had walked down to see the preparations and stood in the school yard watching as the photographer fiddled with screws and tripods. He was tall and thin and kept taking off his cap and ducking under a black cloth to view. Then he'd come out, put his cap on, watched all the time by a curious crowd of faces and adjust the lens at the front. He set up a trail of flash powder in a special metal trough.

Finally the photographer said he was ready and set about arranging the children in rows with Miss Dennison at one end and Herr Ritzema with his ginger handlebar moustache at the other. "Now children, quiet please," shouted the photographer. "You must stay still and look at the camera all the time. Don't fidget, don't move and when I go under the cloth there will be a big flash, but just stay still."

The photographer disappeared under his black cloth and fumbled for a moment or two. Then he shouted: "Right now, keep still, here we go." The children looked frightened and stood stock still, not saying a word. Suddenly there was an enormous flash and a bang and everyone jumped then started to laugh, then remembered they were supposed to be still. John smiled as he watched and his thoughts were filled with how lovely Mary looked.

11
The Daily Mail - 1906/7

The months wore on and Ellen seemed to improve as spring turned into summer and the pattern of the seasons unrolled. John felt happier than he had for many years. Mary's studies were going well. She spent all her time either teaching or studying and gradually isolated herself even further from her former friends. She rarely saw Joe and, if they did chance to meet, they would exchange polite questions and hurry on.

As Christmas approached Herr Ritzema suggested the children should perform a nativity play. The vicar agreed it would be a good idea and Miss Dennison and Mrs. Cowper started making costumes. Even Ellen came down to the school to help. Everything went well and, on the night of the performance there was great excitement. Invitations had been written and sent out to everyone but as the audience were due to arrive only the parents turned up, and often just the mothers, leaving many seats empty.

Revd. Law stood at the back of the school room, transformed at one end into the holy stable with a star above painted onto a dark blue curtain Ellen had found. Mrs. Cowper stood nearby and the vicar asked: "There don't seem to be many people here. Have we chosen a bad night do you think?"

Mrs. Cowper rubbed her hands together and looked worried. "Well no. I think ...well the thing is, I have heard that Miss Alston-Dewbanke is not too pleased. You know she loves doing plays and concerts, and she had arranged one for January you know. I think that might be it."

"Oh that's a shame for the children. You'd think she'd have offered to come and help," said John, realising that they had somehow broken with tradition but thinking all the same what an effort Herr Ritzema, Mary, Ellen and Mrs. Cowper had made and how wonderful the children looked.

With half the chairs empty the play finally started and went off perfectly. Even Ellen seemed to be enjoying herself and smiled at him and clapped when the curtain finally closed. Afterwards John spoke to the children and said how well they had done and handed out oranges to each of them. He congratulated Mary and Herr Ritzema, then he and Ellen walked home, arm in arm. It was a frosty night with no moon, just thousands upon thousands of stars. They did not talk but, as they walked John felt as if he could hear God's universe, hear the cold music of the stars. He felt tiny but part of plan of the immensity.

The next morning frost sparkled on everything. Tiny gardens of frost had blossomed, like white lichen on the wood of the gate and as Fred Douthwaite set off from Skerrygill to go along and water his cattle his feet crunched on the icy ground. Where the sun had shone the frost was beginning to melt but the shadows were still white and his breath steamed in the cold air as he walked up the hill.

He had heard about the nativity play from Nancy. She had been one of the few to attend the school play and she had come home full of how the rumour was that Miss Alston-Dewbanke was put out about not being involved. Now this was a bit of gossip for his friend Tommy Nixon, for that matter he might know a bit more because his bairns were at the school.

Fred walked up the hill, his clogs clinking on the hard stones. He was wearing his old suit, tied round with bailer twine to keep everything together and on top of his waistcoat, an old herringbone coat with many holes in it where the lining showed through. On top of that he had his sack, tied over his shoulder like a cape and round his neck, with another bit of bailer twine which for

93

some reason was always called Michael.

Meg, the sheepdog followed behind, trotting from one side to the other but always behind. Suddenly she let out a low bark as down the hill came the vicar's wife with Rupert bounding in front. She was calling to the dog but it ignored her. Meg wasn't too interested in other dogs but Rupert was ready for a game, a fight, whatever action might be going. As Ellen Law came up she said: "Good morning" and Fred touched his cap and wished her a good morning too. She didn't stop but, shouting for the dog, continued off down the hill. Fred thought she looked a bit funny but you never could tell with folk like that, what they were thinking.

As he came near the church Fred could see Tommy waiting for him, sitting on their "bench" a fallen gate stoop lying beside the road. Clouds of smoke were already going up from his pipe and it promised to be a good crack this morning. Meg, knowing the routine, lay down to wait while Fred and Tommy set about their morning talk. For the last ten years or so this had been the ritual, as Fred walked to water his cattle at Gillses and Tommy walked to look at his sheep in a field up past the church.

"Now Fred, did ye hear aboot this nativity play last night then?" asked Tommy.

"Ay, ah did. Our Nancy was along. Did ye go?"

"No, ah didn't go meself, but the wife went because our Henry was one of t'shepherds."

Fred was busy packing the tobacco down in his pipe, a job that couldn't be rushed. They both waited considering what might be said next. The pipe prepared Fred struck a match and sucked until the bowl was alight and then, taking the pipe from his mouth, said: "Ah met Mrs. Law just now walking out with that big red dog. Ah can't understand it meself. She's always out walking with that dog."

"Ay," said Tommy. "She is. I heard that Miss Alston-Dewbanke is none too pleased about this play. She didn't go and apparently a lot of people stopped away. It was worse with her father being taken ill, that they did not consider to ask her. My Mrs. said she's cross because Camilla is the expert on plays and such like and they didn't even ask her."

"Well I heard something similar. That's what our Nancy said. She said the spot was nobbut half full. The vicar was there and his wife. And there was Miss Dennison and that new German teacher, whativver they call him, and one or two parents and that was all," said Fred. "Seems a bit of a shame like for the kids."

"Ay" said Tommy, pushing his cap back and scratching his head. "It's a bit of a queer carry on like. This vicar, well he is t'church parson, but he's a big heavy man. He's not much like a church parson. That's what I think."

"No thoo's right Tommy. He's not much like a parson and we nivver see much of Mrs. Law. Mebbe she's a gay bit older than him. They don't seem to see eye to eye as man and wife, with her always walking out with that big red dog." said Fred.

"My Mrs. says she hesn't any friends, bar Mrs. Cowper. Now last winter, ye remember them storms, well Mrs. Cowper was up at Vicarage every day and she says Mrs. Law was just laying in bed day after day but there was nowt wrong wi'her," said Tommy peering towards the Vicarage over in the trees as if he might be able to see through the walls.

"Ay, an' they've no family. Mebbe that's the trouble," said Fred, he sucked at his pipe for a time becoming aware that the frost on the stone was melting where he sat and the cold damp was coming through the layers of clothes. "Well I told ye last back end it would be," continued Fred, "I was spreading muck in a field next to t'vicarage there. It was a grand frosty day, just like today, and I saw that school teacher, Miss Dennison, come down the footpath and to the Vicarage wall. Now ye know how long it teks to spread a cart of muck, well I was there over an hour and Miss Dennison stood talking to the vicar all that time. He was leaning on the Vicarage wall. Now I don't know what they could have found to talk aboot all that time."

"Nay I can't say either. It's a funny carry on, that's all I know." said Tommy standing up, pushing his cap up and pulling it down harder on his head. "That school teacher is sek a bonny lass too. She used to walk out with young Joe didn't she? They made a nice pair did them two....Well I'd better go and see to me yows. I'll see yer tomorrow."

"Ay, see yer tomorrow." said Fred as he and Meg set off to walk along the lane past Upmanhowe to the hungry and thirsty cattle waiting in their stalls at Gillses.

Mary Dennison took an innocent pleasure in her growing friend-ship with the vicar. There was a single-minded purpose about her studies. Learning had become an end in itself. Her days were filled with the reality of the class room, her evenings and week-end with ideas and dreams beginning to form. She had read of women who went to university and above all else this was what she had decided she wanted. There were articles in the newspa-per about the Women's Suffrage movement, people laughed at them, but Mary took what they said seriously, though she was careful to keep this to herself.

She had told no one of her dream, not even her father. He wanted her to do well but asking him if she could go to univer-sity might be going too far. One day she had heard him talking about votes for women and saying that could never be right. Mary knew that the only way was to pass her Oxford Senior with flying colours and then apply for a scholarship. She would have to make her own way and could not rely on anyone else to help her. The only person who could help was John Law.

He was her tutor and the key to her dream. She enjoyed their evenings together. She liked talking to him and realised how well educated he was. She studied his gentlemanly manners and occa-sionally he would talk to her about Ellen's health and she was concerned for him. He was a father figure in her eyes, taking over where her own father's experience of life left off and John

Law was the way to take the ambitions, begun by her father, towards the goal she had set herself.

The idea that she might have married Joe now seemed ludicrous to her, she had nothing in common with him. She realised now that life with Joe would have been a short blissful honeymoon and then grinding hard work. Mary wanted something better. She had not travelled further than Darlington or Carlisle, but she knew that out there, past the distant horizon were places of culture like London, Paris or New York, places where women were not chained to fulfil the role of their mothers. As part of their study of political economy, Revd. Law had got hold of some of the suffragette pamphlets from his sister in Manchester. Mary had read these, keeping them secret from her father and step-mother, and at once she had recognised kindred thoughts, women who were like herself.

This knowledge gave her the strength to go on. She would meet friends like Maggie and a distance began to creep into their conversation. She would say the things she knew she was supposed to say, while thinking something completely different, but both would know that she was not telling the whole truth. The further she withdrew from the friends of her own age, the less sympathy there was between them. On the surface with her girl friends this meant nothing more than an insincere conversation.

With the boys it was different. Joe was angry with her and jealous of her studying. He had cut her from his thoughts but when he saw her it still hurt. His friends' reaction was different. One or two of them began to talk of her in leery whispers. Jim Boldron especially talked of her fine ways and her figure but how she was no different underneath. Jim was a wiry young man, not tall but strong as steel. He lived with his widowed father Anthony, the signalman at Barras Station, who went for the midwife the night Mary was born.

One night, as Jim was walking home from the Slip Inn where he had drunk several pints, he saw Mary coming away from the Vicarage and taking the footpath back to the station. It was a

97

moonlit night and he could see she was carrying a parcel under her arm. They were both alone and the gossip from the pub echoed in his ears. He had to follow Mary up the footpath towards his father's house near the station and he studied her shape as she walked a hundred yards or so in front of him. He watched the way her hips moved under her skirt and her tiny waist. When he came to the path leading off towards the Railway Cottages he decided not to take it but to follow her.

He got closer and, realising there was someone behind, she turned and saw him only a few yards behind. She turned and walked quicker, he walked quicker. Panic began to rise in her throat and she started to run. Jim ran too and catching her by the arm said: "I've been watching you, Miss high and mighty. You think you're too good for Joe but he's too good for you. You know that." Mary wanted to scream but just looked up at him. He bent and gave her a kiss that smelled of beer and his hand gripped tight around her waist. "Let me go, let me go, or I'll tell your father you stupid....let me go." Mary struggled and wriggled and finally he let her go. He stood and laughed loud as she stumbled off up the footpath. He laughed and laughed until she disappeared beneath the gloom of the trees near Calva House.

Other men thought of Mary. Tommy Nixon, though a married man with six children, shared Jim Boldron's thoughts. He had begun to think of her differently after his daughter Annie said something about seeing the vicar holding Mary's hand. Tommy did not rationalise the way he felt but, as he went to feed his sheep he could not help thinking about her as he often saw her walking to and from school, or up to the Vicarage. She was always friendly and stopped to say hello and to chat about how Henry was getting on at school. He would listen carefully to her words but as he looked at her pretty face he thought of his youth. She reminded him of his wife when she had been a girl. Her grey eyes, her clear skin and her laugh.

He thought of her when he heard the curlew cry in spring and saw the lapwings crazy flutter. He thought of her as he sat long hours watching to make sure the lambs were born safely. He thought of her when he put the tup in with the ewes in autumn. In the long slow hours of milking his cows, he thought of her as he leaned against the heavy strong warmth of the beasts. She made him feel alive again, even young, and he would notice things like the sunset or the snow glinting on fells far away. He never once mentioned these things to Fred when they met each morning. These thoughts were the only secret he kept from the "Daily Mail".

12
The Empty Church and the Chicken Man - 1907

S ummer's golden days ripened in a harvest of copper, yellow and rust coloured leaves, a defiant display of colour against the oncoming winter. As Christmas approached blizzards blew and hard frosts kept the snow on the ground for many days. 1907 was drawing to a close but this year Mrs. Alston-Dewbanke, not to be out done by the deaf German and the silly young teacher studying so much that no man would marry her, had planned a theatrical extravaganza. The stars of the show were naturally Gerald and Camilla and the production was to be staged at North Stainmore school.

Despite the deep snow and bitter cold everyone turned out for the entertainment which included musical items, sketches, a short play by the school children and a poetry reading by Mrs. Alston-Dewbanke. The school was packed with warm bodies and, as well as parents and friends, Dr. John Abercrombie and his wife, from Augill Castle, had come, as had Revd. Lyde from Brough. Dr. Abercrombie was well known in medical circles and had been a specialist in children's medicine in London before he retired. Now his main interest was local history and he had quickly become a stalwart of the Cumberland and Westmorland Antiquarian and Archeological Society.

After the show was over there was much excitement and everyone stayed for tea, sandwiches and home-made cakes. Dr. Alston-Dewbanke managed to get Dr. Abercrombie in a corner and, pulling his hip flask out, they sneaked sips of brandy together as Dr. Alston-Dewbanke quizzed his friend about how the latest research in children's medicine might be applied to young horses.

There were one or two glaring gaps in the audience and Mrs.

Alston-Dewbanke had noted them with strong disapproval. She could understand why Herr Ritzema and Miss Dennison hadn't come - they wouldn't want to have their last year's nativity play upstaged by this much more lively event. But there was no forgiving the vicar, whether his wife was ill or not. Even Revd. Lyde had come up all the way from Brough and this wasn't even his parish. Mrs. Alston-Dewbanke didn't let her annoyance spoil her enjoyment but this was something she couldn't forget. It really was an insult to the children, especially to Gerald and Camilla who had been so splendid.

John knew he should have gone to the North Stainmore extravaganza but he really couldn't face it on his own. Ellen was in a dreadful state again, now the snow had come. She wandered around the house in her night clothes, never cooked or cleaned up and forgot to eat. She talked to herself most of the time and these days she didn't stop when other people came to the house. Her condition had become an embarrassment to John and he dared not take her to a gathering. He did not know what she might say. He didn't even take her down to church anymore because she wouldn't sit in her pew. The last time she was in church she just wandered around the whole time and kept saying the kneelers needed darning.

He did not know where to turn. Dr. Alston-Dewbanke had been over once to see Ellen but had just said she was as fit as a fiddle and he could find nothing wrong with her. Young Dr. Bainbridge had said the same the year before. There was no one else to ask so John just managed as well as he could and kept his wife away from social gatherings of any sort. During the summer she had spent hours walking with Rupert and this seemed to help her but now the winter was here she spent all her time in the house and gradually became more and more lost in some private world.

John thought he would have broken down himself if it had not been for Mary. Her visits brought joy to his life and took him away from the worries and concerns about his wife's health.

Mary's studies were going well and in the spring she would sit her Oxford Local Senior exam. John felt sure she would pass with flying colours. She was so bright. She grasped ideas and remembered concepts so well. He had always considered many of these things beyond women but Mary was proving him wrong every step of the way.

Since the incident with Jim Boldron, John had made it a habit to walk Mary home after the study session ended. Mary had been greatly upset by the incident and, especially when the nights were dark, she was frightened to walk home in case he should attack her again. Jim Boldron had enjoyed frightening her and bragged about it to his friends in the Slip Inn. He knew which days she had her class with the vicar and he knew what time they usually finished and he started to make a habit of walking home from the pub at a similar time so that he might catch her out again.

Jim Boldron would often see the vicar and Miss Dennison walking home together and he would follow them up towards the station but he could never quite hear what they were saying as they walked along together. Jim's father, Anthony, was the signalman at Barras. He was a widower and had lived for many years in one of the railway cottages near the station. Often Jim would follow the pair up the hill, see them talk for a moment at the station house gate and then the vicar would turn away and head back down the hill.

Jim would carry on up to his father's house. He didn't mention that he had been following the vicar and the school teacher but would just sit and have a cup of tea with his father and they would talk about work or things that were going on or nothing much at all. One day in late winter there was a snowstorm but, as the day went on the wind dropped and the snow fell more slowly and quietly until, as evening fell it stopped altogether. Anthony was a keen gardener and had a greenhouse not far from the station and decided to go out to check that the storm had not done any damage to the glass.

He was expecting Jim home as usual around about eleven o'clock, but there was time just to have a quick look over at the green house before he arrived. He pulled down his big coat and looking out of the door decided he didn't need the hurricane lantern. The sky had cleared and it was a full moon and, with the snow it was eerily bright outside. As he went down the station road he noticed some footprints. One pair were large and the others were smaller, a woman's size.

Suddenly he heard voices and about 300 yards away saw two people coming towards the station. He realised it was the vicar and Mary Dennison. They seemed to be deep in conversation and had not seen him. Instead of continuing to the green house he found himself dropping down behind a wall. He didn't know why he hid. It was a sort of instinctive thing. The top of the wall was covered in snow and gently he scraped a hole in the snow so that he could see the pair. They were closer now and, as they came to the wicket gate that led up to the station they stopped and faced each other. He could see them as clear as day, the moon was so bright, and then, he could not believe it, the vicar took hold of Mary's shoulders, bent towards her and kissed her. He kissed her again and then the vicar turned and strode off down the hill. Anthony Boldron stayed hunched behind the wall hardly daring to breath. After a minute or so he stood up. The vicar was nowhere to be seen but he could see the station master's house and Mrs. Dennison standing in the doorway looking out as Mary hurried inside.

Anthony stood and wondered at what he had seen and soon he saw the figure of Jim coming up the hill following the footsteps he had noticed so innocently fifteen minutes ago. Things seemed to have changed now. Perhaps his eyes had deceived him or what was happening? He hurried off down to meet Jim.

"Jim, Jim, wait," he called.

Jim stopped and looking round saw his father's face and realised that he knew. "Jim have you seen the vicar tonight?"

"Ay" said Jim, "I see him most nights with that Mary

Dennison."

"But what do they do? I've just seen them and I'm sure, well I think they were kissing."

"Ay, likely they were. I've been following them now most of this winter. I've not told anybody but I've kept a book of the times I've seen them together. Once I saw them going into that old derelict house together, you know, at Calva. It was in a snowstorm. But it ain't right. Joe's best off without that one."

"Well no wonder Mrs. Dennison looked so worried tonight. Do you think they know, her parents like?"

"I don't think anyone knows just me and you as well now. A few have suspicions." said Jim.

"Well come on in and get warmed up. I'll make a pot of tea. I was just going down to see the green house to make sure there was no damage you know, when I heard their voices. I couldn't believe it. Do you know Jim, I think the best thing is if we just keep this to ourselves like. We'd best not say anything to anyone. Do you know, I've known that girl since the day she was born. I was there in fact, her father sent me for the midwife and it was a wild night and then her mother died you know. That was a terrible do was that and the Station Master you know he was beside himself and, you know, he thinks the world of Mary. There could be a lot of trouble over this, a lot of trouble."

The strange incident made Anthony Boldron think of something else too. He had never told Jim that he was not his father but his uncle. He could never think of the right words to start to tell him that his brother Harold had got a girl pregnant and he, being married, had taken the child in. It was all so long ago but sometimes he would worry that Jim would find out and might go off the rails. Often Anthony would practice what he was going to say but, when face to face with his nephew/son he could never get the words out. Sometimes he would talk to his brother about it but Harold would just shrug his shoulders and say: "Well ah'll be leaving him me house and the fields. What more can ah do?"

Harold Boldron, spent most of his Sundays in his hen house.

He was a keen poultry fancier and he had various breeds of game - partridge wyandottes, leghorns and buff orpingtons. He had kept poultry since he was a boy and had become fascinated in breeding the perfect specimens. When he wasn't in his hen house he was at work, on the railway, or mending clocks. He had never married but kept himself busy with his hobbies.

It was April, a month since his brother had seen the vicar and the teacher kissing, but Harold had heard nothing about it. He had set two lots of eggs and they were due to hatch on a Sunday. He always tried to set the eggs on a Sunday so that, when they hatched three weeks later, he'd have time to sort out new coops for the chickens. He was busy cleaning out a pen and putting fresh sawdust in ready for the chicks. From the cobweb covered window of his hen house he could see the church. A little earlier he had seen the vicar going in. He heard the bell ring and saw the slight figure of Mary Dennison hurrying down the lane towards the church.

After a little while he thought it was peculiar because nobody else came. After about an hour the vicar and the school teacher left and walked up the road towards the Vicarage together. Harold came out of the hen house into the mild spring air and watched as they walked off up the road. Not far away Fred Douthwaite and Tommy Nixon were sitting in their usual spot and he could see puffs of smoke coming up from their pipes as they sat huddled in conversation.

Harold decided to walk over and ask them about the church. He was curious as to why nobody had gone except the vicar and the school teacher. The Daily Mail greeted him with: "Hello, how is ter, Harold?"

"Ay, I'm well thank you. I've just been up at the hen house. I've some wyandottes hatching today. While I was there, you know, I heard the church bell ring but, do you know, nobody went except the vicar and the school teacher. I was thinking that's a bit funny isn't it? Where's everybody at?"

"Well," said Fred, "We've been asking ourselves that."

105

"Ay," said Tommy, sucking on his pipe, "We've noticed once or twice there's been nobody at church. Sometimes Miss Dennison's parents come but I believe they're away at Darlington this weekend."

"Do you know the vicar comes twice a day on a Sunday to ring that bell but nobody goes to church anymore. There's weeds starting to spring up atween the flag stones of t'path so few feet pass ower it these days." said Fred.

"Well it's a queer carry on if you ask me," said Harold "Mebbe I'll keep an eye on them from the hen house. You know I can see the church from the window. If I see anything worth telling you, I'll pop down again. Anyway I'd better be getting back, as I say, I've got these wyandottes hatching."

"Ay, well we'd better be off too. All this talk doesn't get the beasts fed." The three men all set off in different directions, each with their own curiosity fired about what was going on between the vicar and the school teacher.

Later that day Harold walked home to make himself some dinner. He cut some cold meat and buttered some bread. He was still thinking about the empty church when there was a knock at the door. He went to open it and there was Mary Dennison. Harold felt himself blushing as if she might guess what he had been thinking.

"Hello," he said.

"Hello Mr. Boldron," said Mary "I was just wondering. Do you mend watches as well as clocks? I was at church this morning and I noticed my watch had stopped and I don't want to over wind it. Would you be able to have a look at it for me?"

"Ay, yes I can have a look at it." he said, looking her up and down.

"Well, thank you. How long do you think it will take to mend it?"

"I can have a look this afternoon if you like, after dinner. Can you call back around four o'clock?"

"Yes" she said "I'll do that. Thank you."

He watched as she walked quickly away. She was wearing a green dress with one of those fancy hats and, as she walked across the yard she held her skirt up slightly so that it wouldn't get muddy. After his cold bachelor dinner Harold sat down at his table in front of the window and took the back off the watch. As he thought, it just needed a bit of a clean and he soon had it working again. He went down to check on his hens and was back in good time before Miss Dennison called again. He watched as she came down the path over the fields and towards the house. She was wearing the same green dress and she picked up her skirt again as she came across the yard. He went to the door and opened it before she knocked.

"Hello, Miss Dennison," he said "Come on in. I've managed to fix your watch. It just needed a clean you know."

"Oh, thank you," said Mary "How much do I owe you?"

"Come on in and I'll get it for you." he said.

She followed him into the untidy kitchen. The plates and remains of food from his dinner were still set out on the table.

"Here you are, look, as good as new." Harold handed her the watch and, as she reached to take it, he gripped her hand and would not let go.

"Please, you're hurting me. Let go." Mary wrestled to free her hand.

"I was wondering" said Harold, looking down at her, "whether we should forget payment. I was wondering if maybe you're the sort of girl that might like to come up to my cabin on the railway one day when there's nobody else about. How about it, eh?"

"Let go of me, let go of me. Of course I won't come to your cabin." Mary tried to hold back the panic in her voice and the tears which filled her eyes as she struggled. "Look, if you don't let go of me, I'll tell my father and he'll get you sacked. Let me go."

Harold released his grasp and smirking at her said: "Well I must have been mistaken. I thought you were that sort of a girl. That'll be 6d for the watch repair."

107

Mary struggled in her purse to find the money and hurried to be out of the house. She hated these people. What were they all thinking of? First Jim Boldron grabbing her and now his uncle making suggestions. How dare they? She was angry, frightened and sobbing all at the same time. She had her exams in a few weeks time and all this trouble was the last thing she wanted. She would tell Revd. Law what had happened, he would protect her from these people. He would understand how cruel they could be.

Harold Boldron had a couple of fields. One where he kept his hen house near the church and another further up the hill and nearer to his house, where he kept a few sheep. In the latter field there was a stile and the sheep kept getting out into one of Thomas Cowper's fields where he was letting the grass grow for hay. Harold decided to put a few stones in the stile to block it up but it puzzled him because someone kept moving the stones and the sheep kept getting out again.

It happened once or twice that the stones were moved and every time Harold put them back again. One night he decided to hide behind a wall and watch to see who was moving the stones. He took one stone out of the wall so he could look through and had a good view of the stile. He had a good idea who the culprit might be and about half past nine he was rewarded by the sight of the vicar and the school teacher walking towards the stile. The vicar seemed to have his arm around her waist. "So there is something in it", thought Harold. When they got to the stile they didn't touch the stones but the vicar helped Mary Dennison over and as she jumped down the other side he held his hands up to catch her and, for a moment longer than necessary, held onto her.

"Well, wait till I tell the Daily Mail about this. That'll give them some real gossip to chew on. No wonder nobody goes to church. I never did like that vicar, too high and mighty for me." thought Harold as he stretched himself straight and walked off home.

Jim Boldron continued to collect his evidence too. His notebook was well thumbed and on every single day there was an entry with the time and date. He had become obsessed by the affair. He had said to his father he would tell nobody but one Sunday evening he was out walking with William Hill. They happened to be coming along past the church as evening service was finishing. They saw Mr. and Mrs. Cowper come out, James and Nancy Dennison came out too, along with Mary and they set off to walk home.

Jim and William continued to walk up the road past the Vicarage. They got to the top of the hill and decided to turn around to walk back. It would be opening time by now at the Slip Inn so they would walk back and have a pint and maybe a game of dominoes. They were surprised to see the figure of a woman going back towards the church. Jim said: "Did you see that? That was Mary Dennison. What's she doing going back at t'church?"

"Ay, I saw her. I thought she'd gone home with her parents. But where's the vicar?" asked William.

"Well, he must still be in the church, mustn't he? Come on let's go and have a look." said Jim.

As they got closer to the church they could see there were no lights inside. "Let's hop over this wall and wait to see what happens," whispered Jim. The two young men crouched behind the wall and Jim got out his notebook. "What's that?" asked William.

"It's a book. Well I may as well tell you, since you've seen with your own eyes now."

"Seen what?" asked William.

"Seen the vicar and Mary Dennison. I've been watching them now for six months or so and it's getting worse. It started one night when I just happened to be following Mary, by accident, like. Since then I've seen them out together countless times. That's why hardly anyone goes to church any more. They all sort of know, but nobody's really said anything. Everyone's too frightened to say anything." said Jim.

"Well I didn't know" said William, "but it explains a lot. It explains all that studying and why the vicar's wife is so funny and why Mary threw over Joe, because she and Joe, well we all thought they'd be married once over."

After about half an hour they heard the church door opening. There was still no light in the building. They waited for a few minutes and then risked peering over the wall. They could see John Law and Mary Dennison walking close together away from the church.

"Let's go down to the Slip. I need a drink" declared William. "I can't believe my eyes. I'll have to tell Joe about this. We'll have to do something."

"But what will we do?" asked Jim. "We can't tell the police, what would they do?"

When they got to the pub old Isaac was already settled into his seat by the smokey fire, where he had the luxury to sit every Sunday night. Christopher Fothergill from High Ewbank was there and Thomas Johnstone, but Joe hadn't come down to the pub yet. He wasn't a great drinker and often didn't come down until late. Mrs. Pounder served Jim and William their pints of ale and then they went to sit with Isaac and their friends.

Isaac greeted them with his old joke: "I'd buy thee a pint but thoo'd nivver sup it," even though they already had their beers. Once they were sat down they told Isaac and the others what they had seen.

"What do you think Isaac? Do you know anything about this?" asked William.

Isaac laughed: "Well t'other day when it was blowing a right storm, rain and wind. Well it was such a bad day I thought I'd wait and give old Ted Peacock a lift from the mine. You know we've been friends a long time. I've known him since Alice and me moved in to the cottages under the chapel there. He has always been a good neighbour even though he's tee-total."

Isaac never told a story fast. He would hand out so much information and then stop and stare at the fire for a while or re-fill his pipe. People who didn't know him thought he'd lost the thread of his story or just forgotten but really the silence was for dramatic effect. Isaac knew exactly how long to leave it and then would pick up his words again.

"As I said, it was a cold, wet day and, as we come down under the railway bridge we saw t'vicar and Mary Dennison walking in a field. They had one of those umbrella things and he was holding it over her. Now I had had a pint or two you know up at Tanhill before I set off, just for sustenance like. And well, I thought it must have been the beer and my eyes but it looked like he bent to kiss her under this umbrella." There was another long silence and he took several gulps of beer. The four young men waited knowing this wasn't the end of the story yet.

"Well," said Isaac, "I said to Ted, you know he's as tee-total as a chapel minister. Well I said to him: 'That vicar looks awfully familiar with that young woman. Or was it my eyes?' "

" 'No,' says Ted, 'I'll tell thee sommat. You know that you go to the pub of a night. Well I go to Chapel. Now when there's not Chapel on well I walk up to the station of a night. You see, when I was a lad there weren't any trains and I like to go up and sit and watch the last train come through. It's nice and warm up there in the waiting room. They've always got a roaring fire so it saves coal at home. Well I sit up there and I talk to whoivver's about and I wait until the last train's gone through and then I know it's time to come home to bed. Now often when I'm there Mrs. Dennison is hovering about and looking down the hill to see where Mary's got to. Sometimes she's back before I go but many a time she's not and it's always the vicar walks her home. So I know about it. I've nivver said owt, but I know. I've never seen them kiss afore, but that's what they were doing. As certain as ah'll be at Chapel on Sunday.' "

13
A small boy tells God

In June 1908 Mary Dennison passed her Oxford local senior exam with merit. She was delighted and John felt very proud of his student. She really was very special to him. His life had gone into something of a dream. There seemed to be two distinct parts to reality - one was the awfulness of his wife's illness. Everything which involved Ellen was darkness and depression. Then there was the light and happiness of his friendship with Mary.

John kept the two things separate and could see no way of reconciling them. He felt powerless to change anything. He could not leave his wife. He had to be loyal to her even though his life with her was a terrible mess. He could not stop seeing Mary because seeing her brought him happiness to cope with the darkness of his wife's mental state. It seemed that God balanced things and, the deeper his wife fell into depression the more intense was the joy inspired by Mary.

Mary had started to study for her final certificate so another two years of study stretched before her. John was happy at the prospect of her continuing desire to study because it meant he could see her every day. It was an innocent excuse to continue their relationship which he knew in his heart had become much more than just teacher and student. He dreaded the day when she passed her final exam because he knew then she would be gone. She still dreamed of university and it was quite possible she could go. The only problem would be finding the finances to pay for her education.

John had thought about this and had decided that, if she really did love him, as he loved her, when the time came for her to leave, he would go with her. He would make sure Ellen was alright. He would take her back to her mother and this would make her happy. Then he would just disappear south with Mary and help her get through university. He knew this would mean he would have to give up the church but he could find work of some other sort. If Mary loved him then surely this would bring them both happiness. They would have to be patient, more patient than he had ever been in his life, but he felt sure that God would give them his blessing and understand. Perhaps, even further in the future, he and Mary could leave the country, once she had got her degree. Maybe they could go to Canada or Australia where no one would know their past. He began to feel that God had sent Mary to him to show him how to escape the weight of his circumstances.

He didn't speak to Mary about any of this because he was not certain what she wanted. She was 22 now and her whole life stretched before her. He knew she trusted him and he felt he was her protector, especially with some of these loutish young men around following her when she walked home. If he got his hands on them he would have some stern words for them. They had no respect. He was disappointed that so few people came to church. The enthusiasm he had had when he first came to the parish had drained somewhat and he had come to accept that they were either ardent chapel folk or heathens. He had tried his best to persuade them to come to church and for a time his congregation had numbered a dozen or more, but even these now seemed to have dwindled away.

He would continue with his work but he also had to protect and teach Mary. He had to continue as there was nothing else he could do. He couldn't force people to go to church, but with men like Harold Boldron who made indecent proposals to young girls, well what could you do? He had to protect Mary and then they could both escape to some place where people would leave them alone.

One Sunday in summer Mary's parents were going over to Darlington again to visit relatives. Mary had said she wouldn't

113

go and came down to church as usual. John and Mary were the only people in church. She played the organ and they both sang the hymns. He said the prayers and she read the lesson. Often their eyes would meet but the service went on and, when the final hymn was finished John went over to thank Mary.

"Mary, dearest, I don't know what to do about this. What can we do when nobody comes to church but us?"

"I really don't know what we can do except just carry on." she replied.

"Yes, you're right. It upsets me though that people are so Godless. Look, if your parents are away, shall we meet this afternoon? It's such a perfect day we could have a picnic tea together somewhere. What do you think?"

"Yes that would be nice. But what about Ellen?" asked Mary.

"Well you know how it is. She won't want to come. I've tried everything with her. There's really no hope for her unless perhaps she went back to her mother's for a time. Where shall we meet then?"

"Up in Pratt's wood, that's about half-way isn't it. I'll make some sandwiches and some tea. What time shall we meet?" she asked.

"About two o'clock?"

"Yes, I'll see you then." It had become a habit for them to kiss, just briefly, like father and daughter, when they met or parted. The kiss itself was innocent but behind it lay a sea of passion, dammed up and held back. It was the same if by accident their skin should touch. If her hand should touch his he could feel the hairs on his arms tingle. There was so much pleasure to be with her sometimes he could not bear it yet also he felt it was fated, a gift from God. This was how he rationalised his emotions. God must want him to know about this love otherwise it would not be happening.

Later in the afternoon, as he walked up the fields towards Pratt's wood he felt things would be alright in the end. He whistled a hymn and marvelled at the snowy mountains of cloud in the bluest of skies. It was perfect. He felt happiness was a very short and sweet sensation and had to be taken while it lasted. Like a flower, happiness opened up before you, but you knew it would soon have to close and die. The only thing was to enjoy God's creation as it was here and now. They were glimpses of heaven and they strengthened his faith.

As he came to the wood he did not notice Harold Boldron hidden among the hazel bushes. Harold had not been hiding intentionally. He had come out to get some pea sticks for his garden and was busy cutting them with his knife when his dog growled. Looking up he saw John Law striding into the wood from the vicarage pasture smiling and waving his hand. Coming the other way, down through the wood, was Mary Dennison with a basket over her arm. She was smiling too. He saw them shake hands when they met and then the vicar seemed to bend down towards her before they walked off into the woods, arm in arm.

Down at Mouthlock Chapel, the afternoon session of Sunday School was just starting. The chapel had a new preacher, a Welshman called Edward Jones. The children were terrified of him but fascinated at the same time. He was the son of a Welsh coal miner. He had worked down the pits for a time but then felt the call to the ministry. He had been to a college down in Lancashire and then had gradually moved north until he came to Stainmore. There was something like home about this place and he felt he could settle here.

Edward Jones was a small man, thick set, with dark hair and an intense face. When he smiled it didn't seem as if he was happy, it was more just a lightness between two thunderous statements. His whole life was his religion, from the moment he climbed out of bed to pray until the prayer he said before he climbed back into bed at night. He wanted to bring religion alive for people and the best place to start was the children, so he made

115

his Sunday School as lively as he could.

This was only his third Sunday School on Stainmore but he was pleased to see more and more children were coming. Already his methods were working and the parents approved of his strong words of salvation for the good and eternal hellfire for those who strayed from God's path. Most of the children came to the morning and afternoon Sunday Schools and most of them walked home for their dinner in between. The morning session had been taken up with Edward Jones' favourite subject - sin. His eyes sparkled and his arms flew around in the air as he talked about sin, sinners and redemption. He asked the children to list the ten commandments and he wrote them down on a black board one by one in strong capital letters.

"Laura Fothergill, tell me a commandment,"

"Thou shalt not kill"

"Good, now, Annie Allinson tell me another,"

"Thou shalt not covet thy neighbour's things, I think,"

"That's right,"

"Thomas Allinson, can you tell me one?"

Thomas blushed bright red and shuffled his Sunday clogs under his seat. His mind had gone blank and he couldn't think of anything at all. "Thomas?"

There was a long silence while Thomas sat and looked at his fingers. His friend Henry Nixon poked him in the side and whispered: "Steal". Thomas looked up and said: "Steal, Sir."

"Very good Thomas and Henry, Thou shalt not steal."

Edward Jones was in his element and the lesson was like a dramatic performance. First he would talk very quietly so that all the children sat forward on their seats so that they could hear what he was saying then suddenly he would boom out his message so that they all jumped.

When dinner time came the children were glad to get out of the Chapel so they could let off some steam on the way home. Young Thomas Allinson stayed behind because it was too far to walk all the way to Tufton Lodge and back. His big sister Annie went off with one of her friends and Thomas was left alone with the minister.

"Well Thomas, find somewhere to sit and eat your dinner. I'm brewing some tea, would you like some?"

"Yes, please, sir. Thank you." said Thomas nervous at being left alone with the Chapel minister.

He sat towards the back of the room and looked around while he ate his sandwiches. The new minister had put up lots of pictures with angels and things. One showed a lady with white all draped around her walking along a path with no shoes on and underneath it said: "Though I walk through the valley I will fear no evil." She was clutching something that looked like a book and there were rays of light shining down on her. Thomas thought it was a very nice picture.

There was another one with strange flowers on it, all sort of wound around, and in fancy writing it said: "The love of Christ which passeth knowledge." The minister had gone out somewhere at the back to make the tea and Thomas sat and pondered the pictures. The lady looked a bit like his teacher, Miss Dennison. He had been worrying about his teacher and all the notes she wrote. He had to go to the Vicarage almost every day and the vicar always gave him something to take back for Miss Dennison.

He gave Thomas a penny every time too and, at first, he had given these to his mother but then he had started to hide them under the stairs carpet. It was a red and blue carpet with a pattern on with brass rods to hold it back against the stairs and it didn't quite meet at the edges so it was easy to push a penny under. But there were so many pennies under the carpet now they were beginning to show marks on the carpet where people had stood on them and he knew his mother would find them soon and he would be in trouble. He wasn't sure why.

Thomas put his hands together and found himself saying a prayer. "Dear God, I'm not quite sure how to make up a prayer but I expect it'll be alright if I just say it. I want to know if I

117

should stop taking the letters from Miss Dennison to the vicar and the flowers from the vicar to Miss Dennison. Is it wrong God? I don't want to do anything wrong because of what Mr. Jones says. I don't want hellfire God. Can you give me a sign or something so I know what to do God. Is it one of the commandments they're doing or is it alright? I don't know God and Henry doesn't either. All I know is I've got an awful lot of pennies hidden and I'm worried my mother will find them. I hope you won't mind too much God, because I didn't know I was doing wrong...."

Half a mile away in Pratt's wood, the vicar and the school teacher were walking together hand in hand. A cool spring breeze picked up and Mary shivered. The little boy's prayer passed by unheard. Closer still, in the next room, a curious Edward Jones had finished brewing the tea and hearing the boy's voice had come to stand by the door so he could hear more clearly. When it seemed the boy had finished and was sitting quietly eating a piece of gingerbread. Edward came back in with the pot of tea. He poured the tea out and gave Thomas a cup. As they sat and ate their dinner they talked about their families and Edward told Thomas what it was like down a coal mine. He wasn't so frightening when he just talked about ordinary things thought Thomas. In fact he seemed quite nice really.

As the other children started to come back in, Edward said: "Thomas, if ever you're worried about anything, you know, you can always confide in me." Thomas thought it might be the sign from God.

14
Ellen Runs Away

For the next few months eyes watched the vicar and the school teacher wherever they went and whatever they did but nothing was said. People hardly talked among themselves about what they were beginning to believe was going on - the idea was too incredible. For a time there was a suspension of belief, people thought that the worst could not be true and it must be that the pair were innocent.

Nonetheless rumours had crept into people's minds, there were whispers and giggles. A few people who had seen the pair kissing with their own eyes were sure they were having an affair and some who held a grudge against either the vicar or the school teacher were more willing to believe and to embroider what they had seen or heard.

Some had heard the rumours but had made no decisions, either one way or the other. They were waiting for more proof or something to happen. A few were not prepared to see what was happening under their own eyes and continued to deceive themselves. The truth proved a difficult concept to pin down and depended on which angle it was seen from.

Even John and Mary, who were at the centre of the suspicions, were deceiving themselves. They believed their relationship was an innocent friendship based on teaching and learning as it had been when they first met. This set of words described a safe situation. They had not noticed how emotions had crept up and enveloped them as a mist rising on a frosty morning. John saw himself as a married man, an upright and honest vicar, who looked after his parish conscientiously. He believed himself incapable of being unfaithful to his wife. He felt his love for Mary was more like the love he might have felt for a daughter.

Mary saw herself as an aspiring young teacher, looking for better things in life. She had grown to respect John more than anyone she had ever known. He was intelligent, kind and absolutely on her side. She did not think anything of him being so much older than herself. Her own father had married a woman 20 years younger. In fact the age difference attracted her and she began to feel that, if she was ever to marry, she would marry someone like John. She never let herself think that she was in love with him, because he was a married man, but, in a part of her mind where there are no questions or debates, she knew she loved him.

On both sides the surface innocence of their meetings allowed them to sink deeper and deeper in their own private worlds, into an unspoken love. They would walk along the lane up past Rampson to where the wild garlic grew, the scent so strong they could taste it on the air. They would walk in the woods along the Argill Beck where the ground was a haze of bluebells and the path starred with wood anemones and primroses. In the height of summer when the beck ran dry, withdrawing to some deep limestone passage beneath the ground, they walked along the path of the river through the gorge, searching for wild ferns. A touch, a look, were all that were needed to keep the fire burning on either side, but the words were never spoken so that, what everyone else was beginning to see from the outside, had not been admitted on the inside, so could still be denied in their minds if not in their hearts.

The tangled web of intrigue deepened over the winter of 1908 when Stainmore was a hard place with the winter blizzards ravaging and blowing from the east, the snow knifing past and only stopping if it found a crevice to dig its claws into. Many sheep died in deep drifts that winter and farming people had little time to consider much apart from keeping themselves and their stock alive until the spring when the sun finally turned its gaze to these high meadows.

The bitterness of the winter drove Ellen ever deeper and further apart from her husband. When she had first become depressed she had known why and could rationalise with herself. This didn't usually make her feel any better but at least she felt there was some sense in what was happening. During that last long cold winter when she would wake up to find drifts of snow across the kitchen where it had blown under the door, she realised she had lost her ability to rationalise. She was terrified she was going mad.

She kept dreaming she was standing on the edge of a cliff, dressed only in her nightdress. There was a terrible storm blowing and it kept buffeting her first towards the edge and then away from it. Somewhere there were some twigs, which she could just reach with her fingers, but she already knew they were not strong enough to hold her when she began to fall. She always woke from the nightmare just as she realised at last that she was falling.

Ellen had long since given up the struggle to make the Vicarage into a home. Nothing had worked out right. None of the curtains she had brought fitted properly and she had been unable to alter them. However much she moved the furniture around it always looked wrong. The damp still came through the walls leaving the whitewash permanently stained yellow. She had given up. Nobody came to see her and nobody here would understand or appreciate the town fashion she had tried to bring to her home. Almost everything here was utilitarian, except for maybe a few flowers in the gardens. She thought to herself, what good is a home of my own when there's no love in it?

Ellen no longer bothered to sit in the study when Mary Dennison came. She had tired of the long discussions on philosophy, mathematics or literature. She realised listening to the pair only deepened her depression and emphasised her isolation so she kept to her own room. She held conversations in her head with imaginary friends and she found she no longer cared whether John was well or not.

The harshness of that winter drove her to despair. She wanted to rage and smash things, to shout and laugh, but she could not

121

work out why she should do anything. She could not remember who she used to be. Then something clicked inside her head, as if someone had lit a lantern, in a darkened room. She suddenly saw the way her husband touched Mary Dennison's shoulder as he helped her to put on her coat when she was leaving. She saw clearly how his hand lingered on her shoulder.

He would put on his own coat, his hat and his gloves and would then toss some words over his shoulder towards her: "I'm just seeing Mary home." Then the door would open. In blew some snowflakes and the door would shut and they were gone. Again and again she would see the look of betrayal on John's face as he stood beside Mary when the King came to Brough.

Ellen realised that she had noticed before how John's manner changed in the presence of Mary Dennison. She had always noticed this, from the very first lessons he gave her, but she had thought it was natural, that he was acting the part of teacher and trying to make his lessons interesting. Now she saw with a feeling of sinking beneath wave after wave of despair that this had never been the case. Her husband had always been in love with Mary Dennison. It was just she had never allowed this could be possible so it had not occurred to her.

Ellen knew she was no longer mad. She had never been mad. It was simply she was a nervous person, she had always hated this place and, for the last three years or so her husband had been in love with another woman. Her depression was confusion because she had not been brave enough to let herself see the truth. But, what was she to do? Who could she talk to? Who would understand this terrible thing?

After the clearness of realising the truth she was now faced with even more difficulty and the old insecurity clutched at her and was in a way comforting. It was better not to know such things she thought. But really she had always known. That was why it was an impossible task to make this house a home. That was why John had lost his patience with her and had no interest in her apart from his attempts to get her to see a doctor or go to stay with her mother.

She sat deep in thought, her hands in her lap were blue and white, clenched with cold and tension. When the lantern spluttered and ran out of oil she hardly noticed and just continued to sit, frozen in thought. She did not know how many hours had passed until she heard the door and John came in stamping the snow from his boots. He came in and fumbling for a match tried to light the lantern before realising it was out of oil. He had not noticed his wife sitting. He went out of the room and as he came back in, having found a lantern, he jumped as if he had seen a ghost.

"Ellen, what are you doing? Are you alright? I thought you would have been in bed long ago."

"No, I'm not alright. I have realised tonight what is wrong with me," she said.

"What do you mean?" he asked.

"I've realised that you are in love with Mary Dennison," she said, looking at him to see what reaction her words would have.

For a moment he was silent as if shocked. Then he said: "But that's nonsense, Ellen. You know it's nonsense. I'm just her teacher and I'm very fond of her, but I'm married to you."

Ellen stood up and said: "Well, I just know what I feel in my heart, and that's all I can say. I know I'm not going mad. I'm just lonely and sad. I'm going to bed now. Good night."

"Good night, Ellen," said John and he went to kiss her on the forehead as he had always done when they were first married, and realised it was a habit that had somehow been lost for many years. He felt closer to her than he had felt for a long time. She seemed like an old friend and he wanted to talk to her. She accepted the kiss but hurried past him and upstairs. John returned to the sitting room and, thinking about what his wife had said, began to pray.

The snow lay on the ground through January, February and into March. The frost was deep in the ground and it seemed it would never thaw. Ellen imagined something might change after her realisation and talking to John but everything remained the same. It seemed each person was following their own track, as season followed season, and could not be diverted from reaching their final destination.

Mary Dennison still came to the Vicarage for her lessons; John still walked her home and sometimes, Ellen thought, met her at other times in the week. Ellen knew she was right and John did not come to her to deny it again. The truth made no difference to reality and she remained stuck in the habits of her life on Stainmore. She did not know what else she could do. It seemed the fact that she knew about John and Mary's love for each other made it easier for them and, now she knew what was happening, every word and gesture seemed to add further evidence.

One Sunday, in early April, John knocked on her door and said he was just going down to church. It was just before two o'clock and Ellen knew there was no service that afternoon. She went to the window of the spare bedroom, which looked out across the fields and towards the church. After a few minutes she saw the figure of her husband striding across the field, his black coat flapping in the breeze. She knew what she would see next - the figure of Mary Dennison, pretty in a pale blue dress with a straw hat trimmed with blue flowers and white ribbons, hurrying towards the church.

She saw them greet each other near the church gate and then they disappeared out of sight towards the church. Nobody else went into the church. Ellen knew it was usually empty, but it was bound to be empty that day because there was no afternoon service. She stood by the window and watched for them to come out.

Ellen imagined all sorts of things, some innocent and some hardly imaginable. Her head ached with the throbbing pain which had plagued her so often, but even through this, one thing became clear. She must leave the Vicarage. She could not bear to stay in this house any longer. After almost two hours she saw John and Mary leaving the church. Ellen turned and went to her room to pack a bag with some clothes.

Ellen had not realised but she had been crying as she stood at the window and tears kept dripping onto the clothes she was packing into her holdall. She did not care. She was no longer aware of anything except the urgency to leave before John got back. The only moment of hesitation she had was, when she got to the door Rupert was waiting for her, tail wagging, thinking she was going for a walk. She bent down and hugged him and wondered if she should take him too, but decided she could not because she was not sure where she was going.

She realised John might be back soon and gave Rupert one last hug. As she closed the door she reached up to hang the key where it was always kept and caught her hand on a rusty nail. Blood started to run down her hand from the cut . "I just can't do it. I just can't do it, I just can't do it," she said. The words kept coming into her mouth and she kept saying them as she struggled along the road with the bag which was heavier than she meant it to be. As she walked down towards the church she saw the "Daily Mail", Fred Douthwaite and Tommy Nixon, sitting on their usual seat, the old gate stoup that had long since fallen to the ground, puffing at their pipes. They did not see her until she was quite close. They both looked around at the same time and both saw the tears streaming down her face. They both nodded at her and said: "Hello, Mrs. Law" but she could not reply. She ignored them and hurried past, breaking into a run as she took the little lane down past the church towards Borren House.

The Daily Mail watched until she was out of sight and they had gathered as much information as possible about the whole scene, the distraught look, the tears, the untidy hair, the bulging bag and the way she started to run once she had got past them. "Well," said Fred, "Now what's up do you think?"

"I think she knows. I think she looked like a woman who's

125

leaving home." They sucked at their pipes. Both had gone out so they searched in pockets for matches, sucked again and lit their pipes before the conversation continued.

"As I've said afore, Fred, I think it's queer that she walks out such a lot with that big red dog," said Tommy.

"Ay, you never see her otherwise. But she hasn't got the dog today," agreed Fred.

"There'll be a gay carry on when the vicar finds she's gone. She must know something more than we do, don't you think?"

"It seems like it. There's nobody at all goes to church anymore except the vicar and Mary Dennison. Now that looks queer too, doesn't it. Things is coming to a head if you ask me," said Fred.

Ellen knocked on Mrs. Cowper's door. She thought she was going to collapse. Her legs felt so weak with running and her head was aching. She was sobbing and could not control herself. Mrs. Cowper opened the door and, rubbing flour from her hands onto her apron, seemed to guess the whole situation in one glance. She said: "Come on in, Mrs. Law. You need a cup of tea. Now come on in and sit down."

Mrs. Cowper busied herself making the tea, checking her oven, stoking the fire and nothing was said. Ellen's sobs gradually quietened, soothed by Mrs. Cowper's calmness, as if this sort of thing happened every day. The hot, sweet tea made her feel better and slowly she began to tell Mrs. Cowper what had happened. She told her everything, from her first meeting with John to what she had seen that afternoon. Mrs. Cowper, sat and listened, occasionally nodding or saying "yes" but seeming to pass no judgement on what she heard. After a time she picked up her knitting, so as not to sit idle while she listened to the troubles of the vicar's wife.

Ellen ended by saying: "I'm in great trouble as you see and

now I've left home. I've only got a few things packed and I've nowhere to go, unless I go to my mother. I wonder if I could stay with you for a day or two until I decide what to do?"

When Thomas Cowper came back from mending a wall on the Glebe land which had tumbled in the winter storms, his wife was waiting for him at the door. She said: "Don't go in just yet Thomas. Come outside for a moment, I need to talk to you." His wife looked worried and Thomas asked: "What's wrong? Are the children alright, what's happened?"

"It's nothing like that, just come outside for a moment. I can't talk here. She might hear..."

15
The Argument - April 1909

When John Law got home after walking Mary to her parent's house he did not notice his wife had gone. He went to his study and thought about what Mary had told him when they had met in the church. Her parents were moving back to Darlington. She had not decided whether she should move with them or whether she should stay in lodgings on Stainmore to finish her studies.

John was miserable at the idea of her leaving. He felt unsettled because, even if she did not leave now, it would not be long before Mary had learned all he could teach her and then he was certain she would want to leave. He had not wanted to persuade her one way or another but felt that somehow his wish that she should stay had coloured his words.

He sat in his study, reading, thinking and finally noticed that it was getting dark. Where was Ellen? She would normally have brought him a cup of tea before now. He went and called for her at the bottom of the stairs and then bounded up, two steps at a time, to knock on her bedroom door. He rarely came into this room. She was not there. The wardrobe door stood open, the drawers were open and clothes lay all over the bed. John went downstairs and found Rupert, so knew his wife was not out walking. He set about cutting some bread and making some tea. There seemed no point in going searching for Ellen. It was already dark. She would come back on her own he felt sure.

Later that evening he took Rupert out and went to look in the barns to make sure Ellen was not there. He shouted once or twice but the only sound was a curlew disturbed by his shout. The bird's long complaint died wistfully on the night air. The next morning Ellen was still not home. John decided to walk down to the school to tell Mary what had happened and ask her if she had heard anything. He waited until he could hear the shouts and laughter of the children playing outside at morning break and then set off across the field to the school. The children fell silent as he came into the playground and watched solemnly as he went to the door and into the school. He smiled at the little boy James Davidson, the first child he had christened when he came to Stainmore, who had now started school. His older sister Maisie was obviously enjoying mothering her little brother and was holding his hand as the pair stood looking shyly at the vicar.

John found Mary wiping the blackboard. She did not hear him open the door and he watched her slight figure as she reached up to wipe the word "Africa" from the top of the board.

"Mary," he said and, startled she turned to look at him. "I'm sorry, I did not mean to frighten you. I'm sorry also to arrive unannounced but I'm concerned about Ellen and wondered if you had heard anything?"

"What do you mean? Where is she?" asked Mary.

"When I got home yesterday she wasn't at the Vicarage. She's disappeared. I thought she would have come home by now and I'm worried, given the state of her mind," said John.

"Yes, you must be worried. Look, I'll try to find out if anyone has seen her. We can't talk now," she nodded her head towards the window where John caught sight of three faces before they bobbed down out of view. "I'll come round to the Vicarage this evening to let you know if I have any news."

"Thank you, Mary. You are so understanding. Goodbye until this evening," said John as he left the room. Mary sat down at her desk, her head in her hands. She felt exhausted - the late nights and early mornings were catching up with her, and now this. Where could Ellen have gone?

The children stared as the vicar crossed the playground again and he had the feeling they knew why he had come to the school. He felt sure they knew where Ellen was. As he came round the corner of the church which stood in front of the school he saw

"The Daily Mail" sitting deep in conversation on their usual seat. Instead of seeing them as innocent gossipers it suddenly struck him there was something malicious about the way they were so intent on their discussion. They nodded as he greeted them and walked past and back to the empty Vicarage.

All afternoon John was unable to concentrate. He kept glancing out of the window but Ellen did not reappear. He wondered if she had caught a train back to Ambleside and gone to see her mother. He began to feel certain that this is what she had done, although it was odd that she had not mentioned it or left him a note to say where she had gone. Finally in the evening he heard the door and was not sure if he wanted to see the face of Ellen or Mary as he opened the sitting room door to greet whoever had come in.

It was Mary and she looked worried. For the first time in their friendship, John allowed his natural instincts to act without thought. He did not listen to the old voice which told him how he ought to behave. He took Mary in his arms and held her, drawing comfort from her. He felt he had been strong for so long and now suddenly he felt weak and wanted Mary to hold him.

After a time she said: "John, I still don't know where Ellen is. She didn't catch a train as far as I can gather. I asked Herr Ritzema and he lectured me. I've never seen him so angry and I haven't dared ask anyone else."

"Herr Ritzema has no right to lecture you about my wife. What did he say?"

"Well, I asked Herr Ritzema if he knew where Mrs. Law was and he said no. Then he gave me a lecture about not seeing you. He said that people were beginning to talk and even he, who is as deaf as a post, has heard rumours that we are...."

"We are what Mary? We are just friends aren't we?" asked John, looking down into her face which looked so full of concern. Many times John had given Mary a kiss on her cheek as they said goodbye. Many times he had held her arm as they walked. But always these gestures had remained within the rules of gentlemanly behaviour he had inherited from his parents and his education.

Now, looking down at Mary, the thoughts of her going to live in Darlington, the anxiety about Ellen, he suddenly felt released, beyond the ought and but. His hands, holding Mary's waist, could feel the outline of her hips and his hands slipped further down her back. Mary did not resist. They just looked into each other's eyes and knew what was happening. It was as futile as trying to stop the clouds racing across the sky. They did not talk. If either had started to speak the spell would break and John would have carefully withdrawn instead of carrying Mary upstairs to his bed.

The drought of words continued until they both hurried to dress and, back downstairs, the usual pattern, as if they had just spent an hour in the study, took over and John walked Mary home. A thick fog had settled on the fell and as they walked, though it did not rain, they were soaked by the fine droplets of water. All shapes were lost and distance difficult to judge. It was like walking through a dream. Through the confusion of all his thoughts and emotions, one image kept coming into John's mind - he and Mary were two people alone in a wilderness. Nothing else mattered.

When Ellen first left home, John had felt an anguish of guilt. He had no real grasp of her state of mind. He was not sure if she was capable of killing herself. She might have gone to her mother's or she could have caught a train to nowhere in particular. He was concerned but he felt he would discover soon what had happened to her. He expected to find a letter and, after searching the house and finding nothing, waited for the post to deliver a note. It had not occurred to him that she would stay so close to home at Mrs. Cowper's house.

Two days after she disappeared, he saw Thomas Allinson
131

coming running across the fields with a letter. The boy was out of breath when he got to the door and John said: "Sit down, Thomas, get your breath back while I read this, in case a reply is needed." Thomas sat on a hard shiny chair, not well designed for a small boy to sit still on, in the draughty hall. Thomas watched as the vicar frowned at the letter and then, instead of the usual smile and a penny, he just said: "I'm going out, Thomas. Can you thank Miss Dennison for her letter and say I will see her this evening at her class as usual."

The vicar strode off down the field, towards the school and Thomas had difficulty keeping up. He wanted to see where the vicar was going in such a hurry and in such a funny mood. They got to the school and Thomas lingered by the gate and watched as the vicar went down towards Borren House.

John knocked at the door. He could see Mrs. Cowper setting a large brown bowl of milk onto a shelf in the kitchen before she hurried to the door. She looked worried when she saw the vicar. She had never seen him look so angry. "Is she here?" he demanded. "Yes, Revd. Law, your wife is here. Please come in," said Mrs. Cowper.

"Where is she?" he demanded. He was so angry he wanted to shout at Mrs. Cowper but she just said: "She's in the kitchen. She's not very well, you know, and she's very upset. Why don't you come in and sit down. I'll make a pot of tea."

"Ellen, what do you think you are doing?" John asked as he came into the kitchen where she was sitting at the clean scrubbed kitchen table. Her head was bent and she said nothing. Tears began to splash down dark onto the wood.

"Ellen, go upstairs and pack your things. I'm taking you home. Hurry up." said John tense with rage.

When she had left the room he turned to Mrs. Cowper, who was taking blue and white cups down from the dresser as if normal life could help her keep a grip on what was happening in her kitchen.

"Look, Mrs. Cowper. My wife is going mad. I don't know

132

what she has told you, but she has been ill ever since I married her and she is gradually getting worse. I know her and her madness. You must tell her to come home and never again take her in like this. I had no idea where she was. I've been sick with worry with no letter to say where she was and she was right here, a few hundred yards away and nobody told me."

"Yes, Revd. Law. I'm sorry if you have been worried. I thought you must know where your wife was."

"She is hysterical Mrs. Cowper. She has an affliction of the mind. I have told nobody about this. I have tried to look after her on my own but, over the last year her behaviour has become more and more erratic. She hardly does any housework and she hates Stainmore more than anything else. You must not believe whatever she has said to you. As I say, she is hysterical." said John.

Mrs. Cowper said nothing as she poured the now boiling water into the tea pot. She brought the tray to the table and poured the tea. As she handed the cup to the vicar she said: "I don't think your wife is hysterical. She does have headaches. She has always had those since I met her that first night. But she is not mad I don't think."

"What has she told you?"

"She has told me about her difficulties. She has talked about her family and how she hates the winter months here. She has said that she thinks teaching Miss Dennison is a great tax on your time."

John Law stood up, his huge frame towering over the table and his head almost brushing the beams of the ceiling. "Mrs. Cowper, your husband farms the Glebe land, does he not? Well from now he no longer has the right to the Glebe. I am renting the fields to someone else." He turned and found Ellen waiting by the door. He took her arm and pulled her outside. Mrs. Cowper saw her pale, frightened, face turned to watch her as she said "Goodbye" so quietly she could barely hear the word. Revd. Law was dragging her back up the road. He took her bag from her and marched

133

as she trotted and stumbled to keep up with him.

School playtime had ended but as John walked back across the fields, carrying his wife's luggage and pulling her along he felt sure someone was watching them. This only stirred his anger more. He had never felt such blind rage in his life before. He was angry with everything and everyone. He did not trust himself to say anything to Ellen as he knew his words would be violent. A cold light of rationality shone through his churning thoughts. This is how people must feel before they commit murder or worse. He realised that he even felt angry with God.

Ellen was sobbing beside him, trying to catch her breath. Once inside the Vicarage he took her to the sitting room and asked: "What is the meaning of this stupid behaviour? What did you think you were doing Ellen? I realise now what a mistake I made when I married you. Your mother's ambition and your father's early death have brought you to this. It is your mother's fault, not yours. She wanted you to be something that you are not and she deceived us all. That's why we are not happy."

He took a deep breath and walked to the window. "Don't be frightened Ellen. I am not going to hurt you. I just want to know the truth and, maybe from there, we can somehow rebuild a real life. Do you remember all those letters you wrote to me, full of poetry and how you loved Wordsworth and the wilderness. How you wanted to escape from the chains of your life in Ambleside. Do you remember?"

Ellen nodded and, through tear blurred eyes, looked at her husband.

"Who wrote those letters Ellen? Did you write them or did your mother?"

"My mother wrote them, John. I thought you had guessed that long ago. She only wanted the best for me. She did not think she was doing wrong. My father was a very good tradesman and, when he died, I was all she had left. She wanted things to be better for me."

"It was all a charade and you cannot base love or trust on such falseness. Why didn't you tell me? Why did you deceive me?"

"I didn't mean to deceive you John. I thought you loved me and, part of me thought I might be happy with you. I see now that that can never be. You forget our wedding anniversary, my birthday, I know you have no thoughts for me at all. There is not even friendship left. I can see you despise me because I am weak."

"Why did you run away like that? What have you told Mrs. Cowper?"

"I have just told her how unhappy I am. I haven't told her the reason why. Since we came to Stainmore I have never been happy, but I have somehow managed to bear it, for your sake. I have been so lonely and depressed with nobody to talk to. I know we cannot be close as man and wife but I tried to hold on until, until I saw..."

"What did you see Ellen?"

"I saw the way you look at Mary Dennison....."

They looked at each other. The words had fallen like a pile of stones between them.

"You're right. I do care a great deal about Miss Dennison. But you are my wife and, in my position, we have no choice at all. We have to pretend, as we have always pretended, to be happily married."

"John, I can't pretend any longer. I haven't got the strength to pretend and watch the love in your eyes as you talk to Mary. I can pretend no longer. That's why I ran away. I will leave again but this time I will go to my mother's and I will not come back. I cannot stay..."

"Ellen, Mary will be leaving soon. Her parents are going to live in Darlington and her studies will end soon. She will be going away and I will not see her again. You must let me help her to finish her studies and I will try not to see her at any other time, except when she comes here. I will write to her immediately and give her the letter when she comes this evening. I will also go to see Mr. Cowper tomorrow. I regret my words about the Glebe land now. I will go and thank them for looking after you

135

and....Ellen, look I'm sure somehow all will end well. We just have to be patient. You must come and tell me if you are upset. Never run away like that again."

16
Moving to Darlington - February 1909

John could not sleep. Everything that had happened that day kept coming back into his mind. Mrs. Cowper's words, Ellen's face, the conversation they had when they got home. Then Mary came in the evening and he gave her the note he had written to say that they must not meet again, except on the nights when she came to the Vicarage for her lessons. He gave her the note just before they reached the station gate as he walked her home and her face looked puzzled for a moment. He had turned and hurried home.

All the lamps were out at the Vicarage and Ellen was in bed. John began to think about her and about their marriage. He remembered times when they had laughed together. He remembered especially one day when they had walked through a wood. It had been spring and the woodland floor was covered with celandines and the green promise of bluebells to come. They had seen two red squirrels in a beech tree, chasing one another and had stood together, arms around each other watching the chase.

The more he thought, the less tired he felt and, after a while, he got out of bed and went to his wife's bedroom. He had not gone to her room for years but now he felt he must. It seemed as if to lie with her might somehow save his marriage. There was no sound from her room but, when he tried the handle, the door was locked. "Ellen" he called, "Ellen, let me in." After a few moments she came to the door and asked: "What do you want?" "I want to come in. Open the door, please." She unlocked the door and held it a few inches open. Her face looked frightened and as white as her long nightdress. Her blonde hair was loose over her shoulders. She looked at her husband and suddenly seemed to know what he planned. She pushed the door but he pushed harder. He grabbed her roughly and pushed her onto the bed.

"Ellen, I don't want to hurt you. I just want to try to save our marriage and this is what people do. Don't scream because nobody will hear....."

In the morning John walked down to Borren House. He whistled to himself and was pleased to see a pheasant strolling across a field. He felt confident that he could sort out this tangle and get everything back to normal. He had decided to apologise to Mrs. Cowper and tell her that Mr. Cowper could keep the Glebe land. He had spoken angrily yesterday but now his wife was feeling much better.

He had also decided that the Cowpers might appreciate some extra income and he planned to ask them if they would consider taking Mary in as a lodger when her parents moved to Darlington in a fortnight's time. The idea seemed to counter balance his wife's staying with them and somehow it might diffuse the tension. They were sensible people and Mrs. Cowper was a motherly person who would treat Mary well.

Borren House would be an ideal place for Mary to lodge and was also close to the school. As he expected, all went well with Mrs. Cowper. She was not the sort of person who usually spoke her mind and it was hard to tell what she was thinking. She said in principle the idea of taking Miss Dennison as a lodger was fine but she would have to speak to her husband before making a final decision.

With this news John set off to walk up to the station to discuss the matter with Mr. Dennison. He felt happier than he had for a long time. He felt in control of things and that now he had spoken to Ellen and sent the note to Mary, all would be well. The fog which had been clinging to the hills for days was lifting with a gentle breeze and a watery sunshine kept breaking through the clouds. The train for Kirkby Stephen was just leaving the station as he arrived and he could see the Station Master in his uniform heading back towards the house.

James Dennison noticed the vicar walking up the path and stopped to wait for him. "Good morning, Revd. Law. What brings you up to the station so early?"

"Good morning, Mr. Dennison. I came to see you actually. I wanted to have a word with you before you left, about Mary," said John.

"Oh, well then. Come on into the house. Betty always has the kettle on for when the mid-morning train has left and I go in for my coffee. Come and join us."

The Station Master ushered Revd. Law through into the best room, with its smell of polish and unrumpled air of never being used. From the window there was the most marvellous view out over the Eden Valley and John stood looking out of the window and wondering how he could ever have felt angry with God when there was such beauty in the world.

Mr. Dennison came in and said: "Take a seat, please. Betty is just bringing the coffee. Now, before you say anything, I would just like to say how much I appreciate all you've done for our Mary. You've become a father to her in many ways as well as her teacher and I know how fond she is of you. I always wanted Mary to do well, for her poor mother's sake, and with all these exams and studying, you've given her that chance. I wanted to say something before we go because I've maybe not said thank you in so many words before."

"Well, that's very kind of you Mr. Dennison, and you've touched on the subject I wanted to mention, that is Mary's studying. She has only another few months and then she will have her final exam and then, I'm afraid I will not be able to take her any further. I'm hoping that she may win a scholarship and be able to go on to university. You know a few women do go to university these days and it would be a great opportunity for her," said John. His confidence of earlier in the day began to evaporate as he remembered the scent of Mary's hair and saw the outline of her face somehow shadowed in her father's features.

"Well yes, Revd. Law. We would like Mary to go on as far as she can, although we would not have enough money to pay for a university education. I have every confidence in you, Revd. Law. I feel you have always had her best interests at heart." said Mr. Dennison.

"What I was thinking, Mr. Dennison, was that when you move to Darlington, Mary could perhaps take lodgings locally so she could complete her studies. I've already had a word with Mrs. Cowper and I think they would be happy to have her stay there. What do you think?"

"We were thinking along the same lines, although I had not actually sorted out where Mary was going to stay. She has decided she wants to finish her studies here and so we must find lodgings for her and Mrs. Cowper is a very good sort. We've had so much to do you know, with moving, that we haven't arranged it yet but if you think Mrs. Cowper would be willing, then Mary and I will go down and see her today or tomorrow."

Mrs. Dennison came in carrying a tray with a china coffee jug, cups, sugar, cream and a plate of buttered scones. She was blushing and flustered to have the vicar in her front room. Over the years she had put on weight and even the features on her face seemed to have grown and spread. She put down the tray, smiled at her husband and left the room.

"You know, Revd. Law, I will miss this place. There can be nowhere on Earth with such a view as that can there? I still miss my first wife, Mary's mother. In fact I will always miss her. That's why it will be so hard to leave here. I wish you had known her. She was such a good woman and so elegant."

"Yes. It must be difficult to leave memories behind. But, you know Mr. Dennison, you will always be welcome at the Vicarage, whenever you like and Mary will be able to come to finish her reading and studies, she is such a bright girl," said John.

Outside the door Betty stood silently listening to her husband talking to the vicar. She had known since she married him that he would never love her as he had loved his first wife, but hearing him talk of her still hurt. She had done everything to make him happy but it was all taken for granted. When they fell silent she heard the clink of cups and spoons and then they started to talk again. Their conversation had moved away from the personal and now her husband was explaining to the vicar about the new wooden bungalow that was being built at the back of the station for shooting parties to stay in during the grouse season.

As she became certain they were not going to talk about Mary again and as she began to worry they might come out she crept away to the kitchen. She picked up the freshly mangled washing and some pegs and went outside to hang the clothes out. It promised to be a good drying day and she was washing everything before it was packed so that everything would come out at their new home fresh and clean.

Anthony Boldron, the signalman, one of her only friends since she came to Stainmore, was just coming out of the waiting room with the coal bucket. He'd been in making sure the fire was not too low. Except in the hottest days of summer the waiting room fire was kept burning.

"You'll never guess who's come up here this morning?" she said smiling at him.

"I reckon it'll be the vicar to discuss Mary's education," he said, grinning back.

"Got it in one," she laughed, "and they've arranged that Mary should take lodgings down at Borren House and that everything will go on as before."

"Is that right?" asked Anthony, "Well, I've been hearing a rumour about the vicar's wife running away to Borren House. People are saying there's no smoke without fire, you know. What does Mr. Dennison say?"

141

"Well I've hinted to him what people are saying, but he won't listen to it. He says it's all nonsense and people have nothing better to do than to gossip. He says they're just jealous because Mary is so pretty and clever as well. He says that men are jealous to see a woman getting educated above them. He won't hear anything wrong about the vicar either. I'm just glad we're going and it will have nothing more to do with me."

"Anyway, it won't do for people to see us talking or what will they think?" he laughed. "I'd better get some more coal in and then back to the box before the 11.15 comes up."

The following day Mr. Dennison waited at the school gate at home time until Mary came out talking to Herr Ritzema. She was discussing something in German with him, to practice her language, and he was laughing because she had to shout to make him hear what she said. Her father smiled. He could not help but feel proud of her. She was just like her mother, just as pretty but even brighter. He hoped that she would be alright in lodgings with him so far away.

"Guten Tag," Mary said to her father, taking his arm, and "Auf Weidersehen," she said to Herr Ritzema who climbed on his ancient black bicycle to head for his lodgings at Stricegill.

"Well Mary. Only a few days left until we go. I will miss you, you know," said Mr. Dennison.

"Don't worry father. I shall be over to see you every weekend and, when I've finished my studies I may move somewhere close, it depends what happens."

"Well let's hope it all works out well with Mrs. Cowper. Look she's there feeding her hens. Hello, Mrs. Cowper," he called.

"Hello, Mr. Dennison, Miss Dennison. I had Revd. Law here yesterday and he mentioned about Miss Dennison needing lodgings when you move. Is that right?"

"Yes," said Mr. Dennison, "We thought your house is the nearest to the school and .."

"Yes, well I've discussed the idea with my husband and he says that it will be alright, but we would have to have a rule that she was in by half past nine every night. We all get up early and would not want her coming in later than that. Other than that, the house will be her home. I can make her sandwiches to take to school for her lunch and she can share our meals at other times."

"Yes, well I'm sure that will be fine. Mary wants to come home to us every weekend, so it would be Sunday night to Thursday night, if that was convenient. We will be leaving on 3rd May so perhaps Mary could bring her things down the day before?"

"Yes, I'll make a room ready for then. That will be fine," said Mrs. Cowper. Mr. Dennison added: " Here, look, I'll give you this for a month's rent in advance. Will that be alright? Mary will pay you after that from her wages."

"Yes, thank you. That will be fine," said Mrs. Cowper, as she took the money and put it in her apron pocket.

"Well, I'd better be getting on," she said, "It will be milking time soon. There's never any shortage of work. We look forward to having you to stay Mary and I'm sure we'll get on fine."

Mrs. Cowper picked up the old paint tin she had been using as a bucket for the corn to feed the hens and headed back to the house. She did not know what to make of all this business with the vicar and his wife and now with Miss Dennison coming to stay with her. Maybe the vicar had suggested it because he knew that Ellen could not use her house as a refuge once Mary was living there. It didn't make much sense. She turned and watched as the Station Master and his daughter went up the hill and out of the gate.

Mrs. Cowper had talked to Thomas about what had happened but he had not been able to make much sense of it either. She suddenly felt a need to talk to someone about the whole business. She was not sure she was doing the right thing by letting Miss Dennison have lodgings with her. Perhaps she would go along and talk to Ivy Pounder at the Slip Inn tomorrow morning when she'd finished her work. Ivy was a sensible woman and she might know more about what was going on. Mrs. Cowper felt

143

happier to know that she would have told someone else about Mrs. Law's visit and what was said before Miss Dennison came to stay.

17
The Vicar's Dream

The final boxes were packed and cases standing on the platform waiting for the train to take the Station Master, his wife and the younger children, to Darlington. Both Mary's older brothers, Charles and James, had left home several years ago to go to work. Mary had taken her clothes, her books and her few possessions down to Borren House the day before and now the station house was an echoey, empty shell. Just before he left her father went through the house, looking at the rooms and stood staring from the window.

Mary came in and put her arm round him. "Are you alright, Father?"

"Yes, I'm alright, I'm just saying goodbye to the house. I've been at Barras Station for 38 years and that's a good part of my life. I'm just saying goodbye to it and especially to your mother, Mary. It seems that when I go I must leave her here. Perhaps it's for the best...." He fumbled in his pocket for his handkerchief and kept his eyes turned away from those of his daughter.

"It's almost time for your train, come on, Betty will be getting concerned that you're not going with her. I'll come and see you at the weekend. Do take care of yourself, Father. Don't worry about mother, she is always with us both."

Mary stood on the platform and they waited silently. They could hear the train steaming up over Belah and whistling, as it always did as it came into the cutting before the station. Anthony Boldron had come over to say goodbye. He shook the Station Master's hand and gave Betty a quick kiss on the cheek, whispering in her ear: "I would have liked more of those." She laughed.

Mary held her father's hand and felt like a little girl, going somewhere on her own for the first time. As the train drew near she squeezed his hand and he looked down at her. She could see his eyes were filled with tears. She knew he did not really want to go back to Darlington but wanted to stay here with the ghosts of a past life. The train exhaled a huge sigh of steam and suddenly everyone was busy loading boxes and bags. There was no time for a proper goodbye any longer, just a quick kiss and then Mary felt she was going to cry so she turned and hurried away across the platform and away from the station which was no longer her home.

She stopped at the gate and waited to wave as the train slowly pulled away, puffing as it gathered pace to cross Mousegill Viaduct and then the long climb up to Bleathgill and to the Summit. She waved until she could no longer see the train. As she stood there she suddenly felt there was someone close to her and turning saw Joe standing smiling at her.

"How are you Mary? It's a long time since I saw you," said Joe.

"Oh, Joe, you startled me. I'm fine, thank you. How are you?"

"Oh I'm well as ever. I was wondering, how will you manage now, Mary, with your father gone?"

"I'll be fine thank you."

Joe continued to smile at her, his arm on the fence blocking her way down the path.

"Well, Mary. I just thought I'd come to let you know that a lot of people think things are not fine."

"What do you mean?"

"Well people are talking now Mary. You know before it was just rumours. I'm telling you this for old time's sake. You used to be my girl, Mary, and I still like you, though I know now that you and me can never be together because of what's happened. You've changed Mary and that's what people are saying. I'm just offering you a warning. Now your father's not here."

"I don't know what you're talking about Joe. You always did ramble about things you didn't understand. It's very kind of you to be concerned about me. Perhaps you could let me go home now," she flashed a smile at him to hide her fear and he moved his arm.

"Just remember what I said, Mary," said Joe, "and keep away from that vicar!" He started laughing and she turned and saw Jim Boldron standing at the gate. They were both laughing at her. She was angry and frightened and sad all at the same time. She did feel alone, especially with people like Joe saying such things. She decided not to go back through the wood but to walk back the long way along the road where, if she met anyone, it would be in a reasonably public place.

She felt uneasy and Joe's words came back into her head time and again. Joe worked on the railway, as did the Boldrons, and the fact that her father had been Station Master had held them in check, out of respect for him and fear for their jobs. Perhaps now he had gone they would make her life more difficult. Still, living at Borren House, she would only have a few yards to walk to school and very little danger of any of them accosting her there.

John's letter saying he could not see her as often because his wife was threatening to leave him had upset her too. She believed their friendship was above everything. She loved John and how many times had he told her that his wife was hysterical and suffered from delusions so that he could not have a normal marriage with her but stayed with her because he felt sorry for her. Mary felt threatened too. She needed John's protection and whatever he said in his letter she must see him tonight.

Mary went back to Borren House, helped Mrs. Cowper prepare the tea, ate with the family and then, feeling lonely went to her room to read. At about half past eight she went down the stairs and took her cloak from the hook by the door. Mr. Cowper called: "Where are you off to Mary?"

"I'm just going out for a breath of fresh air, Mr. Cowper. I'll be back soon."

Mary picked up her skirts and ran as soon as she was out of the farmyard. She ran up the lane and across the field to the

147

Vicarage. She did not notice Harold Boldron standing with his beady black eyes by his chicken house as he fastened up his birds for the night. He decided to sit down and smoke a pipe in the shadow of the hen house to see what would happen next. It was a warm May evening and he was happy to sit listening to the sounds of evening creeping in.

Mary arrived at the Vicarage and seeing a lamp lit in the study, opened the garden gate and went around the house to tap at the window. She saw John start and then see her at the window. In a few moments he was outside with her. "Ellen's room is just up there. Let's go round here where she will not see us," he whispered.

"John, I'm sorry I know I'm not supposed to be here but I need you. I'm so lonely with my father gone and Joe stopped me at the station to tell me all sorts of awful things. He said I must not see you, but it's nothing to do with him. I think I need you more than ever now father's gone..."

"Ssh, now, it'll be alright Mary," John said taking her in his arms and stroking her hair. "Everything will be alright I'm sure. I'm here and Ellen will understand how alone you feel and allow me to see you. Everything will settle down and we will be happy again, as we used to be."

"I was never happy John. I can't be your mistress. I can't go on with this pretence. Either you love me or you love Ellen, you must choose....Would you marry me if you could?"

"Yes, without a doubt, I would marry you. I love you more than any other person but I am trapped Mary, don't you see, we are both trapped by our positions. All I can think for us to do is be patient and be very careful that nobody sees us together. When you have finished your studies and you know where you are going then I will drop everything to follow you. We could go to Australia or Canada and start a new life together. I have thought about it. It is our only hope."

"Yes, you are right. I'm so glad we can still dream of a future together," she said.

"Look you'd better be getting back now. Aren't you supposed to be in by half past nine? If you have any more trouble with any of these rough men just tell me. I'll happily sort them out for you. They have no idea how to treat a lady. Cheer up now. Give me a smile and a kiss until tomorrow..."

Harold Boldron did not hear what was said or see the kiss but he saw Miss Dennison hurrying back towards Borren House from the Vicarage. He chuckled to himself and, hearing the noise, the hens shuffled, clucked and settled down again in the hen house. Harold came out from behind the hen house and Mary saw him. "Give us a kiss, Mary" he shouted and she ran faster down the road. When she got back to Borren House her heart was pounding and she was out of breath. Mr. Cowper, still sitting in his chair by the fire, said: "I thought you went out for a breath of air. It seems you've come back with no breath. Are you alright?"

"Yes, I'm fine. I just decided to run down the hill. I'm sorry Mr. Cowper. Goodnight."

As he went back to his study John was not so confident that everything would be alright as he had been before Mary's unexpected visit. He did not like these men who threatened her but there was nothing he could do but be as careful as he could not to be seen with her and yet to protect her from these ruffians. He thought about what he had said to her and wondered if it was completely true. Did he really want to throw away his career in the church and flee to a foreign land with Mary? What future would they have? He could see no easy way out but the only thing to do seemed to be to trust in God and do the best he could day by day, for Ellen and for Mary.

That night John had a dream. He was hot and tangled in his blankets as the dream flickered across his eyelids. He dreamt there was someone in his garden and he had gone to the gate to see who it was. He was dressed in his dressing gown and red carpet slippers. It was night time and yet it was not dark. As he came to the gate he saw a dog lying on the path. It was a strange dog

149

he had never seen before. It was quite a large dog and looked menacing.

Then the dream suddenly shifted to a new level. It was the same dream but the dog was now lying near the gate and John was running down the path towards it. He knew he had to jump over the dog and then put his hand on the gatepost to vault over the gate. He jumped over the dog and put his hand on the post and started to jump and then suddenly he knew he had dreamed this dream before. He knew that what would happen was he would feel the dog's teeth biting his arm. He was frightened and then he realised the dream was déja vu of a dream he had dreamed many times.

18

Empire Day plans and the Methody Man - May 1909

Once a month Hilton's grocer's cart would come up from Brough to deliver groceries and to take orders for next month's shopping. For years Henry Bird had done the rounds and he had a different route for each day of the month.

He enjoyed his work, especially in the summer time. It was good to get out and meet the farmers and their families. He knew many of them through his Sunday job as a Methodist lay preacher. This job also involved him travelling, often setting off before first light to reach a chapel in a far away dale before the morning service. After he had preached he would enjoy Sunday lunch with one of the local families and then take an afternoon service and tea before setting off on the long road home.

He liked the new Methodist Minister, Edward Jones. He liked his sing-song Welsh voice and the way he used volume to get his message across moving effortlessly from a whisper that had everyone sitting on the edge of their seats to a bellowing shout which made them all jump. Henry Bird was pleased to see a new zeal in the local Methodist circuit. Last Sunday Mr. Jones had confided in him, up at North Stainmore Chapel, as they walked to Pennistone to have their lunch, that he hoped to build a grand new chapel at South Stainmore. The idea had inspired Mr. Bird and he was full of it.

Henry knew it was supposed to be a secret plan, which would be announced by the Minister in chapel but, as he reached each farm, he was bursting to tell everyone the good news. On his South Stainmore round he called at Buckles Farm, at the Slip Inn, then down to Swinstonewath and on to Stricegill. He stopped at Old Park for his dinner, a tradition long established, as was the menu which hardly varied throughout the year - cold mutton, mashed potatoes, perhaps some cabbage, a slice of bread, a piece of cake and all washed down with a cup of tea.

Everyone liked Mr. Bird. He was a cheerful character and whatever anyone's troubles he always had a kind word and it was usually the right word. He understood people and liked them. He always wore the same black suit which usually had some white dusty marks down the front where a bag of flour had leaked as he carried it into a farmhouse kitchen. On his rounds he mentioned the new chapel and everyone seemed to greet the idea with more enthusiasm than he expected.

After lunch he made his way to Upmanhowe, the horse going slightly quicker now as the load lessened. Mrs. Nixon came out and after the usual politeness she asked: "Have you heard what's going on at the Vicarage?"

"No," said Henry, "Not a peep, but I can tell you about the new chapel."

"Well come on in for a minute and I'll tell you and you can tell me. It sounds like just what we need up here. A bit more God-fearing."

Armed with the gossip, Henry headed on for Borren House, where Mrs. Cowper told him about the vicar's wife and how Miss Dennison was supposed to be in by half past nine each night but had been out past midnight some nights. At the Vicarage Henry said nothing, but looked long and hard at the vicar's wife and her white, drawn, unhappy face. Each place he called added more information. At Seats he found Harold Boldron was out. Probably up at his signal box, so he opened the door and put the groceries down on the table. He glanced around the room and thanked God he was not a bachelor.

At Great Skerrygill Nancy Douthwaite said her father, Fred, was the one who knew all the ins and outs of the scandal and, as his cart pulled further away from the church and up the little valley to Rampson Gate, Cottage and Farm, the items of information dwindled. Still all this was very interesting and he was sure Mr. Jones would like to know what was going on. Instead of letting the horse amble at its own pace back to Brough, Mr. Bird flicked the reins and urged the horse into a ponderous trot, heading up towards Bleathgill where Mr. Jones had his lodgings. He was anxious to see him as soon as possible.

On Saturday Mr. Jones and Mr. Bird set off from different directions to walk to Borrenthwaite Hall to see Mrs. Alston-Dewbanke. They had several matters to discuss and they had been invited for lunch. Master Gerald was away from home but Miss Camilla and her mother entertained the two clergymen. They were shown to the library where the maid brought in a silver tray with four glasses of sherry. Both Mr. Jones and Mr. Bird declined and Mrs. Alston-Dewbanke laughed saying she had forgotten they were tee-total.

Old Dr. Alston-Dewbanke had died earlier in the year but his widow continued just as if he were still alive. As they waited for lunch they talked about her plans for an Empire and May Day celebration. As they talked Mrs. Alston-Dewbanke drank the glasses of sherry one after the other until she became even redder in the face and even more enthusiastic.

She said: "What we want to do for Empire Day, in conjunction with North Stainmore School, is to get all the children in fancy dress and to have a parade. Master Gerald will lead the parade dressed in military style on a prancing white charger and Miss Camilla will be May Queen. We've already made her dress, all in white and she will be crowned with a garland of white daffodils.

"Now we've invited Mrs. Breeks from Helbeck Hall and Dr. and Mrs. Abercrombie from Augill Castle, and they will be the judges for the fancy dress. What we thought was, there should be some kind of service. Could you arrange that Mr. Jones?"

"Yes, indeed, Mrs. Alston-Dewbanke. At what time of day were you thinking?"

"Well we would have the parade just after lunch. Then we would have the judging. Then perhaps go along to the Chapel for the service and then walk back to the school where there will be

153

a tea followed by sports. How does that sound?"

"That sounds fine, Mrs. Alston-Dewbanke. So we will be at the Chapel at about two o'clock, would that be alright?"

"Yes, that would be just perfect Mr. Jones. And will you come too Mr. Bird and bring your wife?"

"Yes, if I am not needed at Hiltons that day, yes I should be able to come."

The lunch bell interrupted the conversation and they made their way through to the dining room, where the number of knives, forks and glasses, along with the dishes all over the table, made both Mr. Bird and Mr. Jones feel uneasy. Mr. Jones, who worked as a plate-layer on the railway line during the week, felt his social graces were not up to the trial, but his socialist principles urged him not to flinch from the challenge.

Miss Camilla noted their confusion but politely said nothing. In fact she found it hard to say anything as her mother was mostly talking but, as they sat down to eat, Mr. Jones began to speak. At least he did not talk with his mouth full, thought Camilla. He would methodically state a sentence then take a mouthful of soup and bread and, once eaten, say his next sentence. She smiled at the way the drops of soup stuck to the ends of his bristly moustache and threatened to drip as his upper lip moved.

He was telling her mother all about his upbringing in a Welsh valley where his father had been a coal miner. He was saying how he did well at school and how he had been inspired by his Sunday School teacher to go on to become a preacher himself. He told her mother how he had first got a job down the mine and then gone on to work on the railway and how gradually he had moved first east and then north from job to job, always preaching at the local chapels. He then explained how the present Mouthlock Chapel, with its one large room above the cottages, was no longer suitable and how he planned to raise the money to build a new chapel.

He had already got backing from several important people. He had secured the land and had offers of help to build the chapel from local craftsmen and he was now asking, as the largest landowner in the area, would Mrs. Alston-Dewbanke be able to help.

"Well I don't see why not. Camilla what do you think?"

"I think it's a good idea Mama."

"I can perhaps make a donation towards the costs," said Mrs. Alston-Dewbanke.

"We were wondering if you would allow the farmers to quarry the stone from one of your fields nearby?" said Mr. Jones.

"That's no problem at all. Even easier than cash. Just go ahead," said Mrs. Alston-Dewbanke, "If you can help with the Empire Day I'm quite happy to help with the stone for your new chapel. That's only fair. I'm sure my late husband would have agreed."

"Yes, I do believe people should be fair and just. Now that is another subject I want to talk to you about Mrs. Alston-Dewbanke. I cannot abide hypocrisy in anyone. Jesus could not abide hypocrites either as you will know from your bible. Now the worst kind of hypocrite is someone who sets themselves up in judgement of others and then commits the crime he himself tells others is a sin. Do you know to what I refer?"

"No," said Mrs. Alston-Dewbanke, "You are talking in riddles. I believe in calling a spade a spade. Don't you Mr. Bird?"

"Yes, of course. I think what Mr. Jones is trying to tell you is that there is evidence of a quite compelling kind. There is evidence of wrong-doing and it's not right Mrs. Alston-Dewbanke. I've heard it from several people and it seems things are going from bad to worse." said Mr. Bird.

"I'm afraid I still don't understand. Do you Camilla?"

Camilla giggled and said: "I think Mama, they are referring to that awful vicar. You know the man who could not be bothered to come and see our Christmas play when I was playing Spring. It was so good that wasn't it Mama?"

"Oh, the vicar. Revd. Law, the one who knows nothing about horses, or hunting, or whisky and calls himself a country vicar

155

and his wife is so drab, isn't she Camilla?"

"Yes, Mama. She seems a frightened little mouse," agreed Camilla, enjoying the conversation.

"Well what has he been up to this vicar?" asked Mrs. Alston-Dewbanke.

"Well," said Mr. Jones, "He's having an affair."

"An affair. Good God, who with?" asked Mrs. Alston-Dewbanke, shocked at this news.

"He's having an affair with the school mistress, Miss Dennison," said Mr. Bird, his eyes sparkling.

"But that's dreadful," said Mrs. Alston-Dewbanke, "for the Church and the School, and the children, for everyone. We must put a stop to this. How do you know he's having an affair?"

"People have seen them walking out together. I lodge up at Bleathgill and young Joe Stephenson lodges there too. He has told me all sorts of things about what has gone on and then, not long ago, a small boy confessed in chapel that he had been carrying love notes from one to the other. The only people who go to church now are the vicar and Miss Dennison," said Mr. Jones.

"But this is awful. We must get the Chapel built as quickly as possible."

Mr. Bird added: "I saw Anthony Boldron, you know the signal man who lives up at the station cottage. Well he has known Mary Dennison all her life. Her parents have left you know and gone back to Darlington and things have got worse since then. Well Mr. Boldron told me he saw them near Calva, you know that old house, and they were there for twenty minutes or so, kissing and cuddling. He said he heard them arrange to meet the following night."

"I cannot believe this. I've never heard anything like it," said Mrs. Alston-Dewbanke, looking genuinely shocked.

Mr. Jones said: "And the vicar's wife, she ran away to Borren House, and that's what really put the nail in the coffin, because she wouldn't do that now if there wasn't something very wrong, would she? And, worse still, people have seen them going into

156

the church and staying in there with the door shut alone for nearly two hours. I hardly dare say this, but that was on Good
Friday..."

"My dear man, we must call a meeting as soon as possible. I
want you to get these people who have seen this vicar and the
school mistress to come here one evening, late. Preferably after
dark. I want to hear what everyone has to say and then we must
make a plan," said Mrs. Alston-Dewbanke.

"That's a good idea," said Mr. Bird. "I can see everyone when
I go round with my deliveries and let them know the date."

"What about the new chapel, Mr. Jones, when will you start to
build it?" asked Mrs. Alston-Dewbanke.

"Well we were thinking of having a stone-laying ceremony,
perhaps next month. I think we said 10th June, didn't we Mr.
Bird?"

"Yes, that was the date and you and your family would be very
welcome to attend Mrs. Alston-Dewbanke."

"Yes, I'd be glad to attend and I think we should have the
meeting soon after the stone laying ceremony. I'm going to be so
busy with this Empire Day and you will no doubt be busy with
the stone-laying plans, but let's have this meeting soon. Nothing
like this has ever happened on Stainmore before and we should
put a stop to it.

"In the meantime I think you should warn everyone to keep a
careful eye on what they get up to. It's shocking, Camilla, quite
shocking. I've never heard of anything so dreadful. My late husband would turn in his grave if he knew about this. He would
take his hunting whip out to that man. He would not stand for
such nonsense."

During this conversation the maid had come in to collect the
soup plates. She had lingered over the task as much as she dared
and then stood at the door for a few moments to hear more. She
could not believe it either. When she brought back the main
course she again waited at the door until she caught what was
being said and then, after laying out the plates and dishes, she
157

hovered over the sideboard, sorting cutlery and cruets, in a haphazard way so that she could hear as much as possible. She could not wait for her day off and then she would walk over to Oxenthwaite to see her friend Maggie Towers to ask her is she knew any more details and to tell her what she had heard.

19

The Stone Laying - June 1909

For the next few weeks the stout form of Mr. Jones in his long black coat was seen flitting here and there all over the parish, like a blackbird feeding a nest full of youngsters, as he called to see people to raise support for the planned chapel. He was full of a vehement enthusiasm which infected everyone he spoke to as he gathered promises of practical or financial help. The plan became a mission and he felt guided by God to build this chapel to right the wrongs of the vicar and restore faith in the goodness of people.

One of the first visits he made was to J. Irving Mawson's office in Barnard Castle. Mrs. Alston-Dewbanke had suggested that, as her family's trusted solicitor, he would be able to give advice of the best way to proceed, both with the building of a new chapel and with what to do about the vicar. Mr. Jones caught the early train to Bowes from where he set out to walk to Barnard Castle.

He found Mr. Mawson's office in the main street and was impressed by the efficient air of business the clerk and secretary gave, sitting at their desks in a rather dark room, lined with books and rolled up documents stacked to the ceiling. On one of the desks was a sturdy typewriter and on the other ledgers and piles of papers. He was led up a narrow flight of stairs to Mr. Mawson's office.

Mr. Mawson proved to be a man of substance. Exactly what Mrs. Alston-Dewbanke would recommend. The buttons on his waistcoat strained to hold in his well-fed solicitor's stomach and his gold watch and chain spoke of a well-fed bank account. He had one of the biggest, blackest beards Mr. Jones had ever seen. It looked like a thicket of black thorn, but his head shone through the thinness of his hair and there was a line across his forehead where the tide of weather stopped at the brim of the black bowler hat he usually wore.

Mr. Mawson greeted Mr. Jones with a strong handshake and asked the secretary to bring in a pot of tea. He said: "Now, Mr. Jones, I've had a letter from Mrs. Alston-Dewbanke, our mutual friend, and she has laid out the situation and the problems you have. If what she says about this Revd. Law is half true then you have got problems, believe me and I have every sympathy."

The tea pot and a plate of biscuits arrived after a polite knock on the door. Mr. Jones decided he could respect Mr. Mawson as a man who would get things done, a man to trust. He began to tell him about the need for a new chapel in simple practical terms but gradually found himself confiding in this burly man with his intelligent eyes. Even the biscuit crumbs in his beard did not detract from his seriousness of purpose.

Mr. Mawson listened, nodding his head occasionally and, by the time they were on their second cup of tea he said: "Now Mr. Jones, what you are doing is absolutely right and I am prepared to organise everything. I have a friend, a Mr. Hilton, who can draw up the plans, he will get the chapel built and I am prepared to give substantial financial help. All you have to do is organise the stone laying ceremony and get as many sponsors as you can." Mr. Jones left Mr. Mawson's office feeling full of strength and confidence that everything would work out nicely with Mr. Mawson in charge.

The morning of 10th June dawned with the clearest of pale blue skies and innocent white clouds on the far horizon over the Lake District. Mr. Jones was down at the old chapel by 9am where he met Mr. Bird and they set about putting up a temporary stage. Ivy Pounder from the Slip Inn had also arrived early and, like a general in a military manoeuvre, was organising cups, plates, cutlery, tables and food for the celebration tea.

The new Mouthlock chapel to seat 180 people was to be built almost next door to the old chapel but nearer to the road. Mr. Bird was setting up a table and chair where he could sit with a large book in which he would write down pledges for subscriptions to the chapel fund or to provide materials or labour. On the corner of the table was a pile of sheets with the order of service specially printed by Braithwaites, printers in Kirkby Stephen.

The architect, Mr. Thomas Hilton from Bishop Auckland and his daughter Amy had arrived on Stainmore the day before the stone laying ceremony and had stayed at Borrenthwaite Hall by invitation of Mrs. Alston-Dewbanke. For Mr. Hilton the drawing of the plans had been a special task because his grandfather had been one of the founder members of the original Mouthlock Chapel built in 1831 following the visit by the famous Methodist preacher Hugh Bourne.

Mr. Hilton and Amy had rather an odd evening with Mrs. Alston-Dewbanke. She had not met him before but she had heard he was a man of culture who had travelled Europe in his youth to see works of art in all the great cities. Mr. Hilton was a tall and tidy man and Amy was well dressed in the way people who live in towns and keep in touch with fashions are, which left Camilla feeling uncomfortably that all her clothes were slightly shabby and out of date.

Mrs. Alston-Dewbanke did not pay too much attention to these details. She saw the visit as an opportunity to revel in culture and to have a party. She had organised a recital for after dinner with herself, Camilla and Gerald singing songs, playing the piano, acting out tableaux from history and reading poetry. Mr. Hilton and Amy were the captive audience and clapped politely. Amy did not dare look at her father as she knew she would start to giggle if she saw the look on his face.

On the morning of the stone-laying ceremony Mr. Hilton and Amy set off early to walk across the fields to the chapel. He carried the plans in a large roll tied up with red ribbon. Mr. Jones had written to ask if he would bring the plans so that they could be put up for display for all to see.

Isaac had taken the day off from hauling coals as had Ted Peacock, the old miner. After a dinner of potatoes and cold mutton washed down with sweet tea, they brought out their kitchen chairs and their clay pipes to sit in the sunshine and watch the proceedings. Once the dinner plates were washed they were joined by Alice and by Edith Ingham, who were both in cheerful mood and looking forward to an entertaining afternoon.

The crowds started arriving after dinner with some coming on foot, others in horses and traps and a large crowd arrived by the 12.30 train from Kirkby Stephen. Everyone wore their smartest clothes and there was a holiday mood of excitement and the buzz of conversation as people who had not seen each other for some time met. The vicar and the school teacher were conspicuous by their absence and many a huddle of conversation touched on the subject of the rumours.

Mr. Irving Mawson's black bowler hat, black beard and his air of property made him stand out from the crowd. He was talking to a group of young men including Joe Stephenson. The conversation looked serious as he asked a question then waited, beard nodding encouragement for their replies. Occasionally Mr. Mawson would scan the crowd as if looking for someone, as in fact he was. He was waiting for Mrs. Alston-Dewbanke. Mr. Mawson was a widower and Mrs. Alston-Dewbanke was now a widow. Mr. Mawson had not drawn any further conclusions than that Mrs. Alston-Dewbanke was wealthy and of a similar age. He was quietly trying to impress her but was not ready to make a direct approach as yet.

Mr. Mawson was the main sponsor for the new chapel and he, along with all the other more substantial sponsors, would lay a stone ready to build the first wall of the chapel. The stone for the chapel was to be quarried, by permission of Mrs. Alston-Dewbanke, from a field near Gillses and the farmers had

162

promised to cart all the stone to the site free of charge. Mr. Mawson was looking forward to seeing Mrs. Alston-Dewbanke and even more to seeing Borrenthwaite Hall and spending the evening with her and her family.

As two o'clock approached Mr. Jones climbed onto the make-shift stage along with Revd. W. Watson from Carlisle. Mr. Jones had never spoken to such a large crowd before and he was uplift-ed by the sight of so many supporters. He welcomed them with a sincere seriousness and enthusiasm before announcing that the ceremony would start with a hymn. The crowd shuffled and cleared their throats before following Mr. Jones' loud and clear voice in singing and, as they sang, the significance of the event seemed to settle warmly on their backs with the afternoon sunshine.

The hymn ended and Revd. Watson asked everyone to kneel in prayer. As people knelt on the ground and Revd. Watson's deep voice said the words of the prayer the people of Stainmore who had allowed doubt to enter their faith as they watched their vicar walking out with the school teacher, now felt that doubt cast aside in a new conviction symbolised by the chapel.

After the prayer ended people rose to their feet and above them the swallows dived and swooped in the warm air. Revd. B. Hanley then climbed carefully onto the platform and led the crowd in singing psalm 84. As they chanted the words wound around the event, and mixed with what many people knew or suspected about Revd. Law's behaviour, and left them with a feeling of goodness and conviction in the rightness of building the chapel.

"O how amiable are thy dwellings: thou Lord of hosts!
My soul hath a desire and longing to enter into the courts of the Lord: my heart and my flesh rejoice in the living God.
Yea, the sparrow hath found her an house, and the swallow a nest where she may lay her young: even thy altars, O Lord of hosts, my King and my God.
Blessed are they that dwell in thy house: they will be always
163

praising thee.

Blessed is the man whose strength is in thee: in whose heart are thy ways.

Who going through the vale of misery use it for a well: and the pools are filled with water.

They will go from strength to strength: and unto the God of gods appeareth every one of them in Sion.

O Lord God of hosts, hear my prayer: hearken, O God of Jacob.

Behold, O God our defender: and look upon the face of thine Anointed.

For one day in thy courts: is better than a thousand.

I had rather be a door keeper in the house of my God: than to dwell in the tents of ungodliness.

For the Lord God is a light and defence: the Lord will give grace and worship, and no good thing shall he withheld from them that live a godly life.

O Lord God of hosts: blessed is the man that putteth his trust in thee."

Mrs. Pounder and the ladies who had been preparing tea had all come outside to listen to the ceremony and stood at the back of the crowd, near the old chapel. Jane Johnstone had been helping and she stood to one side of the group of women. She had not noticed Joe making his way in the gaps between the prayer and hymn around the back of the crowd and towards her. She had been trying to see him and could make out some of his friends, William Hill from the Slip Inn and her brother Thomas, but she couldn't see Joe and began to worry something had happened to him if he wasn't here.

Then, just as the psalm finished, a hand slipped through her arm and she turned to see Joe smiling down at her. For the first time she felt sure that everything would work out between them and she felt proud to be standing at his side as Mr. Mawson made his way through the crowd and up onto the platform to make a speech.

She could hear the swallows as they skimmed overhead and a

curlew far away but she didn't hear what Mr. Mawson said. She heard the words but their meaning seemed to escape her. She almost felt as if the ceremony was a blessing on her love for Joe and she was sure that he had come back to her and forsaken all thoughts of Mary Dennison.

In front of the platform a space was cleared where the foundation had already been dug and the stone layers came forward. Mr. Cowper and Mr. Nixon were standing, trowels in hand, with a pile of dressed stone beside them. They helped Mr. Mawson lay the first stone, followed by the architect's daughter Amy and a shy girl called Miss Winter who blushed salmon pink to match her dress as she came forward. Mrs. Alston-Dewbanke moved forward to lay her stone followed by Miss Alderson from Calva and Miss Beckwith from New Hall.

Mrs. Pounder had realised rather late that she was one of the stone-layers and came pushing through the crowd, wiping her hands on her best pinafore, ready to put down her stone. Fred Douthwaite from Skerrygill was next and Miss Cowper from Borren House. Young John Alderson from High Ewbank came forward to lay his stone and the final stone was laid by Mr. J. W. Dent from Barras.

Over behind the platform Mr. and Mrs. Allinson from Tufton Lodge were standing with their large family and Mrs. Allinson was bending down comforting young Thomas who had started to cry after the first hymn was sung. He was trying to tell her about the pennies under the carpet on the stairs but she didn't understand what he was saying. Mr. Jones noticed the boy crying and went over to talk to his parents and told them what had happened in the chapel. Thomas quietened down and said: "Mam, I didn't know I was doing wrong. The vicar gave me the pennies and I just took letters or flowers from him to Miss Dennison. Henry knows all about it. I told Henry and asked him what I should do but he didn't know."

Mr. Allinson said: "Well how much money is there Thomas?"

"I don't know, Dad. I never counted it, I just hid it," said

Thomas his head hanging in shame.

"I remember a year or more ago he brought some pennies home from school and he said they were from the vicar but I never thought anything of it then," said Mrs. Allinson.

"Well there's a lot more there now and I knew it was wrong and Mr. Jones told me it was wrong at chapel," said Thomas.

"Well, Mr. Jones. I think when we get home we'll take the stair carpet up and whatever we find under there will go to the chapel fund. What do you think Thomas?" asked Mr. Allinson.

"Yes, Dad, that's what we should do," said Thomas.

Mr. Jones said: "That's very kind of you Thomas. Come with me, I'd like your help, just for a minute."

Holding Thomas' hand Mr. Jones went up to Mr. Mawson and explained quickly what had happened. Everyone was watching and Thomas felt himself blushing and a trickle of sweat run down his forehead. He remembered he'd been crying and tried to rub his face to get rid of the streaks of his tears. He thought he might start crying again.

Mr. Mawson said to the crowd: "We've got one last stone layer. A very important young man who has donated all his savings to the fund. Step forward Thomas." The crowd, sensing this gesture had something to do with the vicar and the school teacher, clapped and cheered as Mr. Cowper laid the wet mortar and Thomas struggled to lift the heavy stone into place.

Revd. Watson then climbed back onto the platform and made an address. The afternoon heat was beginning to tell on the smaller children who were fidgeting as the sermon wore on and was followed by a collection. The ceremony ended with Rev. W. Whiting from Appleby pronouncing a benediction and then Mr. Jones announced that tea would be served outside the old chapel and in the school room for those who wanted to sit down on a chair rather than on the grass.

After tea people began to drift away. Mr. Hilton and Amy set off for the station where they were catching the afternoon train back to Bishop Auckland. Farmers and their families set off for home to get back for milking time but most of the clergymen, along with Mr. Mawson, stayed behind for a public meeting in the old chapel in the evening. The clear sky of the morning began to fill with huge white towers of cloud as the afternoon drew on. After milking quite a number of the farmers came back for the meeting even though the clouds had churned and thickened and there was a distant rumble of thunder on the air.

Revd. Hanley presided at the meeting at which everyone congratulated each other on the success of the day and made detailed plans and dates for the building of the chapel. When the business was over there was a supper of all the left-overs from the afternoon which Mrs. Pounder had tidied onto plates and covered with clean tablecloths.

Outside the thunder rumbled closer and rain began to pour down. They waited for the shower to end before the meeting broke up and people headed home feeling happy that some action had been taken. The chapel would be built and it would be a symbol of the goodness of the people of Stainmore in the face of a threatening, glowering storm of divisive chaos.

20
Making Hay at Calva - June 1909

Work started the next day on quarrying the stone for the chapel. Stone masons on the site were dressing and laying the stone and Edward Jones found time to visit every day to check on progress. Mr. Mawson came over once a week by train to inspect the work and usually walked over to Borrenthwaite Hall for his tea before returning to Barnard Castle.

The sturdy grey walls growing out of the ground were a sign of growing confidence in the Chapel and of distrust of the Church. Now that Mary's father had moved away, there was never anyone at John's Sunday services except himself and Mary. He felt powerless to change anything. He realised he had given up on his wife ever being able to share his life. His church was neglected and he felt everyone was turning against him. All he could do was continue to try to do the right thing by his wife, his church and by Miss Dennison - she was the one good thing. He could help her on a path to achieve great things. He kept telling himself he had chosen his own path and he must stick to it but he could help Mary find her way to a more fulfiling life.

John spent hours pondering on his love for Mary and on how true it seemed and how right with God. He felt torn apart by his belief in Christianity and by his marriage vows. There was little to do in the church and no congregation to visit. He spent as much time as he could out of the Vicarage and away from Ellen. She had again lost all hope and had no interest in anything. He found her company depressing. She found his company distressing, so they went their separate ways and one or the other would take Rupert out walking.

Since the thunder storm on the day of the stone laying ceremony the weather had been hot and dry and everywhere was dusty. One day, towards the end of June, John decided to walk up to High Ewbank and beyond into the wilderness of the fells where a ruined cottage stood on the hillside, a reminder of more prosperous days. The heat became oppressive and he was glad he had brought a bottle of cold tea. He decided if he drank it he would fill the bottle with water from higher up the Belah beck where it would be fresh and cold. He watched a skylark as it climbed into the heavens until he could no longer see it but could hear it's magical music spilling back to the ground.

As the afternoon heat reached its peak clouds began to gather again and churned upwards in pillars of white. There was no thunder just torrential fat drops of water falling straight to the ground. By this time John was near High Ewbank. He did not want to go and trouble the Fothergills for shelter. He had seen them a few days before and their greeting had been cool. The look on Mr. Fothergill's face was barely polite and full of unspoken accusation.

There was no shelter on these high pastures barren of trees so John just stood in the rain. He thought he could hear the ground gasping as the first drops soaked into the baked ground. Far away down the Eden Valley he could see where the sun was still shining. The shower did not last long and afterwards everything seemed washed and clean.

John walked back towards home above the railway and down past Bleathgill Edge, the quarryman's cottage sheltering in trees, where the views were stupendous. He could see the shoulders of the Pennines beginning at last to take on their coat of summer green. Below was a buzzard's view of the lush Eden Valley and then away to the west the Lake District fells blue in the distance.

The longest day was fast approaching and, with the shower of rain, the grass seemed to grow as he watched it. John had collected a few specimens of hay meadow plants as he walked and was thinking he would do a special class at the school about the plants the children could see in the fields around them. After the difficulties with Mr. Cowper when Ellen ran away earlier in the

169

year, the event had been smoothed over and Mr. Cowper had continued to farm the Glebe fields. Early in the year he had kept his lambing ewes in one of the fields but now they were knee high with grasses, herbs and flowers - buttercups, ragged robin, dog daisies and orchids.

John's mind was still full of the inspirational view over "The Plains of Heaven" as John Martin had titled his painting of the Eden Valley from Stainmore. His soul felt cleansed by the dramatic experience and his natural optimism restored. As he reached the Glebe fields he thought that this year, as a token of friendship, he would offer to help Mr. Cowper at hay time and resolved to walk round by Borren House straight away to let him know. By the time he had called to speak to Mr. Cowper school would be just finishing for the day and he could see Mary and let her know about the school project to study the flora of the hay meadows.

Mary was busy sorting out piles of books when John went into the class room. As she looked up to see who had come in her face beamed with happiness. John thought she could not smile like that unless she felt the same about me as I do about her. He felt full of joy too but somehow it was a joy made more vibrant by the knowledge that sorrow was its shadow. Like seeing the perfection of a fragrant rose in full bloom and knowing that tomorrow the petals would have fallen.

"Mary I've been for the most wonderful walk today to that ruined cottage up above Heggerscales. I spent some time there thinking and wondering who had lived there so many years ago. I was even day dreaming that it could have been our home! Then I got caught in the rain and the views across the valley with the sunshine and showers falling together across the land it was so beautiful and I kept thinking of you and wishing you were there beside me," as he spoke he looked down at Mary's face and she seemed shy and laughed a little.

"Perhaps we should meet later John and go for a walk across the fields. We haven't really seen each other except for my lessons and in church. We haven't had a chance to talk together as we used to when my father was still here and you used to walk me up to the station. What do you think?"

"What about Mrs. Cowper? What will you say to her?" asked John.

"I'll tell her the truth. I'll say I'm going out for a walk after being stuck inside all day in school it seems a perfectly reasonable thing to do."

"What time shall we meet?" asked John.

"Perhaps eight o'clock. I'll meet you half way between the Vicarage and the school. Will that be alright?"

"Yes. Perfectly alright. Oh, and I thought today about doing a class with the children on the flora of hay meadows. They are so simple yet so wonderful. All the children must be familiar with them but we could study how many different species there are in one field."

"Yes, that sounds a lovely idea."

John bent forward and kissed Mary gently and whispered: "Until later..."

The hours until their meeting seemed to drag slowly past. John realised that it was the first time they had arranged to meet which did not seem entirely innocent to both of them. On every previous occasion they had met or been together they had been protected from guilt by a valid excuse. He had walked her home all those nights to protect her from the threat of attacks. The innocence of the excuse had been easy to hide behind even when he realised more than a year ago how much he cared for Mary and how much he wanted to be with her all the time.

He had begun to feel recently that circumstances were forcing them together. People did not come to his church. His wife was not quite sane and, though he had tried, he knew he was not the right person to cure her if she could be cured at all. He had no friends in the parish, in fact he had begun to feel that people disliked him. The feeling had changed since the stone laying ceremony. Before that the locals had seemed indifferent to him.

171

Polite but non-committal. Now some of them were hostile. He could not put his feelings down to any particular incident and sometimes thought it was his own paranoia. Whatever the cause, whether it was imagined or real, he was left with Mary as his only true friend.

He was waiting in the lane as Mary walked up to meet him just before eight o'clock. She had changed into a pure white dress with a sash of blue around her waist. On her head a plain straw hat tied with a matching ribbon of blue. Her dark hair framed her pretty face and as she came nearer he realised the blue of the ribbons brought out the blue in her grey eyes. He thought, 'If Mary was a flower she would be a violet. Shy, perfect, curved and exquisitely beautiful.'

Arm in arm they set off to walk on the path they had used so many times before up towards the station. There was a new warmth between them and a new equality. They were both aware that they had met because they loved each other and for no other reason. They had tried to hide their feelings. They had known from early in their friendship but had continued to deny it, hiding behind the small certainties of everyday life.

Even when John had carried her upstairs to his bed in the Vicarage it had seemed like a dream and neither had spoken of what happened since. Now it seemed, in the clarity of the evening light with all the dust washed from the atmosphere and the world sparkling with a deeper meaning, their love had suddenly come into bloom. They could no more stop it than they could stop the grass growing.

They did not see Harold Boldron, standing leaning on a hoe in the corner of his garden, watching as they walked absorbed in each other's company, towards Calva. Harold Boldron looked at his pocket watch which gleamed in the late evening sunshine. He went back to his work, weeding out the nettles and docks between his rows of peas. The picture of the vicar and the school teacher walking through the long grass, her head bent up towards his and his down towards her, kept coming into his mind. The midges were beginning to bite but he would stay out until it was dark to watch to see what time they came back.

John and Mary walked through the wood in silence and towards Calva, an abandoned house on the edge of the wood. It was now used as a barn and was already half full of new mown hay. The over-powering sweetness of the dried grasses engulfed them as they entered the semi-darkness of the old house.

Mary was late home that night. Through the blissful, swallow rich, evenings of late June she took to walking out every night to meet John. They began to meet later, when it was almost dusk so that the risk they would be seen was less, but Harold Boldron was always on the look out, either near his hen house or in his garden. Each night he consulted the pocket watch he kept in perfect working order so it never lost a second, and every night he would see John and Mary coming back from Calva later and later.

Ellen was at the bottom of an ocean of despair. She had been sinking for years and now she saw clearly what was happening. She saw a new look on John's face and for the first time detected guilt. The more she understood and the clearer she saw the less able she was to do anything. In her thoughts she realised she was saner than she had ever been. Her mind was like a forest of unconnected and tangled trees, all springing up and trying to demand the light of her attention but now a clearing had opened in the forest, with a little tumble down cottage beside, and in this clearing she felt strong.

She felt she knew the truth, but the more clear it was, the less able she was to explain to anyone else how to get to this clearing. How to put her thoughts into words. Every few minutes she would think about going to see Mrs. Cowper again but, as soon as the idea had come into her head, she felt hemmed in by the dense forest again, tangled and lost.

One night, as the grandfather clock in the hall struck eleven o'clock, she decided to go outside and look for her husband. She had been in bed and was dressed only in her night clothes but this did not occur to her. She went out of the house not noticing that Rupert was barking at being left behind. She knew where to walk and set off towards the clearing in her mind. She had not gone far when she saw two figures coming towards her. A tall man and a slight woman, arm in arm. They did not notice her at first. She stood and waited in her white nightclothes in the gloom. All three were shocked when they saw each other.

Ellen began to shout and scream, her long blonde hair falling wildly over her face. Mary began to cry quietly and John suddenly became furious and started shouting at his wife: "You're hysterical. What do you think you are doing here? You've gone completely mad. You've always been mad and there is no hope for you." He had grabbed her roughly and was dragging her screaming back towards the Vicarage. He kept telling her to be quiet but she just yelled louder. She was not shouting words just noises which woke the curlews who started crying their long sorrowful warnings. Somewhere a dog started barking and an owl screeched.

It was very late when Mary got back to Borren House. She noticed the lamp was still burning in the kitchen and knew that Mr. and Mrs. Cowper were waiting for her. She paused to compose herself and wiped her face in case her tears had left marks on her face. She wondered what she could say and could only think of telling the truth. That there had been a disturbance at the Vicarage and she had helped Revd. Law calm his wife.

Mr. and Mrs. Cowper looked worried as she came in and Mrs. Cowper said: "Mary you just can't keep flouting the rules like this. Do you realise what time it is? It is nearly two o'clock in the morning and Thomas has to be up again soon to start milking the cows and tomorrow we will be starting to cut the Glebe hay. We can't have our lives disturbed like this. We agreed with you and your parents that you would be out no later than half past nine at night."

"Yes, I'm sorry Mrs. Cowper. I know. I can explain," Mary told them what had happened at the Vicarage and they listened in silence.

"The thing is Mary," said Mrs. Cowper, "we have young children and we can't have them seeing you behave like this. You're a teacher and you should know how children are and how we as adults must be. If you can't be in at a reasonable time then we will have to give you notice to leave."

"We're responsible to your father for you. We will give you one more chance but, if you're late in once more you must leave," said Mr. Cowper.

The following day, after the cows were milked and walked unhurrying to their pasture, Thomas Cowper went to harness up the bay Clydesdale mare with the grass cutter and made his way to the Glebe field. The vicar saw that hay making had started and, after changing into some old clothes, went over to offer his help. The oldest of Thomas' sons had been kept off school to help and one of his cousins had come up from Kirkby Stephen. They were busy raking the newly cut swathes of grass into rows and John went over to help them.

The rattling of the grass cutter, the rhythmic work of raking the hay and the growing heat of the day were soothing to John's troubled mind. He put all his attention into his work and after a while even began whistling "Immortal, invisible," one of his favourite hymns. The lads working alongside him said very little and, when they did speak only spoke to one another. The vicar began to feel that his presence had spoiled their fun. Still he kept up his work cheerfully and tried not to think of Mary or Ellen.

Driving slowly round the field, sometimes flicking the reins, Thomas was deep in thought. He was troubled by what Mary

175

Dennison had said the night before and by her staying out so late. He felt responsible for her and wondered if he should write to her father but could not think what words to use. He had heard the rumours and he suspected they were true, but he had no proof to offer the girl's father.

It was a bad business and he thought perhaps the best outcome for the sake of his own family was if Mary was late in again and then they could ask her to leave. She was a nice enough lass but he had to think of his own children and also what others were saying. He couldn't be seen to condone what might be going on.

Late in the afternoon Joe and Jim Boldron arrived. They had finished their shift early and were helping out with hay making, like many of the younger men, wherever a farmer needed a hand. By this time the vicar's tanned face was showing a hint of red from long exposure to the sun and the exertion of his day's work. He waved at the young men and continued his work. They started turning the grass raked earlier into rows so that it would begin to dry underneath.

Unlike the two younger boys, Joe and Jim, continued to talk and laugh and at one point the vicar heard them say something about "Riding the Stang" at which they had to stop raking because they were laughing so much. Thomas Cowper had gone to take the horse back and then to milk his cows. The vicar decided he had done enough for the day and made his way home to wash and change.

Mary crept quietly out of Borren House just after nine o'clock that night and, as soon as she reached the church could see John walking quickly towards her. As he walked along the side of the Glebe field he had been surprised to see that Thomas Cowper was still working. The others had gone and Thomas was finishing off the last row of grass so that it would be ready to dry in the morning sunshine.

They had stopped to talk briefly and Thomas had thanked him for his help. He wanted to say more to the vicar who he knew was going to meet Mary Dennison but, Thomas thought, how can you tell a vicar how to behave? They above everyone should know what is right and what is wrong. In a way he felt sorry for them, but he could not agree with them.

John and Mary took a different path towards Calva so that they would not meet Thomas Cowper but, as he straightened his stiff back from turning the last sheaf of grass, picked up the rakes and put them over his shoulder, he saw the unmistakable outline of the vicar and Mary Dennison on the horizon. He walked home to tell his wife that they would have to ask Mary to find somewhere else to lodge as soon as possible.

In the sweet smelling shell of Calva, which had no glass in its windows, just a view of the summer stars, John and Mary held each other close. This place was their haven against all that was wrong with their world. Here there was just the truth of simple things. They had made a vow that, within the walls of this old building, they would not talk about any of their troubles. There was little need for words as they lay entwined and entranced in the bed of hay. Time seemed to stand still, even to connect with other times before or in the future, rather than in its proper relation to the next hour.

Finally Mary began to dress though John insisted on kissing every part of her before she was again hidden beneath her clothes. He dressed hurriedly and then Mary said: "I can't find my necklace. It's the one which belonged to my mother. Oh John, the clasp must have come undone and it is lost in the hay. Oh no."

"Stand up. Look, you stand over there and I'll feel carefully everywhere. I'm sure we'll find it. Don't worry."

They spent over an hour groping in the darkness trying to find Mary's necklace and finally she was persuaded to abandon the search when John promised he would come to look again first thing in the morning when it was light.

When Mary got back to Borren House it was midnight. The lamp was burning in the kitchen again but this time only Mr. Cowper was waiting for her.

177

He said: "It's no good Mary. You will have to find somewhere else to stay. You can't stay here. We want you to leave tomorrow."

21
A Plot is Hatched

Mary Dennison went to Darlington most weekends to stay with her father and step-mother. She did not tell them that she was moving from Borren House or that there were any problems. She did not want to worry her father who seemed to have become frail and aged since he retired and moved away from Stainmore. Privately he told his daughter he wished he had never left and that, although he had been brought up in the town, he now hated the streets and houses and longed to look out from the Station House windows and feel the ghost of his first wife walking through the house.

Mary did not want to add her problems to his sadness so she was always cheerful when she saw him and spoke confidently about her plans to complete her studies and go on to university. She wanted him to be proud of her and she wanted him to be happy. The visits became a strain of keeping up a pretence and several times she almost told her father but then she imagined the look of anguish which she knew would crumple his face and she could not bring herself to say anything.

On the train home as she gazed out over the bleak moors of Bowes she would think about the situation and how to resolve it. There were three certainties - she loved John, she wanted to continue her studies and she did not want to upset her father. She had to be brave, find new lodgings, keep working and finish her studies. At that point things would change. John had promised that, once she had completed her exams, they would leave Stainmore for good and head south for a new life. He had said he would leave the church and get some other work and support her through her studies and that eventually they would be married.

Mary had asked Mrs. Nixon if she could lodge at Upmanhow.

She had enquired at Old Park, at Stricegill, at Gillses and at Swinstone House. For one reason or another no one was able to offer her lodgings. Mrs. Cowper finally suggested that she ask at Great Skerrygill so Mary walked along one afternoon when school had finished.

Fred Douthwaite was scything thistles in the pasture when he saw Miss Dennison come walking down the road. He leaned on his scythe as she came over to speak to him. Fred was one of the few men who was the same height as Miss Dennison and she found it odd speaking to a man and looking him in the eye. She was used to men being so much taller than herself.

She explained that she needed to find new lodgings and wondered if there was room at Great Skerrygill. Fred said: "Ay, there's room. But how much rent will you pay?"

"I was paying Mrs. Cowper two shillings a week for bed and board. Would that be alright?" asked Mary.

"Well, I don't see it would be a big problem, so long as you don't want anything fancy like. Come on over and we'll ask our Nancy because it will be extra work for her."

Mary was shown into the house with its white-washed walls, ancient oak beams and stone flag floors. Fred was right. There were even fewer comforts than in Mrs. Cowper's house. It looked as if everywhere needed a good clean.

Sides of bacon hung from the ceiling in the kitchen and buckets stood on the floor. A cat sat on the table looking disdainful, as if this was the usual place sit. There were sacks of animal feed piled up by the wall and a huge pan of unsavoury looking bits cooking in a pot on the fire. Nancy noticed Mary looking at the pan and laughed: "That's for the pigs. Mr. Bird fetches us a bag of stuff that's gone off and I cook it up for the pigs. You'd have to take us as you find us. We're not posh folk but we're decent and honest," said Nancy.

Fred decided he would leave the negotiations to the women and went off back to his thistles thinking that if Mary Dennison moved into his house he would have all the gossip he needed to keep "The Daily Mail" going and he wondered if he should maybe take a walk along to see Tommy Nixon that night to tell him the news.

Meanwhile Nancy was showing Mary up the stone staircase to what would be her room. Mary had prepared herself for a room full of cobwebs and old sacks on the floor but found a pleasant bedroom with an old iron bed and a wash stand with a pretty jug and basin.

"It's very nice, thank you," she said to Nancy.

"Well, when do you want to move in?" asked Nancy.

"Well, if it's alright can I move in today? I haven't got a lot of things to move, just my clothes and a few books. Will that be alright?" asked Mary.

"Fine," said Nancy.

"I can pay you a month in advance if you like." said Mary.

"Yes, I think that would be best. I'll sort out some sheets and get the bed aired for you. It hasn't been slept in for a long time." said Nancy.

At first Mary felt comfortable with Nancy. She had seen her at church before, a few years ago when people used to go regularly, but had not spoken more than a few words to her. The room was fine and she felt that Nancy and her father would not ask too many questions about where she was going and what she was doing. The lodgings might not be as good as Borren House but she would manage.

As she walked back up the road Fred Douthwaite was still scything thistles, his sheep dog lying in the grass nearby, ready to be on duty if needed. Fred raised his arm and waved to Miss Dennison and she noticed that his trousers were all tied up with string around the middle. 'They're an odd couple,' she thought, 'but they seem quite friendly. It must be difficult for Nancy, living with her father and having to look after him. She may end up never marrying and never having children of her own.' Mary did not know that Nancy had been engaged to marry for the last eight years. She was courting Tommy Nixon's oldest son but they had

181

decided not to marry while old Fred was alive and needed his daughter to stay at home and look after him.

Nancy was not the only Stainmore girl waiting patiently to be married. Jane Johnstone was still working at the Slip Inn but now, finally, there seemed some hope that Joe would settle down. He had officially asked her to marry him and she even had an engagement ring. Most of the time she wore it tied to a ribbon around her neck so that it would not get damaged when she cleaned out the fires, scrubbed the floors or washed the pint mugs. She had a fear that the ring might slip off when she was washing or churning the butter and she would lose it so only allowed herself to place it on her finger at night before she went to bed.

Joe had proposed to her after the chapel stone laying ceremony and they had begun to plan for their wedding. It wouldn't be a big affair but the difficulty was they couldn't have Revd. Law to marry them. They had decided to walk down to Brough the next Sunday to have a word with Revd. Lyde and ask him if they could be married in St. Michael's Church. The only problem was their illegitimate child and whether they would be allowed to be married in church.

They had even discussed what they would say to Revd. Lyde about why they did not want Revd. Law to marry them. They had asked Mrs. Pounder if they could have a reception at the Slip Inn and Jane was busy making her wedding dress. Joe was trying to find them a place to live and, even if they couldn't find somewhere on Stainmore, he knew of a little house in South Road, Kirkby Stephen, where they could lodge with his uncle.

Joe and Jane's little boy, Joe, who still thought his grandparents were his parents, would come to live with them. He had just started school and Jane was so proud of him. He was going to

North Stainmore school as she would never want him to be taught by Miss Dennison.

Other parents had begun to feel the same way and, at first Mary put her smaller classes down to parents keeping their children off to help on the farm as they often did. Then she realised that some of those children were not missing school at all but were walking all the way across to North Stainmore school. It was like the church. The vicar had been shunned and now people were shunning her. She realised this was the case but pushed the knowledge aside as she could not let it worry her. She had to concentrate on her studies and work hard. That was the only way a future with John could be guaranteed. That was her one goal and she had stopped worrying about what people might think of her.

On the day that Mary moved from Borren House to Great Skerrygill, John helped her to carry her bags along the road. As they came down the road towards the house, surrounded by old ash trees, they met Fred Douthwaite walking up the road, pipe in his mouth and stick in hand. He stopped to say "Good morning" and gave the vicar a long hard look. The vicar and Miss Dennison said "Good morning" and then, with nothing much else to say carried on down the road. Fred called after them: "Nancy's in the garden round the back. Give her a shout."

Fred and his dog, Meg, carried on up the road, his clogs clinking on the stones. He somehow felt slightly angry with the vicar and the school teacher. He decided that it was because they had set themselves up as better than the rest of the ordinary folk and yet they were carrying on like, well like, he couldn't think of who they were like but he knew it rankled him that they thought themselves somehow better and yet he was sure they were in fact worse than others.

As he came down towards the church he could see Tommy sitting on their seat, puffing at his pipe and waiting to hear what news he had. Fred told him that the school teacher had moved in and that the vicar had come along with her to carry her bags.

183

Tommy just looked as if this sort of thing was to be expected. He said: "Well I nivver," and puffed some more on his pipe.

"That roan cow calved last night. A good strong bull calf." said Tommy.

"Ay, that's good then." said Fred.

"What d'you think it'll be like having her living in your house then?" asked Tommy after a while.

"Well I don't know, but she's paying two shillings a week for the privilege. We've not spoken about any rules of what time she comes in an' sek like. We'll maybe just leave her to do as she wants. Nancy thinks she'll be alright with us and that this will all blow over but I can't see it myself."

"My wife wouldn't have her after what she did to the Cowpers. Not with young children in the house." said Tommy.

"No, well it's different with us. There's just Nancy and me now, and we've plenty of room." said Fred.

"Ah know what it was I was going to tell you. Fred, there's to be that meeting tonight alongside the new chapel building. They're going to discuss how the chapel's coming on and what we can do about the vicar and I think we should mebbe be there. You'll know most about what goes on now. If you see Arthur Anderson from Rampson maybe you could let him know as well."

"Who told you about the meeting?" asked Fred.

"Well I think it was Mr. Jones that suggested it but Joe came round telling folk about it. It's at seven o'clock tonight and I think some will be following it with a pint or two down at the Slip Inn." said Tommy.

"Well, maybe I'll walk along then. Shall I call in for you?"

"Ay, do that," said Tommy. "See you tonight."

That evening John walked along to Skerrygill to meet Mary. She was standing waiting for him, leaning against a tree with her hat in her hand. Nancy was getting the washing in and watched the pair as they set off up the gill beside the massive rock of granite, knocked off the top of Shap Fell and carried to Stainmore by

184

the last glacier thousands of years before. They followed a little footpath up between two hills and then struck off to the right towards Seats and out of Nancy's sight.

As the vicar and school teacher walked up through the trees with the moon already visible as an almost transparent disc in the sky, the meeting at the new chapel had begun. Mr. Jones was sitting on what would be a door step and about twenty men who had gathered out of curiosity or conviction had found themselves uncomfortable seats on bits of timber or building stone.

After talking for a few minutes about progress with the building of the chapel Mr. Jones began to ask if there was any new information about the vicar and the school teacher. Harold Boldron stood up and said: "I've seen them many a time on an evening. Before he used to walk her home up to the station after she had had a lesson at the Vicarage. You could sort of understand that, not letting a pretty young girl wander around late at night on her own. But, since her parents have gone, they've taken to walking out together. I've seen them many a time walking up to Calva of an evening."

Joe stood up and said: "Well you all know that Mary used to be my sweetheart. Well when that vicar came and she started having lessons she got all high and mighty. I blame him for taking her away from me. I've seen the way they look at one another. I saw them in Brough when the King came and I know what's going on."

William Hill said: "I know old Isaac is not here tonight, but he's seen them kissing each other at the station gate. I think Ted Peacock has seen the same."

Tommy Nixon, took his pipe from his mouth and said: "Well I heard screaming coming from the vicarage one night not so long ago. It was awful. I thought someone was being murdered, but I think it was mebbe Mrs. Law. Fred and I saw her that day in an awful state running down to Borren House."

Mr. Jones asked: "Mr. Cowper did anything untoward happen when Mary Dennison was with you?"

185

"Ay, well, we did have some trouble. She was never in at night by half past nine. Sometimes it was after midnight so we said she had to go. I've seen them walking out together, just once at hay time and my wife talked a lot to Mrs. Law. She's a very unhappy woman."

Others added more information until the discussion turned with Anthony Boldron to the death of Mary's mother in child-birth and the night he had gone to get the midwife. Mr. Jones interrupted: "We seem to be getting away from the point here. I've got three things to add. One is that the Allinson's boy came to confess to me that he had been taking messages from one to the other and that seems to me a terrible thing to use an innocent child for such a purpose.

"The second thing is Mr. Bird, on his grocery rounds, has picked up a lot of information from different people about what the vicar has been getting up to. Everyone knows about it. People stopped going to church long ago because of this and this chapel here," he stopped to thump the stone beneath his feet as if it were his lectern, "this chapel here is being built because people on Stainmore are God fearing people. What else can they do when their vicar stoops so low. He is supposed to guide them to live a Godly life and look at him."

Here he stopped to look dramatically at his audience. No one said anything, though one or two nodded their heads. "Now the question is what do we do? We can't just sit back and watch his wife suffer, our children suffer and have to be taken out of their school because parents fear what that woman might be saying to them. We have to take some action. Has anyone any ideas? What do you think Fred? I know she's staying with you now."

Fred cleared his throat and rubbed the stubble on his chin. "Well, I think we need proper proof of what they're up to before we do anything drastic. What can we do anyway?"

"Well," said Mr. Jones, "I've been thinking about it. First we should do as you suggest. We need proper proof. Then, if we've got the proof, we have to tell the school governors and the church authorities. That's what we must do."

Joe stood up and said: "I'll volunteer to be a watcher and try to get proof." "So will I," said Harold Boldron. "Ay, me as well" said William Hill from the Slip Inn. Most of the men gathered volunteered to keep an eye on the vicar and the teacher.

Mr. Jones said: "If you have a notebook then write down what you see, where they are and what time of night it is. If we all collect details like that then that is proof for whoever might still doubt. Now, I've talked to Mrs. Alston-Dewbanke about this, and Mr. Mawson for that matter, and they suggest that our next meeting should be at Borrenthwaite Hall. We can't meet here again it's too public a place. Only those who agree we should take action against the vicar should come. If you talk to anyone else who agrees ask them along too.

"The more people we have the better and Fred, you can be our chief witness because you'll be closest to her. If you think they suspect anything is going on come and tell me right away. We all have to be careful not to be caught but we have to get the proof. Remember this is the Lord's work. We are not doing anything wrong. If they are innocent then we will soon find out and then all will be well. If not, then we will decide at Borrenthwaite Hall what to do next."

"When's the meeting?" asked Mr. Cowper.

"Well we need a few weeks to gather our evidence. I would think the middle of August would be about right. Let's say 15th August at the same time, seven o'clock, unless you hear any different. I'll have to check with Mrs. Alston-Dewbanke that the date is alright for her. Thank you all for coming and, remember, take care you are not caught. There are plenty of us so you need not take risks to get too close to them."

The men started to get up to go. Mr. Jones raised his voice above the talk that had begun: "Wait a minute, before you go, let us kneel down and say the Lord's prayer."

The men stopped and kneeled where they were among the stones, barrows and buckets of the builders and said the Lord's prayer. Above them the moon had gathered strength and was no longer a pale disc but a full globe with a thin finger of cloud outlined against the silver light.

22
A Meeting at Borrenthwaite Hall

Mary Dennison did not spend much time at Great Skerrygill as she moved in just as the school summer holidays were starting. She stayed there after she had her lessons with the vicar but much of the time she went to Darlington to spend with her father. Mary didn't mind Fred Douthwaite. He had a very dry sense of humour and once she got to know him a little she found the things he said very funny. His daughter Nancy was not so funny and Mary had begun to find it difficult to have a conversation with her. Nancy didn't have much to say. She was always working and seemed in a world of her own filled with a set of weekly chores which never ended. She also had a critical manner which Mary could feel though nothing was said.

When Mary went back to Darlington she found her father seemed to have shrunk. He was thinner and Betty was even bigger, larger than life. It made Mary sad to see her father and realise he was not happy. But there was no going back for him. He seemed to have lost interest in life and, even seeing his daughter, and hearing her talk of a bright future did not cheer him.

During the weeks of summer when Mary was often away, John Law would catch the train from Barras to Winstone near Darlington where he would meet Mary. These days were blissful. They could walk openly together without looking over their shoulders. People were strangers and did not know their circumstances and did not ask.

They did not do anything in particular. They just met, usually in the morning, and spent the day walking together, talking and laughing, holding hands. Often Mary had brought a picnic and they would find somewhere to sit in the shade where they could eat. It was like a dream, unreal and unattached to their ordinary lives. One day they had walked for miles in blazing sunshine and arrived back too early for the train. They were both hot and thirsty and, though neither of them usually went into inns they decided to get a drink in the Winstone Public House at Edgeholme.

Above the door was a sign saying that Ruth Hildreth was the landlady. Inside it was cool and dark and empty. They had to ring a bell to get the landlady to come and, when she came into the room she looked as if she had been sleeping off the afternoon heat. She looked at them, curious to see a vicar in her pub with a girl who looked half his age. "Could we have a glass of beer and two pence of cream, please?" asked John. "We have beer, sir, but no cream," replied the landlady. "What will you have Mary?" "Do they have lemonade?" she asked, "I'll have a glass of lemonade, please."

The couple sat down on a sofa near the window and the land-lady, yawning behind her hand, started putting glasses away where she could keep half an eye on them. She saw they were holding hands, the girl resting her head on the vicar's shoulder. They didn't seem to be talking but seemed rather subdued. After a time the vicar got out his pocket watch to check the time and the landlady surmised that one of them was catching a train. Soon afterwards they left and, though she had no idea who they were, the visit left an impression on her.

Back on Stainmore the message about the meeting at Borrenthwaite Hall had reached every house. There was an excitement in the air and a sense of importance between people as they whispered about the affair. Before the idea of a meeting was suggested, most people knew something about the affair, but kept quiet, not sure what to say or to do. Once the idea was open-ly discussed it took on a life of its own. It became a fact rather than an individual fiction.

Mr. Jones spoke to many of the local farmers. Some said they would go to the meeting, some said they would like to hear what happened at the meeting and one or two said they would rather have nothing at all to do with it, sensing some hidden danger of what a crowd with a mission might do. Mr. Cowper at Borren House was one of those who shook his head and said it was a bad business and he would not be able to go to the meeting. He promised Mr. Jones that he would not say anything to anyone about the meeting and would not tell Mrs. Law, even though his wife often saw her. It was a difficult decision for Mr. Cowper because some of his fields were rented from Mrs. Alston-Dewbanke but he decided he would have to risk her displeasure.

The meeting was for the men of the parish and many of the railway workers and some of the dozen or so coal miners from Borrowdale pit, who hardly knew the vicar or the school teacher, were planning to go along. The women knew about the meeting but it was understood this was no place for a woman. The only woman present would be Mrs. Alston-Dewbanke. Annie, the maid, had promised her friend Maggie Towers, that she would try to listen at the door to hear what was said. Maggie had even asked Mr. Henderson if she might take the next afternoon off. She had said she needed to go home to help her mother but planned instead to meet Annie to hear what was happening. She would then call in to see Jane Johnstone at the Slip Inn so that they could talk about what had been said.

Long shadows walked before the men as the evening sun glanced towards the horizon. Groups of men, mostly in their working clothes could be seen walking across fields towards Borrenthwaite where Mrs. Alston-Dewbanke and Mr. Jones were already waiting. The largest room had been cleared and as many seats brought in as could be found. There was a table at the front with two chairs for Mrs. Alston-Dewbanke and Mr. Jones and they were busy discussing how to handle the meeting.

There were some fifty or sixty men squeezed into the room with its ornate wallpaper and fancy plaster work ceiling, when Edward Jones stood up and cleared his throat. "Now, gentlemen,

191

first can I thank you all for coming. I had never expected such a good turn out which only goes to show how strongly we all feel about this affair. You all know to what I refer and this meeting has been called at Borrenthwaite Hall by kind permission of Mrs. Alston-Dewbanke to decide what should be done. Some of you may not know all the facts of what has been going on, some will be only too well aware. For the last few weeks we have been keeping a special eye on the vicar and the school teacher, so that we have evidence of their wrong doing. Before we go any further does any body have anything to report?"

Harold Boldron stood up, scraping his chair back, as he did so and said: "Well I've seen them many a time. You see my hen house is just near the church and I'm often down there, special- ly on a Sunday. Now I'm a God fearing man and I've always gone to church but not since Revd. Law came. I've seen him meet Mary Dennison at the church when there's no service. They've gone into the church and stayed there on their own for two hours and nobody else went in.

"I've known Mary Dennison since she was born. Her father's an upright, a good man, but he was never the same after Mary's mother died. Mary's been led astray by this vicar. I've seen him walking up in the woods, trying not to be seen. I was getting pea sticks for my garden and the dog growled. Then I saw the vicar coming down the pasture and soon after Miss Dennison. When they met they held hands and then he bent down to her. I could- n't see what he did but it looked like he kissed her. Then they went off into the woods and I didn't see them again.

"Another thing is, when she was still living at the Station House he used to walk her home and they would walk up through my field. The sheep were forever getting out over the stile so I kept putting a stone in and someone kept taking it out. One night I hid behind a wall to watch and it was the vicar. It was about half past nine at night and after they'd got over the stile they carried on walking and he had his arm around her waist. As I say I used to be a church man, but how can you go to church to listen to a man like that, with his wife left at home all on her own?"

"Thank you, Mr. Boldron," said Mr. Jones, "Does anyone else want to say anything?"

Joe stood up and said: "Well you all know that Mary used to be my girl. We had plans to get engaged and everything until the vicar came along and started teaching her. She changed then and that was it. She would have no more to do with me. I've never seen them together much but I know what's going on."

William Hill from the Slip Inn stood up and said: "Joe's right. Mary was his girl. She had been for years. We were all at school together and she did change when this vicar interfered. I remember one Sunday night there was only four or five people went to church and after the service they all came out and went away. About fifteen minutes later the vicar came back from one direction and Mary from another and they went back into church for more than an hour. There was no light in the church the whole time and, when they came out, he set off to walk with her up towards the station."

One of the labourers who worked on the farm at Borrenthwaite Hall, a man called Happy Teasdale who lived at Rampson Cottage, stood up and taking his cap off, held it twisting between his hands, and said: "I've seen them too but I can't say more than that."

More men stood up and someone shouted: "We should lynch him!" Everyone started talking and shouting at once until Mr. Jones stood up and, shouting above the noise, said: "Enough, enough. Nobody can hear. Now look, sit down all of you, sit down. Mrs. Alston-Dewbanke has a few words to say and then I have a suggestion."

The men fell silent as Mrs. Alston-Dewbanke, looking very stately and authoritative, slowly rose from her chair. Before she began speaking she glared carefully at a few of the men in the front rows. "If my husband was alive today, he would know exactly what to do about this disgraceful behaviour on the part of the vicar and the school teacher, people we entrust our children to, people who should know better.

"Now, I've never liked this vicar much and I thought, when we started to build the new chapel it would bring him to his senses and he would think about what he was doing. It doesn't seem to have worked. In fact, from what some of you are saying tonight, it seems to have got worse. Now, what I want to say is that, if there's any trouble I would be prepared to help financially. There could be trouble over all this. There could be fines. Some of you could be taking a very big risk. I'm prepared to help to get this matter settled but you must all remember," and here she stopped to glare even more piercingly at some of the men who shuffled in their seats under the heat of her look.

"You must remember," she said, "that what I've said about money is in strict confidence. That means that whatever happens my name must never be mentioned. If it is then I will deny this meeting ever took place. I have one more thing to say but I will leave it until Mr. Jones has explained his idea."

"Well, my idea is that we catch them red-handed so to speak," said Mr. Jones, "where they cannot deny that they are seeing each other and when we've got the evidence against them. I'll be there and I would like to quote some of the bible to Revd. Law. I would like to stop him in his tracks. Now, the way we'll do it is, if you all agree, the family men, those with wives and children, they can be the look outs and signal men to watch for them coming. The young men with no family yet, such as Joe and William, we just need a small group of them and they'll actually catch him and then the rest of us can come along and we'll read the bible to him. The important thing is we will not hurt them physically. There's to be no violence only the truth of the word of God."

The men looked at each other and cheered. Fred Douthwaite stood up and said: "Well you know that I meet my friend Tommy Nixon every day, and we've seen a few things, like when Mrs. Law ran away from home. Well now, Mary Dennison is lodging with us at the moment, when she's not staying with her father over at Darlington.

"Our Nancy has been keeping an eye on her at home but we've not let on that we know anything about anything. When she's at our house, she goes out every night about nine o'clock to see the vicar. Their favourite walk is up from our house at Skerrygill up through two fields. Now the second field is called Cuddy Wife. Now from that pasture, before you get up to yon barn, there's a stile - a gap in the wall with a hurdle in it. Well atween that gap and that building there's a road turns off to the right, a footpath, and it goes across towards the church through the fields. Well that's the spot to catch him, when he's coming over that stile out of that field and into this one where the barn is."

Mr. Nixon stood up beside his friend: "We'd have to pick a night with no moon so they couldn't see us. The moon's waxing at the moment so that's no good. We'll have to wait till September until there's no moon."

Mr. Jones said: "Are you all agreed that we should go and try to catch the pair of them? If anyone disagrees with this plan they should leave now, if they don't want to get involved. But remember, we are sworn to secrecy about what happened here tonight." He looked around the room and all stared back or nodded their heads and nobody left the room.

"Well then, all you married men will need to act as look outs. We'll draw up a plan and tell you all where your hide out is somewhere along where we think they'll walk from the church to Skerrygill. You all realise we could be in trouble for this. We don't know how the vicar will take it or what will happen so you have to be careful. Not a word to anyone.

"Now I need six or seven strong young men willing to take a risk. They'll be the ones to catch him. Nobody else will lay a finger on him. If any of you young men are willing then can you stay behind after the meeting so we can talk about the details. Now, before you all go, Mrs. Alston-Dewbanke has something else to say."

195

Mrs. Alston-Dewbanke, throwing formality to the wind, her double chin wobbling with enthusiasm, stood up and said: "Before the day we're to have a dance. Everyone here tonight can come along, with your wives and girl friends. We'll hold it on the last day of August and it will be a "Raising the Wind" party and we'll dance and sing like the good old days when my husband was alive. I still remember the party we had when young Gerald flooded the cellar with beer and was using a barrel like a boat. How we laughed....those were the days.

"We'll have the dance in North Stainmore School rooms. I've already spoken to the master and he has agreed the date. The Johnstones will play the fiddle and we'll have Brough dance band too. The ladies should bring refreshments and we'll dance and sing like the good old days. So, gentlemen can you ask everyone who wants to raise the wind, before the storm, to come along. "

The men cheered and, laughing and talking, left the room and set off to walk home. Left behind were a group of young men who were not laughing or smiling - there was John Boustead from Park House, Richard Boustead his cousin from Augill Head, Jim Boldron from Mouthlock, Christopher Fothergill from High Ewbank, William Hill from the Slip Inn, Joseph Stephenson from Bleathgill, Thomas Johnstone from Dowgill Head and James Smith from Light Trees.

23

Raising the Wind - August 1909

In the next two weeks a silence fell over Stainmore. The birds feeding second nestfuls of young were too busy to sing. The sheep and cattle in the fields lay sleeping silently in the shadows of walls through the heat of the summer days. The hay had been gathered into pikes and then carted to barns where its sweet smell hung on the air. Summer was at its height and on the farms the seasonal cycle had reached a quiet time which stretched until the cooler autumn days brought sorting and selling of sheep. People could be seen out walking, meeting and talking, but the innocence of these meetings was betrayed by the glances aside and the too casual gestures. Time and place slowed and were trapped in an unnatural heat and a sticky silence.

Mary Dennison sensed the change. It seemed to her that Fred Douthwaite had an extra twinkle in his eye when he joked with her and that, whenever she left the house, Nancy was standing at a window watching her. Sometimes she would even turn to look back but, in the darkness of the old house it was not possible to see anyone; she felt as if a ghost followed her wherever she went.

Sometimes Mary walked up the road, away from the Vicarage towards Rampson, the next farm along, where the Andersons lived. She liked Arthur and Edith Anderson. There was something about them as if they understood more than other people. Often when Mary walked that way she would see Mrs. Anderson working in the garden in front of her house and they would talk. They would not discuss anything of great importance but Mary felt that she could say anything to Edith. She felt she could even talk to her about the vicar, though he was never mentioned.

Arthur and Edith had three sons, Clifford, Edward and Anthony. Mary got on well with them all. She sensed that they respected the church and education and yet, at the same time, had a much less strict view of how life should be lived. These were all impressions gathered from the gaps between words, not the words themselves, and Mary did not think consciously about their views but she felt at home with them.

North Stainmore's school was founded as a council school and was not linked to the church in the same way as South Stainmore school. It was built some fifty years before for the children of North Stainmore who previously had to walk several miles to get to South Stainmore or have no education. The newer school had a special relationship with the chapel and its spiritual leanings were towards non-conformism.

John and Mary heard nothing about the dance that was planned. The temperature of excitement was rising all over the parish but the secret remained hidden by walls where men watched every evening, whispering plans among the nettles and moving stones to make spy holes. Those who were involved were busy, those who had not gone to the meeting held their silence and watched the watchers.

The Andersons knew what was going on and felt sorry for the vicar and the school teacher. At night in bed Arthur and Edith talked before they went to sleep and wondered if they should warn the pair but realised that retribution would come their way if they did. Their lambs would not fetch as much at auction and, if they needed help with anything it might not be forthcoming. They could not put themselves outside their circumstances but decided to ask Mary Dennison if she would come to lodge with them, where at least they could help if help should be needed.

Mary was happy to move up the road to Rampson, though Fred and Nancy Douthwaite seemed concerned when she said she was moving. Their concern convinced Mary even more and, though she had paid her rent until the end of August, she moved sooner, carrying her bags to the new, bigger and airier room at Rampson. The day after she had told them she was moving, Fred was sitting at his meeting place near the church, impatiently waiting for Tommy Nixon, who seemed to be late and walking slower than usual, so slowly that Fred decided to walk to meet him. "You're in a hurry this morning, Fred, what's up?"

"She's moving to Rampson. Mary Dennison's moving today to live with the Andersons. I don't know if she suspects something or what, but you'll have to get the news out. Can you send one of your lads up to see Mr. Jones?"

"Ay, I should say I could. But it won't make any difference her moving will it?"

"Well it might," said Fred. "She might start taking a different route to meet the vicar. We might have to change our plans. I would think the best thing is to have extra eyes out for the next few nights so we can see where they go and what time. In case there are any changes."

"Yes, ay, you're right Fred. I'll get our Henry to run up to Mr. Jones this morning. You'll be all ready for the dance tomorrow?"

"Oh, ay. Nancy's busy baking and that's one good thing. Having Mary Dennison in the house meant we had to be careful all the time about what we said and did. Now Nancy can get on with making her pies with nobody to bother her. Well, I won't hold you up this morning. We'd best get that message out as soon as we can. See you tomorrow."

"Ay, see you tomorrow," said Tommy as he set off up past the church to have a quick look over his nicely fattening lambs.

Meetings had been held every week, all through August. They were always at Borrenthwaite and Annie the maid hovered somewhere near the door to see who came and to try to hear what was said. The Cowpers did not go to any of the meetings and nor did the Andersons. They kept away sensing danger. They were church folk and long traditions, the deeper meaning of belief seemed to go against the grain of what was happening. It was a moral dilemma and many preferred to wait on the sidelines to see

199

what happened. Some privately thought it was wrong to plot against the vicar, God's representative, while others thought it was the only right thing to do but, while the parish conscience was split, they all had one thing in common - keeping the issue private from the vicar and the school teacher.

Mary felt happier after moving to Rampson. It seemed that whatever shadow hung over her was lifted. Every night she would go out and walk to the Vicarage because she could no longer bear not to see John, even if it was only the briefest of conversations over the garden wall. Most nights he would walk her home, concerned for her safety after the threats made to her.

Ellen had the feeling of a thunderstorm brewing. She felt the days oppressive with heat. Her headache was constant. She felt like a wire being stretched, thinner and thinner, the tension growing. She no longer had the strength to leave her husband. It seemed an impossible thing to be able to find a suitcase and then to put clothes in it.

Whatever she thought of doing was a huge obstacle, insurmountable, impossible. She just stayed in the relative cool of the house, knowing her husband was in love with a girl half his age, knowing that at some point she was to be abandoned on some high tide, but waiting for a miracle, for fate to push her to her destiny or just for death. She did not care which.

John was polite to Ellen. He made sure she ate something each day and he tried to make conversation with her. He could never quite abandon such a helpless creature. Sometimes his passion for Mary seemed like a cruel vision of another life he would not be allowed to lead. At other times the dream seemed real and they would talk and make plans for their future, once she had completed her final exams.

The longer their love affair went on, with only dreams to sustain it, the more unrealistic it began to seem. John was filled with indecision which gradually began to pull back towards the security of all that he knew and all that he was. If he ran away with Mary, what work would he do? Where would they go? What would happen to Ellen? How long would Mary, young as she was, be happy with him? Would he in turn be abandoned?

He prayed to God consciously and subconsciously for the most part of every day to give him a clear answer. He knew the bible's view but felt an all-forgiving God would be kinder. Often he would walk with Rupert down into the gill he had visited on his first day on Stainmore. He would find a rock to sit on near the river and would sit, praying, waiting as if for a sign. He would try and stir his life-long interest in plants and nature into an enthusiasm which would overwhelm him in something aside from his love for Mary. He could not hurt either woman. He cared for them both.

Mary was sensitive to many things beyond what she understood rationally. She knew John's first intense passion had begun to fade just as the leaves on the trees were looking dusty and tired on the mid-summer trees. She felt he was beginning to distance himself from her. Where once she felt she had come first to him above all other things, now she realised there was the hint of an excuse in some of the things he said. Occasionally he said he could not meet her because he had some work to do and doubts would fill Mary's mind.

Mary tried to be strong. She tried not to think of him, but he had become her life line. She had lost all her old associations, even her family were now far away. Joe was no longer a friend and she had heard he was engaged to Jane Johnstone from the Slip Inn. Her friendship with Maggie Towers had evaporated. John had become everything to her - teacher, friend, lover, father. She had trusted everything he had said about them leaving together. This was the ambition that had grown out of her mother's death, and through her own childhood. Her insecurity made her more desperate to see John and, even if he said he would be out, she still walked to the Vicarage so that she might see him.

On the night of the dance, when half of Stainmore was at North Stainmore school, whirling and dancing in the sticky summer heat, with the fiddle music entwined around them holding

201

them fast in its spell, John had walked down to Brough to see Revd. Lyde. The meeting had been arranged some time before to discuss parochial church council business. The date of the dance had been arranged at the same time so that Revd. Law would have less chance of seeing the revellers and becoming suspicious.

Mary knew that John was out, so planned to sit at home with the Andersons reading by the light of a lantern. The light attracted midges and moths into the house, through the open window, and occasionally the flame would flicker as a tiny body was incinerated. Mary felt restless and, once the three boys had gone to bed, Arthur and Edith were strangely quiet and concerned.

At about 10.30pm they made their way to bed and Mary said she would go up too but, once in her room, she could not settle. She lay down on the bed and stared out of the window looking at the stars through the open curtains, wondering what weird life might exist out there millions of miles away. She wondered if another creature at the other side of the universe might be trying to sleep and looking across the emptiness of space back at her.

After a time the house became silent. Mary felt an irresistible urge to be close to John. She felt he was somehow threatened. She crept out of the house and almost ran the half mile or so along the road to the Vicarage. It was very late and she saw no one. When she got to the Vicarage all was silent. She opened the garden gate and silently went into the garden where she sat on the lawn looking at the blank, black, windows of the house and imagining John sleeping within. She realised there was no external danger. Everything was quiet and peaceful, the turmoil was in herself.

She sat on the lawn for what seemed ages. The turmoil subsided and she tried to think clearly about what was happening but her rational mind was overcome by something like a trance. She was loving John through the walls of the vicarage, willing him to wake up and come to her, waiting for him to dream how much she loved him.

Mary sat on the grass loving John as she had never loved him before. A pure love like the light of the stars. She could no longer see any wrong or right, just how much she loved him. She sat for what seemed hours. A breeze had started up and the first grey light of dawn was beginning to lighten the eastern sky. She shivered and the emotion that had kept her warm began to settle and condense as starlets of dew on the grass around her. As the cold crept into her she shivered and felt a darkness of loss. Her clothes were wet with dew and the breeze was raising itself into a wind.

She was unaware of the quiet feet walking across fields as the tired and subdued dancers made their way home from North Stainmore, their pact sealed and the date set for the act of retribution on the vicar and his mistress. She did not hear Joe walking with his arm around Jane Johnstone, bending often to kiss her. Only God heard as two cells fused and genes miraculously mixed to bring Jane and Joe's second child into being.

The couple were talking quietly as they walked, making plans for their wedding day. Jane wanted to be married in church but, after their visit to Revd. Lyde, now knew this would be impossible because of their illegitimate son.

Joe turned to her angrily and asked: "So what good is the church then, if it cannot marry us? If we want to be married in church, we should be married in church, and our love should be blessed. You know Jane how they preach on and on about forgiveness. Well it's all just hot air. Worse, it's lies. The church is for God's people, like the chapel. Who do you know who is so pure they have never sinned? Who is this vicar that he thinks he can judge us?"

24
Riding the Stang - September 1909

The wind was raised and now those involved in the plan felt an intensity of purpose as the hours drew ever closer to the darkest night in the moon's cycle on 13 September.

The men who watched gathered in groups of five every night to watch for the vicar and his mistress. Fred Douthwaite, Tommy Nixon and Harold Boldron were in the same group and would spy from the hen house near the church, lying belly down in the long grass to catch a glimpse of the vicar walking with his arm around the school mistress. The fire was being stoked up piece by piece.

Two nights later they glimpsed the pair again at midnight walking together across a field. On the same night Thomas Parsley from Bleathgill decided to call at Rampson to see the Andersons and to note what time Mary Dennison came home. As she walked through the door he glanced at his pocket watch it was quarter to one in the morning.

The oppressive heat of summer broke on the day Mary decided to go over to Darlington to see her father. She left on the Friday evening train and planned to return on the Sunday when John would meet her from the quarter to nine train and walk her home.

John went to the church in the morning to find no congregation at all so he walked slowly back to the Vicarage. It was a perfect September day but there was a chill in the air out of the direct sunlight. He noticed the trees were full of crows which had begun to flock for the autumn and he thought how unpleasant they were with their beady black eyes, their croaking voices and scruffy black feathers.

He went back to the gloom of the Vicarage where Ellen was

still lying in bed and decided to spend the day in his study until it was time to meet Mary. After a supper of bread and cheese he set out to walk with Rupert over to the little shop at Blue Bell where he collected some groceries, including a small box of chocolates tied with a blue ribbon for Mary. He walked back to the Vicarage unaware of eyes watching from barns, from behind walls and between trees. Once he had left the groceries in the kitchen and checked that Ellen was alright he set out again for the Station to meet Mary from her train.

Mary's train arrived just before John got to the Station and she was walking down the road to meet him, looking tired but smiling to see him. As they walked Mary thought she heard voices and once they stopped to listen but all they could hear in the gathering darkness was an owl and the plaintive cry of a curlew disturbed. She felt nervous and said she was sure the voice she had heard was Jim Boldron.

The sky was clear and, now the sun was almost down, it was getting very cold. John put his arm around Mary's waist and held her closer as they walked under the trees of Pratts Wood. Five pairs of eyes watched from the darkness of the trees as the couple picked their way slowly along the path.

Further down the hill Fred Douthwaite and Tommy Nixon hid in a plantation by a wall near Seats. They heard the couple coming as it was nearing dark. One of the first frosts of the year was beginning to bite in the air. The vicar and the girl were alone so they need not pass on any warning to the men who waited further along the path.

The couple walked slowly, hardly talking but feeling close and eternal as the rocks beneath their feet. The last shafts of sunlight were glancing over the Lake District as night fell softly like a blanket on the earth. They were happy with a deep content of certainty about the rightness of their love and to be close again after Mary's visit to her father.

Above them countless stars began to prick out of the black sky. As the bright planet Mars rose in the east, the green planet of Venus was setting in the west. John and Mary reached the stile above Great Skerrygill on the path back to Mary's lodgings at Rampson. John helped her climb the stile and she was half-way over when from out of the deeper shadows behind a wall eight men, with blackened faces, suddenly appeared and made to grab the couple.

John shouted: "What is the meaning of this? What have I done that you should attack me like this?" None of them answered and Mary screamed as two of the men grabbed her and the others tried to pull John to the ground. A shot was fired into the air and someone was blowing a whistle constantly like a scream of pain.

John was a big man and struggled with the men who had difficulty getting him down as their feet slid on the frosty ground. One of the attackers wore a mask, another was dressed as a policeman and all had their faces blackened by soot so that their angry eyes shone out from circles of white. At last amid the confusion Mary could hear a voice she recognised as a lad called Thomas Parsley shouting in desperation: "If you just keep quiet nothing will happen."

A voice shouted: "Sit on him" and a voice of a man wearing a mask shouted: "Put your boot in his mouth." Mary stared from the wall in petrified horror, recognising the voice as that of young Christopher Fothergill from High Ewbank. John was still struggling violently with the men but with the whistle and the gun shot more people were coming running from all directions and eventually John was on the ground and being bound with ropes. Mary sobbed hysterically as she recognised Joe who now sat on the vicar to hold him down.

The frost began to ache into John's bones, crushed as he was under the weight of the man and with his hands and feet tied. He looked around and could see there were maybe 40 or 50 men and youths. It was too dark to see faces clearly but he recognised some voices, including Fred Douthwaite and Thomas Cowper. He was lying quietly now trying to work out what was happening and what to do.

Edward Jones was talking to a group of the men slightly further away. John thought that they were trying to decide what to do now that the vicar had fought with them instead of coming quietly with them as they had planned. Joe sat on John's chest and occasionally spat on the ground near John's face, while others shouted curses at him and threatened to bash his head in. They jeered and taunted mixing words from the bible with curses. Thomas Cowper watched and felt sorry for the vicar and for the sobbing girl, whatever they had done he felt there should not be this hatred in men's eyes.

The indecision about what to do sat in the air but Joe, feeling the cold earth and the man beneath him lying in the churned up, frozen mud, suddenly felt his mind filled with words. Looking straight at Mary, his eyes level with hers, he started to recite part of the service for the burial of the dead.

Mary wept silently and the men fell quiet, their heads lowered as Joe's words rang out: "Man that is born of a woman hath but a short time to live, and is full of misery. He cometh up, and is cut down, like a flower: he fleeth as it were a shadow, and never continueth in one stay.

"In the midst of life we are in death: of whom may we seek for succour, but of thee. O Lord, who for our sins art justly displeased?" Joe picked up a handful of mud from the ground beside the vicar and dropped it on his head. He stood up and, turning his back on Mary, disappeared into the throng of men.

The crowd stood silent around the fallen man the only sound Mary's frightened sobs. The Methodist Minister then stood forward and said: "Let us sing the hymn, Lead Kindly Light." The men shuffled their feet and then, with the strong, musical, voice of Edward Jones leading they began to sing. The men stood in a circle round the prone figure of the vicar and the girl, standing near his feet.

Lead, kindly Light, amid the encircling gloom, Lead Thou me on;

The night is dark, and I am far from home, Lead Thou me on.
Keep Thou my feet; I do not seek to see
The distant scene; one step enough for me.

I was not ever thus, nor pray'd that Thou shouldst lead me on;
I loved to choose and see my path; but now Lead Thou me on.
I loved the garish day, and, spite of fears,
Pride ruled my will: remember not past years.

So long Thy power hath blest me, sure it still will lead me on,
O'er moor and fen, o'er crag and torrent, till the night is gone;
And with the morn those Angel faces smile,
Which I have loved long since, and lost awhile."

As they sang the words gradually calmed the crowd. At the same time it brought courage to them and the singing grew stronger and louder. The stars above watched impassive, cold and silent, and the vicar tried to recognise the voices and the faces of those around him, looking to catch the eye of one of the men he recognised.   Eventually he could discern old Fred Douthwaite in the darkness, and after a time he came up close to the vicar. John said: "I beg you Fred, cut the ropes, they are cutting into my wrists. For the love of God, cut the ropes Fred and do not let them hurt Mary."

Fred shook his head and said: "I am here, Revd. Law, but I have not laid a hand on you. I cannot cut the ropes or they will punish me too".

"If you cannot cut the ropes then loosen them, quickly," pleaded John.

Arthur Anderson from Rampson was standing listening just behind Fred. He struck a match to light his pipe and John saw his face.

"Arthur, you cannot stand by and watch this happen. You are a good man and you are Mary's guardian. Please, cut these ropes, before anything else happens. I'm afraid what they will do to Mary."

Coming closer Arthur said: "It is really too bad, sir. I will release you, but don't let the others know." He began to search in his pocket for a knife but Joe was watching the two men talk to the vicar and came over and asked: "What are you two doing talking to him? Leave him be."

John looked up and saw the hatred in Joe's eyes and felt fear for the first time. What were these men capable of doing? If they could assault him and bind him like this what else would they do? He tried to see Mary but from where he lay he could only see the dark bodies of the men who seemed to be arguing among themselves with an occasional curse spat in anger and then quieter soothing words. He remembered that he had a knife in his waistcoat pocket and began carefully to twist his cramped arms to try to reach it. After several minutes he managed to get the knife out but William Hill saw a momentary flash and twisted the knife from the vicar's frozen fingers.

Joe had a bottle of carbolic acid used for treating sheep in his pocket. He took it out, removed the cork and poured the oily liquid onto the vicar's head and chest. The strong smell made John retch and cough. He began to feel desperate and then saw some men carrying a gate towards him. They laid the gate on the ground and roughly pulled him onto it and bound his hands and feet to the gate.

The eight men with blackened faces then picked up the gate and lifted it shoulder high and set off to carry the vicar over the fields. The crowd followed and two men dragged Mary behind. The Methodist Minister walked alongside John and said to him: "Mr. Law we are taking you back to your proper place, the Vicarage. That's where you should have been all these nights." He continued to talk to John but his words were drowned out as some of the crowd began to sing "For he's a jolly good fellow." They continued to sing all the way to the Vicarage where Ellen Law lay tangled in a white nightmare of sheets.

By the time they reached the Vicarage it was nearly midnight.

William Allinson from Tufton Lodge, older brother to Thomas who carried the love notes between the vicar and the school mistress, said he would go and get the vicar's wife. He hammered on the door until finally it opened and Mrs. Law stood before him, her shocked face as white as her nightgown. William asked: "Where is your husband? Why is he not here at home with you at this time of night?" She stammered: "He went out after supper, at about half past six. I don't know where he is."

"I think you have a good idea where he is and who he's with. Come out and see who is here, lying on your lawn. Come and see your husband," said William, his voice a little less stern. Shaking with fear Ellen followed William round the corner of the Vicarage where she saw a man tied to a gate and a large crowd. The only other woman there was Mary Dennison who was being held between two men, her head bent to the ground.

The men looked at Mrs. Law and in the silence Edward Jones walked up to the vicar and kneeling over him he began to recite the ten commandments. Suddenly Ellen turned and staggered back into the house, slamming the door and bolting it behind her.

John lay silent tied to the gate. His mind was racing, trying to think and plan, though he was in pain. The ropes were so tight that his hands and feet had become swollen. His head hurt where the fluid had burnt into his skin and a nail on the gate had cut into his leg. He was cold but no longer frightened. The horror had escaped somewhere as the men carried him down to the Vicarage and now that they were turning and leaving John began to feel angry.

The Methodist Minister took a knife and cut one of the cords which held the vicar and now he and Mary were suddenly alone again as the men disappeared quickly into the darkness. "Mary, Mary, are you alright?" called John and she, suddenly looking up, realised everyone had left. She came to help free John from the ropes and with her handkerchief tried to wipe the oily carbolic from his face.

She was crying but there were no longer any tears. When he

was finally free John stood and looked around. He wanted to beat someone but all the men had fled and he could not run, his leg hurt too much and his head was throbbing.

Despite his injuries John said he would walk her home to Rampson. Though Arthur Anderson had been in the crowd, he had not harmed the vicar or Mary, and had been the only one to offer to cut the rope. John said: "You will be safe there Mary and then I will walk to Kirkby Stephen to inform the police of this assault, these hooligans. Those men will pay for what they have done. I cannot believe that they could do this to me, their vicar, or humiliate you, the school mistress..."

Finally John and Mary arrived at Rampson where a lamp was still burning as if they were expected. Before she went into the house John took Mary in his arms. "I will come back tomorrow Mary. Don't go to school tomorrow. We have to sort this out and these men must be charged. Just rest tomorrow and I will come to see you. This nightmare will soon be over and God forgive those men. I am so angry at the ignorance, the stupidity."

"I'm so frightened John. What will happen to us now? I'm scared of everyone and terrified at what could have happened," said Mary tears still in her voice.

"They won't do anything else. Not once the culprits have been brought to justice. Don't worry Mary. Perhaps this is for the best but, look, I must go now my darling. I must report them as soon as possible." John kissed her and held her. He heard the door of the house open but ignored the sound. Arthur Anderson stood, the lantern light behind him and smoke curling up from his pipe, watching them. Finally John looked at him. They stared at each other for a moment, saying nothing, then John turned and walked back up the road.

It was four o'clock in the morning before John finally arrived at Kirkby Stephen police station. He was exhausted and could barely speak. The police sergeant on duty could hardly believe his ears as the vicar recounted what had happened and showed him the cuts on his ankles, his swollen hands, to prove his story.

211

The vicar made his statement, naming all those he had recognised and reporting that he had lost his knife, his purse containing 25s had been stolen, he was injured and his clothes were damaged beyond repair.

25
The Principle of Virtue

The day after the attack on John and Mary dawned bright and sparkling as the sun rose on a new made world. The people of Stainmore carried on their work as if nothing had happened although gossip spread between the isolated farmhouses like a plague consuming all the facts and rumour from one place before moving on to the next.

The local constabulary arrived in force with three officers calling at farms all over the parish to gather information. When the police had finally completed their investigations and gathered evidence, summonses for assault were served on eight men who were considered to be the ring leaders. John Law was now isolated from almost everyone in the community who turned their backs on him. The police kept him informed of the progress of the slow business of gathering evidence and John bought the local newspaper to read about what was going on.

When the summonses were served the local newspaper report described the ring leaders as: "without exception belonging to respectable families, the majority of them being sons of farmers. Some of them are actively connected with religious bodies, either as local preachers, Sunday School teachers or as Christian Endeavour workers. One young man is a prominent footballer in the North Westmorland League."

The newspaper went on to say: "The district is in a state of excitement such as has not been experienced during the present generation." John put the newspaper down and wondered, for the thousandth time, what the outcome of all this would be. It seemed inevitable that he would have to leave the area for good but, in the meantime, he had to carry on with his life as before. If he changed anything he would appear guilty. So he kept visiting Mary at Rampson and occasionally even walked out with

213

her. He continued to live at the Vicarage and continued to hold services in the church, mostly with no congregation. For the same reason he tried to persuade Mary that she must, at all costs, continue to teach at the school. Mary could not face the idea of standing in front of her class. She imagined the children's direct looks, their questions and their sniggers. In the end she had no decision to make as Mrs. Anderson told her the school managers had requested, and been granted, a police guard at the school because she would not be allowed in.

On the morning after the attack, though exhausted, John walked up to see Mary. She was still in bed but he waited in the front room with its smell of polish and long disuse. They spent two hours together as he explained what the police had said and how he planned to find out the names of all those involved and bring charges against them. Mary cried silent tears thinking she could not believe there were so many tears inside a human heart. Her face was flushed and swollen. John kissed her gently and kept saying she must not worry.

He returned the next day to bring her a bottle of curative emulsion he had bought from Dr. Bainbridge in Brough and to let her know that he had written to her father. John returned in the evening to sit with Mary and they sat holding hands and talking quietly in the sitting room for more than two hours while in the kitchen Arthur and Edith Anderson sat together and wondered what they should do.

The next day the vicar was back at Rampson again. This time he had brought a bottle of wine for Mary and this time he went up to her room. Again he stayed for almost two hours and the week continued in the same pattern, with the vicar calling every day to bring Mary a present - a bottle of sherry, some toffees, and to sit with her for the best part of the evening.

Finally Edith Anderson felt she must say something and, as the vicar came down the staircase at half past nine, she was waiting for him in the kitchen. "Revd. Law, please may I have a word with you?"

"Yes, of course, Mrs. Anderson,"

"It's just I do not think it's right for you to visit Mary like this. She was not injured in any way by the assault. She is quite well in herself and I am looking after her. I really don't think it's proper that you should visit her like this in her private room, in my house," said Edith wishing her husband was not out that evening.

"Mrs. Anderson, you must understand. My visits are quite innocent. I've taught Mary for several years now. She is my student and I promised her father when he moved to Darlington that I would take care of her. Some of these young men have threatened her and after what has happened she is very nervous."

"But, you must also see Revd. Law, what people are saying and they will know that you are here bringing her presents and staying for hours at a time. People will think that I am condoning your behaviour and, it's difficult you know in a close community like this. We can't be seen to take sides."

"Yes, Mrs. Anderson, I do see your problem but it is scandalous that people should insinuate that their vicar, a married man, could behave in anything less than a proper manner, especially with a young lady." With that the vicar picked up his hat and left, feeling his anger rising and wanting to avoid letting it escape in the presence of this farmer's wife who would no doubt misunderstand the cause of his anger.

Revd. Law's church services were suddenly better attended than they had been for several years with many curious people or press men finding their way to the remote fellside church so they could see for themselves the vicar who was quickly becoming notorious, not just locally but all over the country. The church had fallen into disrepair since the first enthusiasm of Revd. Law's ministry and now the vicar kept the door locked because souvenir hunters had started to remove items, even pieces of furniture, from the building.

The day before the trial of the eight accused the congregation at Matins numbered twelve - nine of them were journalists.

Revd. Law walked down as usual from the Vicarage but today he was accompanied by three young men, friends from Manchester. He unlocked the church door and prepared for the service. Five minutes later the curious press men heard the door open again and in walked Miss Dennison, looking pale and pretty, in a grey suit with matching hat decorated with pink rosebuds at an angle to compliment her features and her dark brown hair.

As they had done for years, the vicar tolled the bell and Mary Dennison played the church harmonium. There was no choir so the vicar led the singing, heartily accompanied by the men from the press. After the Litany and Holy Communion Mary Dennison left the church and the vicar took a text from St. John on the effects of virtue.

John explained to the patient journalists: "The principle of virtue and its effects are totally distinct. One is the root and the other the leaves and flowers. The Apostle taught that worship must be accompanied by activity in doing good and in a life of innocence. Pure religion manifests itself in this way."

He looked long and hard at his congregation and continued: "Those who do not desire to cultivate a life of innocence will try to persuade themselves that they can make amends for wrong doing by what are generally held to be good deeds. But that, according to St. John, is not possible. Pure religion is to visit the fatherless and widows in their affliction and to keep oneself unspotted from the world.

"What is the root of all evil? Is it not sin, the work of the devil? To continue in sin is to continue in that from which all human misery sprang. The Apostle declared that morality itself was the service and ceremonial of Christian religion. It was not a religion that despised one world in order to get to another. Attention to outward acts of religion ought to make people more sympathetic with those who mourn and ought to make them go out into the world with a larger and more sympathetic heart to spread rich flowers of joy and gladness on the sorrowful path of the world's journey."

The men from the press, including Mr. Braithwaite from Kirkby Stephen, listened solemnly to the vicar's monologue. They scribbled surreptitiously, hiding their note pads behind the backs of the pews. The men tried to look as though they were in church out of devoted loyalty to God rather than human interest in the vicar's morals. Only one, a man with greying hair and a purple coloured nose that looked like the sort of fungus to be seen growing on the side of a tree, smirked occasionally at the vicar's words.

After the service the vicar locked up the church and chatted outside for a time with the press men and submitted good humouredly to the inevitable photographs. Then he left and walked back up the hill to the Vicarage with his three friends.

The pack of press men dispersed in different directions, all looking for additional material to make their story the most colourful. The journalist with the bulbous nose who worked for *The Star* made for the Slip Inn, where the cause of the grotesque nose became plain as he ordered three whiskeys one after the other.

He bought a whiskey for William Hill who sat by the smokey fire and, after a while they started talking. The journalist, delighted to meet one of the accused, worked the conversation around with whiskey, precision and delicacy until he had gained William's trust and a first-hand account to add colour to his story.

As soon as he felt he had enough material the journalist left the Slip Inn. Smoke clouded out of the chimney as he shut the door and William coughed, and began to wonder whether he had told the stranger too much. He was worried about the court case and the other seven accused would be gathering at the Slip Inn later, so they could have a final session of courage from a bottle before the trial.

There had already been meetings at Borrenthwaite Hall with Mrs. Alston-Dewbanke and with the appointed defence counsel, Mr. Irving Mawson. At these meetings what the accused should say in court had been discussed and agreed. It had also been

217

agreed that Mrs. Alston-Dewbanke would pay Mr. Mawson's fees of £50 and that, if the eight men were found guilty, their fines would be paid by public subscription with Mr. Jones organising the collecting of the money. All who attended the meetings were sworn to secrecy.

The court case was to be held in Kirkby Stephen Magistrates Court, a substantial Victorian grey stone building to the rear of the police station and above the cells. Access to the court room was by two steep staircases.

The town had experienced nothing like this before and there was great excitement. People were divided in their sympathies. Old friendships were strained by arguments about the case while festering enmities broke out anew. Feelings in the town immediately prior to the case reached fever pitch and the police feared their could be public disorder so an extra dozen police officers were drafted into the town under the supervision of Supt. Dickinson from Appleby.

The court room was only about thirty feet square, quite sufficient for dealing with the usual petty crimes of the area. There was a press desk to accommodate one, sometimes two, journalists but for this trial more than thirty reporters were expected from London, Leeds, Manchester, Preston, Darlington, Newcastle and many other places.

The chief constable of Cumberland and Westmorland, Charles de Courcy Parry made a special request to police Sgt. Storey to make provision for the journalists with tables and chairs in an L-shape around the room. The chief constable personally checked the arrangements the day before the trial. In appreciation to Sgt. Storey for his help the journalists had a collection among themselves, presenting him with an envelope containing a crisp new £5 note.

The Post Office too made special provision for the journalists. The sleepy office in Victoria Square normally dealt with two or three telegrams a week. Now they had been given notice that they would need to transmit some 30,000 words, chiefly to the evening newspapers, immediately after the court case. In order to cope with this the post master had sent for extra telegram instruments and a staff of twelve experienced operators were travelling to Kirkby Stephen from Carlisle and Preston. The post master had a nerve wracking few hours when he heard that two goods wagons had been derailed at Oxenholme Station and the five telegraphists from Preston would be late.

Finally all the preparations were ready. The arguments about the case stopped. Crowds gathered outside the court house with one mind - to hear what would happen to the eight young men and whether there would be any more details of the affair between the vicar and the school mistress.

26
Eight Young Men - September 1909

The court was due to open at mid-day on Monday 27th September but long before that the streets of Kirkby Stephen were filled with curious people. Some had travelled from neighbouring towns, others had taken the day off work so that they could enjoy the spectacle and catch a glimpse for themselves of the vicar and his mistress. It was Market Day in Kirkby Stephen, so all the farmers had planned to be in town anyway to attend the auction while their wives did a little shopping. Some of the farmers and their wives managed to squeeze into the court, thinking it would provide good entertainment and the auction could wait until later in the day.

People making their way into court jostled through the crowds to the steps leading up to the court room where a police officer checked their identity before they were allowed into court. The first case to be heard that day was of a man from Musgrave charged with being a passive resister. This was followed by the signing of the jury lists and applications from local publicans for occasional licenses to sell alcohol at Brough Hill Fair.

The court room was full of journalists. The accused men were gathered in the police station and the court waiting room was full of people who had been called as possible witnesses. Just after twelve o'clock Revd. Law and Mary Dennison arrived, accompanied by two solicitors.

The crowds outside fell silent as they passed. As soon as they had disappeared inside the court house people began talking among themselves. Miss Dennison was wearing a dark blue tailor-made costume, pinched tight at the waist with a matching blue hat trimmed with red roses. Revd. Law wore his long dark coat, his white dog-collar showing at the neck and carried a black umbrella.

Jane Johnstone and Maggie Towers were standing in the crowd, both wearing their Sunday coats and hats. After the couple had entered the court house Jane said: "Did you see her face? She looks ten years older. She's definitely guilty or she wouldn't look so nervous."

"Yes" Maggie agreed, "but the vicar looked full of himself, didn't he? He wants to make them pay you can see that. He'll paint a very black picture of what happened I can tell you. Mr. Henderson says it's a very bad do you know. They think the worst of everyone on Stainmore because of this you know."

"Well they are toffee nosed people who don't understand anything, aren't they?" said Jane, thinking of Joe and praying that all would go well for him.

Inside the court an expectant silence fell as the court clerk shuffled his papers and then called for the usher to bring in the eight accused. The bench consisted of magistrates who were pillars of the local community, chaired by Captain Grimshaw. The magistrates all wore self-conscious expressions of impartiality, in the face of the media audience and such a high profile case.

The magistrates were Dr. T. H. Gibson, Mr. R. B. Thompson, Mr. W. Hallam, Dr. Walker, Mr. J. A. Atkinson, Dr. Abercrombie, Mr. J. W. Fothergill, Mr. W. Jackson, Mr. J. G. Reynoldson and Colonel Mason. Preceded by a police officer the eight young men filed into court. They were all dressed in suits and each man carried his cloth cap in his hand. The men stood in a line, shuffling their feet, as they listened to the clerk.

He read: "Your honour, I have before you eight men who are all charged with assaulting and beating Revd. John Law and Miss Mary Dennison on the night of 13 September. Could the accused please raise a hand as I read out your names - John Boustead, aged 21 from Park House; Richard Edward Boustead, aged 22 from Augill Head; James Thomas Boldron, aged 24 from Mouthlock; Christopher William Fothergill, aged 21, from High Ewbank; William Hill, aged 24 from the Slip Inn; Joseph P.

221

Stephenson, aged 24 from Bleathgill; Thomas James Johnstone, aged 23 from Dowgill Head and James Smith, aged 21 from Light Trees. All these young men are farmer's sons, save Mr. Stephenson who is a railway employee. These men are represented by Mr. J. Irving Mawson assisted by Mr. J. W. B. Heslop. Mr. Mawson how do they plead?"

Mr. Mawson, dressed in a formidable black suit, with his gold chained pocket watch stretched across his ample front, stood. He looked briefly at the line of young men and smiled before turning to the bench to say: "Not guilty, Sir."

Prosecuting solicitor Mr. C. H. Allan, from Penrith, then stood and said he was representing Miss Mary Dennison. He was a sandy haired man, with spectacles and freckled, nervous hands which trembled as he held his papers. He explained to the bench that it may cause confusion if both Revd. Law and Miss Dennison's cases were held at the same time. The bench agreed to hear the cases separately and Mr. Allan sat down to listen closely to the arguments of Revd. Law's solicitor, Mr. C. E. Robinson, from Kirkby Stephen.

Mr. Robinson rose with a theatrical air and bowed to the bench and to the journalists before opening the prosecution case against the eight men who now sat, fidgeting slightly, on hard wooden chairs. Mr. Robinson began by describing the parish of Stainmore with its wild fells and lonely farmhouses. Between each sentence he gave a slight pause to let his words sink in. He would look at the floor and then raise his head slowly so that his eyes met those of the magistrates. He would lean on the table, one hand on his hip and gesture with his free hand.

Mr. Robinson worked through the events of the night of 13 September, gradually winding himself up towards his climatic conclusion. In his most serious voice he said: "All the circumstances show that the assault was premeditated and carefully prepared and reflect the greatest discredit upon this large community. The future position of the assaulted parties could hardly fail to be seriously affected."

Mr. Robinson said that although Revd. Law only recognised one or two of the men on the night of the attack, he had since managed to identify the others by making enquiries. The men had been interviewed by the police and had admitted the offence took place.

He added: "I submit that it is your duty to administer such punishment to these young men to show that there is no excuse for them going about for the purpose of assaulting innocent people who are walking along public footpaths in a lonely place like this and who have not in any way given any cause for this conduct.

"Sir, it was a perfectly proper and gentlemanly act to escort a young lady home. What happened that night proves how essential it was for the vicar to offer his protection for this young lady. Your honour, if there had been any misconduct by the vicar, and I hasten to add there are no grounds to suggest there was, then any lay person would be perfectly entitled, because he was a clergyman, to bring their suspicions up under the Clergy Discipline Act of 1892.

"Under this Act there is provision that a clergyman alleged to have committed an offence can be prosecuted by his parishioners. If these people had a grievance against their vicar, they did have a remedy and they did not have to take the law into their own hands. This was a violent and cowardly assault.

" Revd. Law stands out as a man of considerable courage and as a gentleman. These are the facts of the case and I submit that they are such facts and the circumstances are such, that it is your imperative to take a very strong view of it and show these men that they must not go about the country at night to do harm to people and property as they have done in this case."

At this point the court adjourned for lunch. Everyone stood and stretched stiff limbs. Revd. Law and Mary Dennison, who had been sitting to one side of the court were escorted out by four police constables who followed them and their solicitors, in case of any trouble, down to the Kings Head Hotel where they had ordered lunch in a private room.

At two o'clock everyone was assembled again and Revd. Law was called to the witness box. As the vicar put his hands on the front of the box the journalists sitting closest to him noticed that the wounds on his hands and wrists where the ropes had bitten in were still to be seen. John gave his evidence in a calm, clear voice.

At one point the discussion moved to exactly where the assault had taken place and Ordnance Survey maps were spread on the solicitors' table. Mr. Robinson and Mr. Mawson each had a map and, after a few minutes confusion, discovered that the fields were numbered differently. Mr. Mawson quipped: "Ah, my map has number five on the field in question. That's because five boy scouts were stationed there."

John told the court in his own words what had happened, confirming the story outlined by his solicitor. But he added: "Some of the men quoted scripture and used the most abusive language. The most sacred names in scripture were associated with foul and abusive epithets."

Mr. Robinson then asked Sgt. Storey to bring various items into court as evidence. The first was a black bottle which was passed along the line of magistrates so that they could smell the strong odour of carbolic. The ropes were also brought into the court. The gate, which the vicar had found the following day about twenty yards from his door, was in the police station if any of the magistrates wanted to inspect it. Sgt. Storey also produced the vicar's pocket knife which he told the court had been handed in at the police station a few days after the attack by one of the defendants, William Hill.

Mr. Mawson then rose and stood, swaying slightly from one foot to another as he began his cross examination of the vicar.

John Law, looking Mr. Mawson squarely in the eye, said: "I did not hear any talk of undue friendliness between myself and Miss Dennison and I do not think I did anything to create any suspicion of undue friendliness."

Rubbing his beard, Mr. Mawson then asked the vicar: "Did you not go to the Anderson's where Miss Dennison lodges with a long knife strapped to your wrist and say that if you met anyone on the road there would be bloodshed."

The vicar replied: "No." Mr. Mawson continued his line of questioning about Revd. Law's relationship with Miss Dennison and, to each question, the vicar shook his head and refused to answer saying that the information requested did not relate to the charges being heard in court that day.

Mr. Mawson said: "These young men took upon themselves a very arduous task. They are all respectable young men, farmers' sons in the main, and they realise fully the gravity of the charges against them. However, they also realised the gravity of the improper conduct of a clergyman. This immoral behaviour had been talked of for months beforehand in the district and was widely known."

At this point the chairman of the magistrates, Captain Grimshaw, interrupted Mr. Mawson and said that peoples' opinions outside the case being tried that day were not relevant.

Mr. Mawson nodded and then continued, looking hard at the vicar, who had so far refused to show any hint of weakness in his composure. Mr. Mawson asked: "Revd. Law, on the night of the attack you visited the police station and then you walked back to Stainmore where the first thing you did was not call on your wife, but visit Miss Dennison. You arrived at her lodgings at Rampson at around 8.30am and stayed with her for two hours in a private room. Am I correct?"

Revd. Law said: "It was an hour."

Mr. Robinson rose quickly, scraping back his chair, and said: "Your honour, I object to this line of questioning. These matters are immaterial to the charges of assault against these men.

225

Mr. Mawson argued: "On the contrary, your honour, this is precisely what this case is about. I trust that you will allow me to continue this line of questioning."

Captain Grimshaw consulted in whispers with his colleagues and then said: "Mr. Mawson it looks as if you are fishing for material for an ulterior object. However if you keep your questions to matters relating to before the assault then we will allow them."

Mr. Mawson then asked the vicar: "Did you meet Miss Dennison, by appointment, on the Wednesday before the attack so that you could see her home?" John said: "Yes, I did."

Like a ferret after a rabbit Mr. Mawson then went down what at first appeared to be an empty tunnel of questions. He twisted and turned through a labyrinth of words, at once both quick and cautious and, twenty minutes later he had laid his trap to prove that what Revd. Law had said about what he was doing before the attack was not true and that, in fact he had been in Pratts Wood with Miss Dennison.

Around each corner Mr. Robinson was waiting to jump on Mr. Mawson. He harried him at each turn until the chairman felt the arguments were going in circles. As it was now around tea time the magistrates retired, to drink tea and eat biscuits, and to decide how wide they would allow Mr. Mawson's questions to go. Mr. Mawson was calmly satisfied that he had already been allowed to do a good deal of damage to the prosecution case and was content to be told that from that point on he could only ask questions about events on 13 September.

At this point Mr. Mawson called on his first witness. Old Fred Douthwaite, wearing a new pair of clogs and a suit which was two sizes too large, stood in the witness box and, after swearing to tell the truth, set about telling the magistrates the whole story, as if he was sitting on the gate stoup with Tommy Nixon. He was quickly brought back to the point by Mr. Robinson. Fred told the court that he had seen Miss Dennison and Revd. Law at around 9.45pm on the night in question, coming down the road towards his home at Great Skerrygill.

Thomas Parsley was then sworn in and told the magistrates he had seen Revd. Law walking with his arm around Miss Dennison at about half past nine on the same night. They were walking towards the stile where the attack took place. He was followed in the witness box by Tommy Nixon who said he was with Thomas Parsley in Pratts Wood and had seen the vicar walking close beside the school teacher.

Mr. Mawson felt no more witnesses were required. He had achieved his object and thrown sufficient ammunition into the hands of the press to show that the eight young men had every justification to act as they did. He concluded: "Your honour, the defendants' desire was to put an end to what had become intolerable in the parish and they came into court knowing that thrice armed was he that had his quarrel just."

Both sides of the case had now been heard and the court adjourned while the magistrates considered their verdict. Those left in the court room relaxed and began to talk quietly among themselves. John noticed that Mary looked agitated and was on the verge of tears as she talked to her solicitor. The strain of listening to all the evidence and the insinuations which had been so clear were taking their toll on her. John went over to sit beside her.

With a handkerchief screwed up in her hand she looked at him and said: "John I can't go through with this. I can't stand in the box and be strong like you. I will break down, I know I will, after listening to that awful man and the things he was suggesting."

John said: "Mary you must be brave. You must take this forward or it will look as if we have something to hide. Mary, please. What do you think Mr. Allan?"

Mr. Allan pushed his spectacles further up his thin nose and said: "I do think it will be hard for Miss Dennison. Everyone has heard the evidence and we can see the defence are trying to colour the magistrates' judgement. I think the best thing would

227

be for Miss Dennison to take civil proceedings against each defendant. That way she would not have to face this public humiliation."

Just then the door opened and the clerk said: "The court will rise." Everyone stood and John made his way back to his seat. The chairman remained standing to read the verdict. He named each of the men and said that each would be fined £5, including costs with half a guinea out of every man's fine to be paid as a prosecutor's fee to Mr. Robinson. The alternative, if they did not pay their fines, was one month's imprisonment."

Captain Grimshaw made no further comment. The eight guilty men and the vicar showed no emotion but Mary's crying was obvious, her body shaking, her head down. The chairman then asked Mr. Allan to outline his case against the men on behalf of Miss Dennison.

There had been no time for John to impress upon Mary how important it was that she also pressed charges. He prayed that her solicitor could see this too but moments later he heard Mr. Allan saying that his client had decided to withdraw her case against the eight young men because of the insinuations as to her character already heard in court. Instead his client would take civil proceedings against each of the defendants.

Suddenly the case was over. The magistrates withdrew. The journalists hurried out and headed for the Post Office to tele-graph their stories, or the station if they were making their way home. They had the copy they wanted. A police officer stand-ing on the stairs passed the message to the patient crowd outside who cheered as the eight young men came down the stairs, wav-ing their caps and feeling as if a huge weight had been lifted from them. Jane jumped up and down, waving to Joe but he could not see her among the sea of faces.

When the Revd. Law and Miss Dennison came out of the court a few voices were raised to shout and whistle but the police moved in quickly and stopped any disorder. Mary set off to walk up South Road to the North Eastern station, followed by uniformed officers and a few curious civilians. Soon afterwards John set off up the same road, meeting Mary at the station. They caught the 5.23pm train and travelled together, enclosed in their carriage and in their own thoughts, until they arrived at Barras Station.

27

A Teacher Dismissed - October 1909

Following the nightmare vision of her husband tied to a gate on the Vicarage lawn, Ellen was in a state of shock. Her despair sank deeper than ever before. She felt all light had left her life and she had fallen into some deep pit in the earth where she wandered, blind, stumbling over rocks, with no understanding of where she was or where she was going.

When John spoke to her she looked at him as if he were a stranger. She did not understand what he said. Other faces came into focus before her eyes but she knew none of them. The rooms of the Vicarage were the tunnels and caves in the pit of her despair. The only thing she recognised was her dog Rupert who would rest his head on her knee, his brown eyes looking up as if he understood her sorrow.

John had told Ellen about the trial but the words had no meaning for her. After he had left the house, on the day of the court case, she pulled on her best coat, her white gloves, the hat she had worn when she first met John and her best black suede boots. She opened the door and set off across the fields, following the path her husband had so often taken to meet Mary. Blindly she crossed the stile where the attack took place. The muddy soil stuck to her boots, the fine drizzle soaked through her coat. Nobody saw her as she walked, ever upwards towards the wild moors, for everyone was down in Kirkby Stephen at the court case.

Struggling up the railway embankment, catching her dress on thorns she tripped so her knees and gloves were covered in mud. She walked blindly driven by some force she did not understand, and as she walked she felt as though, with every step, the years of indecision, of floating in a mist of confusion, were being left behind. It was as if she had at last discovered a map of the tunnels of despair and there was one, but only one, way out.

A goods train driver whistled a warning as he came thundering down the tracks towards the woman who seemed deaf to the noise of the train. The brakes squealed but the woman was already climbing on her hands and knees up the embankment on the other side of the tracks, up towards the moor.

Seven miles away, down in the valley, argument was piling on argument as the case against the eight men was built into a stone wall of truth. This wall was then pushed over and argument was added to argument to build a new wall of facts against her husband. Ellen's mind raced, she began to sob with the effort of walking. She was now on the moor, the reeds tangling in her skirts, the black peaty soil squelching in her boots, the violent green moss of the boggy land all around her.

Ahead she could see wave after wave of moorland, a desert with no living thing except a few Swaledale sheep. The only sign that humans had ever touched this bleak landscape was a tumble down building, no more than a pile of stones.

Ellen's hair had come loose and blew across her face. Her coat and dress were torn and one boot was lost, sucked off into the boggy ground. She finally collapsed, exhausted, near the pile of stones which had once been the entrance to an old coal mine, part of the workings of the Tanhill seam, abandoned fifty years before. Ellen lay semi-conscious on the cold wet ground. She clutched the mud and stones between her fingers, fighting with the last remnants of her love for John and her ruined life.

Over a nearby crest of moorland a horse and cart came plodding slowly into sight. Old Isaac Wilson whistled a tuneless melody which escaped from among the few teeth left in his mouth. He was day-dreaming about the events of the last few weeks when the horse pricked its ears to a wailing sound, like the whistling of wind through the reeds. "Woah, there Bessy, now what was that?" he asked the horse, which was well used to these one-sided conversations. Man and horse stood, the cart creaking

231

a little, until the inhuman sound came again. Isaac stood up on the cart and scanned the moorland for any sign of man or beast.

He loosened the reins to let the horse graze on the tough wires of grass. "Stay there Bessy," he said, knowing full well she would go nowhere without him and knew the daily route better than he did anyway. Isaac struggled over the tussocky grass and reeds until what he thought he had seen was confirmed. A woman was lying on the ground beside the old pit head. She was so still she could be dead, he thought, and then remembered the wail. He went up to her and carefully rolled her over so he could see her face.

"Mrs. Law! What is t'doing here? What a state thee's in. Hold on, ah's got some brandy somewhere in a flask." He fumbled in the folds of his several coats until he found the flask. The woman's eyes were open but she did not seem as if she could see him. He pulled her upright into a sitting position and propped her against the broken down wall.

"Come on Mrs. Law, now, have a sip of this. It will warm thee through. Come on now," he coaxed and held the flask up to her lips until she took some of the fiery liquid. "Ah, that's better," said the old man, as he took a gulp himself, wiping his mouth on the back of his hand. "Come on now, missus, it's not far to walk to the cart and ah'll give thee a lift home." His arm round the woman's waist, he helped her over the ground. He kept talking to her all the way as he half carried her back to the cart: "Thou's like a bird. A bag of coals weighs more."

On 5th October Ellen Law left Stainmore for good to go home to Ambleside. She left the Vicarage at 11.20am with Rupert following on his lead. John stood at the door to say goodbye to her. She ignored his proffered hand, the look in his eye. He had pleaded with her once, the evening before, not to leave but they both knew it was too late. Ellen had a new determination and dignity. She had packed quietly and her last words to her husband were spoken with icy calm: "I am leaving you because your mother is coming."

Ten minutes after Ellen had left Mary arrived at the Vicarage. Jim Boldron was feeding his uncle's hens and had seen the vicar's wife leave and the school teacher arrive. He decided to wait to see how long the visit would last. By one o'clock Jim's stomach was grumbling and he headed home for lunch. Mary was still in the Vicarage.

Later that day Jim Boldron met the couple walking up towards the station. The vicar had his arm around Mary's waist. Jim kept his eyes on the vicar's face, staring at him as they came closer. For a moment he thought the vicar was going to hit him as he loosened his arm from Mary's waist. Anger shone in the vicar's eyes but then the couple linked arms and walked away. Mary was catching the last train for Barnard Castle and then would travel on to her father's home.

The following day John Law's elderly mother and his sister Eleanor arrived to stay at the Vicarage. Mrs. Elaine Law and her late husband Thomas lived in Richmond, Surrey, when they were first married but had lived in Manchester for many years where Thomas had worked in the book trade. John's sister was married to William Foster and lived at Bolton-le-Moors and would be returning home after a few days.

John's mother loved reading and though concerned at the circumstances of her visit to her son was looking forward to spending her spare time in his library reading all the books she had not already read. Queen Victoria was her role model and in dress, etiquette and manners she was strict, even formidable. She had never thought much of her daughter-in-law and was secretly pleased when a private deed of separation arrived from Ellen's solicitor, in which she declared she could not live with her husband any longer because of the weather on Stainmore.

Mary returned to Stainmore a few days later. The vicar met

233

her from the train and arm in arm they walked down the hill to the ruined house at Calva. Mary said: "My father is so upset about all this. I think it may kill him. He's had letters from people here saying terrible things about us. He gets angry with me and then cries and says how sorry he is.

"The final straw was yesterday I had a letter from the school governors. John they have asked for my resignation or they will take proceedings to dismiss me. My father doesn't know yet. I don't know how to tell him."

"Oh dear," said John "That is harsh of them to take this out on you. But I suspected it might happen. Some of the governors are the same men who served as magistrates at the hearing the other week. They have no sympathy for us. They could never understand."

"But, John, everything I've worked for, everything I've dreamed of.... all of it is breaking piece by piece before my eyes. My reputation is in tatters and that is everything for a woman, education or no education. Don't you see John? You will walk away from this. I am forever tied to it. I could try to take legal action against them if they dismiss me but then they will go over everything again, like they did in court. It could be even worse. I can see no way out."

They had reached Calva by this time and went into the darkness where the hay was stored in what had been a kitchen. He took her in his arms and began to kiss her slowly beside the old range full of pieces of stone and dust which had fallen down the chimney. Above them was a hook where an oil lamp had hung, the beam above blackened by many years of smokey light. To one side was the cupboard where generations of people had kept their tea and sugar, stored near the fire to keep dry. It was a ghost of a home but the only place John and Mary had where they could be alone, together. They slipped into the past or the future. They were no longer tied to the present and they felt eternal as they lay side by side, their clothes scattered across the hay.

The present came sharply into focus later as they walked back towards the station. Jim Boldron was standing at the gate, talking to his father. They let the couple through and then strained to hear what they were saying as they stood on the platform waiting for the train. Jim watched as they kissed and then, as the vicar turned, he heard him say: "Good night dear. I will look all the way back and try to find it for you."

John had a lantern and it was easy to follow him back down the path as the train pulled out of the station, puffing huge clouds of white steam and smoke as it strained up the side of the hill. The lantern light bobbed along the path ahead and then Jim watched as John Law went into the old house at Calva and spent ten minutes or more searching for an earring in the hay.

On 18th October 1909 a special sub-committee meeting of the Westmorland Education Committee was called at the Town Hall in Kendal when the council members Mr. Nanson and Mr. Willink met with managers from South Stainmore School. Present on behalf of the school were Mr. R. C. Boustead, Mr. B. Raine, Mr. S. Anderson and Mr. J. P. Boustead.

The six men discussed the situation and the managers reported that they had been planning to take action against Miss Dennison even before the assault. Miss Dennison knew about this and, following the assault she had tendered her resignation. The committee unanimously agreed that the secretary should write to Miss Dennison to accept her resignation on condition that she did not return to school during school hours so as not to upset the children any further. She was also to be instructed to return her key to Herr Ritzema by post and remove any personal belongings outside school hours.

The school managers were not happy about these suggestions and argued that stronger action should be taken against this woman who had so blatantly disregarded her moral duties as a teacher and as an instructor to their children. The managers argued that she could not be trusted and deserved none of the niceties of a polite letter.

In deference to the managers' concerns the committee agreed that if Miss Dennison did return to the school during school hours, the managers should telegraph immediately to the secretary of the Education Committee so that immediate action could be taken. They agreed that an advertisement would be placed to find a replacement for her. The meeting was closed and the minutes signed as a true record of the decisions made.

At this point Mr. Boustead stepped forward and said: "I speak on behalf of myself and the other school managers here today. We as managers hereby resign from our positions because, Mr. Willink and Mr. Nanson, we are disappointed that you have not taken stronger, more appropriate action against Miss Dennison. We will put our resignation to your committee in writing." With that, he picked up his hat and the four men walked out, leaving the council officials puzzling over why the managers had been so angry.

28

The Bishop's Inquiry - January 1910

After her dismissal from South Stainmore School, Mary stayed for longer and longer periods at her father's home. She had moved all her clothes and books away from her lodgings with the Andersons at Rampson who had decided to give up the farm and let Mr. Anderson's sister Isabella and her husband Joseph Bell take over the farm.

In November Joe and Jane were married in the Chapel by Edward Jones. The celebrations lasted all day and their first son, Joe who was now eight-years-old, dressed in sailor's suit, was the shy page boy. At first Joe and Jane lived in the Slip Inn but, just before Christmas, old Mr. Peacock died. Joe and Jane had a home of their own at last and, with another child on the way, their cup of happiness was filled.

Life seemed to have returned to its quiet round and, even at the Vicarage, a kind of uncertain peace had settled until John received a letter from the Bishop, requesting that he attend a meeting at the Bishop's residence at Rosehill, near Carlisle. The meeting did not go well. Behind the formalities and the affable smiles of the Bishop, John could sense a frosty chill.

The Bishop, sitting at his gilt edged table with a splendid view of the River Eden through the window behind, asked John questions while his secretary noted down the vicar's answers. An hour later John walked back away from the Bishop's splendid mansion knowing the inquisition had hardly begun.

On 2 January 1910 the five day Ecclesiastical inquiry into Revd. Law's conduct began in Kirkby Stephen magistrates court. On the morning of the inquiry John made his way up to the station to catch the early train. It was bitterly cold and the ground was hard as rock, the grass crisp with frost. Looking to the east the sky was banked high with menacingly yellow clouds, heavy with drift after drift of snow.

His was the only case to be heard that day at a special sitting. The charge read by the registrar to John, now standing alone in the dock, was: "There are grounds for this inquiry into the scandal or evil reports concerning the Revd. John George Law as having offended against the law ecclesiastical by having been guilty of conduct unbecoming of a clerk in Holy Orders and tending to evil example and impurity of life."

The inquiry was chaired by Mr. G. A. Rimington, chairman of the Cumberland Quarter Sessions. Members of the commission of inquiry were Canon Shepherd from Appleby, Canon Hall from Wreay, Mr. B. Heywood Thompson from Nunwick Hall and Mr. John Nanson from Appleby.

The arguments now needed a finer edge than that used in the criminal court for the eight young men. Representing the Bishop of Carlisle were Mr. H. E. Mellor, Kirkby Stephen, and Mr. H. D. Crawford, barrister, instructed by Mr. J. Irving Mawson.

The rows of smartly suited men also included barrister Mr. Gordon Hewart from Manchester, instructed by Mr. C. E. Robinson, acting on behalf of Revd. Law and Mr. G. Gatey, solicitor from Ambleside, watched the proceedings on behalf of Ellen Law.

The press desks were laid out as before in an L-shape and twenty journalists attended to report on the case which had by now captured the nation's attention. Before the evidence was heard, Mr. Mellor reported that he would be calling 25 witnesses for the prosecution. Mr. Hewart then asked that the hearing should be in private, with the press excluded, because the evidence might affect a civil case which was being brought by Miss Dennison against the attackers. The chairman and members of the commission discussed this request among themselves for a few minutes before the chairman announced the hearing would be public.

Mr. Mellor opened the case against John Law by explaining

that the fellside people did not know how to deal with a situation such as this in a proper manner. He argued that, even had they known of the proper channels for such a case, they would have not been able to use them without incurring a great deal of expense.

"Instead," said Mr. Mellor: "They did what had been done in Cumberland and Westmorland before - they tied Revd. Law to a gate and no doubt treated him very roughly." Mr. Mellor added that he thought the vicar's conduct had been "perfectly scandalous."

The first witness called by Mr. Mellor was Harold Boldron from Seats. He said that he had previously been a church man but, after seeing the vicar and the school mistress together so often, had stopped going to church. He told how he visited his hen house near the church twice every day and so had been one of the first to realise there was something going on between the vicar and Miss Dennison.

Mr. Hewart then stood to cross examine the witness. His first question aimed to take the man off guard. "Mr. Boldron, how many illegitimate children have you?" Mr. Mellor lodged his objection but Harold Boldron, looked straight at Mr. Hewart and said: "I am not afraid to answer. I have one. He is your next witness."

Jim Boldron then made his way up to the box, touching his father's arm as they passed each other. Jim told the commission how he had kept a notebook of the times and dates he had seen the vicar and his mistress together. He had continued to keep this record, even after the assault and the couple were still meeting.

John had been impassive to this point but looked puzzled when the next witness took the stand. She gave her name as Ruth Hildreth, the landlady of the Winstone Public House. She told the commission she had recognised Revd. Law's picture in the newspaper. She said: "They were in my pub two or three times. I remember one time he ordered 2d of cream and a glass of beer."

Mr. Hewart intervened: "But, Mrs. or is it Miss Hildreth,

Revd. Law is a teetotaller. He is a total abstainer." Mrs. Hildreth looked bewildered but Mr. Mellor stepped in to say: "I have proof that Revd. Law was in Winstone that day. I call my next witness."

John W. Walker, another unknown face to John Law, took the stand and said he was the booking clerk at Winstone Station, which was situated between Barnard Castle and Darlington. Standing with his hand on the bible he said: "I saw this man, Revd. Law with a young lady, at Winstone Station on 11 and 18 August. They booked from Winstone to Barras. I remember them because they weren't an ordinary sort of couple."

Witness statements continued through out the first and second days of the hearing. The amount of evidence became over-whelming and privately Mr. Hewart told his client he thought the case was going very badly indeed. Outside the snow flakes were hurtling through the air, driven by a blizzard from the east. On one side of the building the windows were covered by snow leaving the court room in an eery grey light. Outside on the streets there were no crowds. The only people to brave the weather hurried, heads down against the blast of snow-filled wind. On Stainmore houses, walls, sheep, were slowly buried in deep drifts of dazzling white snow, sculpted by the wind into voluptuous shapes, like sand in a desert.

Anxious glances were cast at the windows from time to time in the courtroom as people wondered how they would get home and how long the blizzard would take to blow itself out. The boiler was heaped with coal but even so, cold draughts blew under the doors and people took to wearing their coats inside the courtroom.

When the time finally came to present the case for the defence, Mr. Hewart began by saying: "The seriousness of this case must not be forgotten. My client's reputation and career are at stake. I want you to consider this case through the eyes of wisdom, untainted by emotion or rumour.

"What we have here is a case which arose solely out of suspicion. We are dealing with a population of some 140 souls and, for some reason, suspicion arose among them about the relationship between the vicar and the school mistress. Once it had arisen the whole of Stainmore became a huge whispering gallery.

"You have heard evidence of how people watched through peep holes, exactly in the frame of mind to see what may never have happened. Revd. Law was quite rightly acting in "loco parentis" to Miss Dennison and she was seeking to better herself by being taught by him. He is, as you can see, a gentleman of education and taste.

"However, once a suspicion had grown in the minds of a small group of more or less ignorant villagers that the relations between the married vicar and the young school mistress were not proper, what followed? The most ordinary incidents and the most ordinary courtesies of life were twisted into something wrong.

"Stainmore men, women and I am sorry to say, children, had implanted in their minds that there was something improper going on so that mere handshaking, the mere fact that the two went together to church - the most ordinary events of daily life between vicar and parishioner, vicar and schoolmistress, vicar and organist, tutor and pupil, friend and friend, became so much material to bolster the suspicion.

"Sirs, I do not for a moment think that the witnesses you have heard were telling lies, but that their minds were so poisoned by odious suspicion, that they actually believed what they saw and what they wanted to see."

At this point John was called into the witness box to be cross-examined by Mr. Mellor, who gave the vicar a cursory smile, as opponents in the boxing ring might, a moment before the fight began. The vicar denied that anything improper ever happened between himself and Miss Dennison. Mr. Mellor asked: "Do you think, Revd. Law, as your lawyer does, that this was a conspiracy?"

John replied: "I think to call it a conspiracy would be taking it

241

too far. It was a suspicion."

"Revd. Law, I would like to ask you to tell us, when were you married?"

"I'm sorry, I can't remember the date," said John

"But you must remember the month and the year?"

John merely looked at the man in front of him who after a few seconds said: "Really Sir, don't play with the court. When were you married?"

John said: "I cannot tell you the year.... My wife was not well. She was in fact extremely erratic because of an illness of the mind. She has left her home and has now filed a private deed of separation on the grounds that she cannot stay on Stainmore during winter."

Mr. Mellor, eyebrows raised, asked: "Was that the only reason?"

The chairman then intervened saying: "Mr. Mellor I do not think the wife's reasons for leaving are material to this case."

Mr. Mellor nodded: "I take your point Mr. Chairman, however I do think it is significant that the vicar and his wife are now separated."

Mr. Mellor now turned his clever eyes back to the vicar and said: "Now, Revd. Law, as to your relationship with this young woman. Did it never occur to you how it might look to your parishioners to be seen escorting a pretty young lady all over your parish?"

"I did not escort her everywhere. Before the assault I would see her home some nights, especially if it were dark, because she was afraid. I did what any gentleman would have done to make sure a lady in his care was safe. Miss Dennison was threatened by one of the farmer's sons one night and I have experienced the same sort of threats. In fact one of the farmers once threatened to shoot me."

Mr. Mellor laughed: "In that case it would be more dangerous for Miss Dennison to be with you than to walk on her own." The journalists laughed and John realised which way the dice had fallen.

The chairman then adjourned the hearing. Only ten minutes passed before the commission returned and the chairman reported: "We have listened carefully to the evidence on both sides of this case. The point of this inquiry is to establish whether there is a prima facie case into which there should be further inquiry. We have unanimously agreed that there is enough prima facie evidence for instituting further proceedings against the Revd. John George Law."

29
The Vicarage Vandalised - May 1910

In the months that followed, as winter loosened its iron grip on the land and warmth returned to the sun, John felt increasingly despondent. He turned his attention more and more to his garden, seeking solace in the feel of the earth between his fingers and watching the flowers and vegetables in his garden grow.

He could not escape from the knowledge that his wife had deserted him and the strain of all that had happened had divided him from Mary. They rarely saw each other and, when they did, the sweetness was tainted by a bitter hint of argument. Mary blamed John saying if he had been more careful then nothing would have happened and she would not have lost her job and her reputation.

John was angry with Mary because she had not stood by him in court on that first occasion when, he felt, if she had loved him, she would have had the courage to pursue the charges against the eight men. If she had done this and then carried on with dignity as if justice had been done, then they could possibly have faced the storm together. He needed her support in these court cases. Her presence symbolised innocence. If she stayed away they both looked guilty, but Mary was not willing to be humiliated in court again. John knew that, once divided from each other, they were weakened, and now it looked as if both their careers would be ruined.

Occasionally he would travel to Darlington to see Mary. They could not be seen walking together, even in a place like Darlington, because both of them were known. It was impossible to see each other any longer except in the presence of other people, Mary's father or John's mother. They no longer felt safe together, wherever they were.

They wrote to each other frequently and John treasured the letters, even then holding out a distant hope that somehow everything would work out. He was working hard on preparing his case which was to be held in the Chancery Court in York in two months time. He had little enough money left after paying solicitors for two court cases, so was gathering together the necessary paperwork in order to save legal costs.

Mary felt abandoned in Darlington. John's visits to her were now so infrequent. The periods in between his visits were dull and desperate. She wrote to him of her heartache, asking him to visit her more often. She then decided that the best course of action would be for them to run away together, as John himself had suggested all that time ago. She wrote to find out about the cost of tickets to Canada or Australia. She even went to the Post Office to get a passport.

The plan was explained in a letter to John and she asked him to reply soon so that she could book the tickets.

John wrote back to her, a short note which read: "My dear Mary, I think you are letting your daydreams run away with you. I cannot possibly leave Stainmore under this cloud. I must stay to fight for our innocence. I cannot run away or it will seem I am a guilty coward. We could not live with that shadow over us. Please can you stop pleading for me to visit you. It only adds to the pressure when I am working so hard on the paperwork for the case I must face in York. I am still hoping that you will be able to have the strength to come with me to York. If you love me, Mary, you must understand. Your dearest friend, John."

Mary was hurt that he should push her away like this and that he did not consider how she felt. She was certain she was the more injured party. She wrote by return to him: "Dear John, You do not know how much your words hurt me. My father is worried sick about the future. I have nightmares about the past. You know that I cannot come to York with you. I think it best that we should not see each other again until all this is finally over. Perhaps it would be best if you did not write to me either

245

if all you can say are words to hurt me. I would be grateful if you could forward my books and things to Darlington. Yours ever, Mary."

When this letter arrived, John paced up and down the kitchen, the letter in his hand, the cold words in the familiar handwriting wrenching his heart. He wanted nothing more than to be with her. Why couldn't she understand that it was impossible because of all the circumstances and everything that hung over him. She was being unreasonable, he decided, and he wrote back:

"Dear Mary, It seems you are equally good at writing words which can stab where they will cause most pain. You know I will always love you, but I do not need to be at your side for you to know that. It is a fact as certain as summer follows winter. But it can only harm us for us to be together now. I cannot be with you until, as you say, all this is over. You must be patient and stay quietly with your father.

"We should not see each other again, I agree. Even our letters could harm things further. So, if you wish, I will not write to you again until we are both free. You can never know how sad I feel that I cannot be with you, the only joy in my life. Perhaps you could come to collect your things, next Tuesday or Wednesday, so that we can meet for one last time before this dreaded hearing in York. Truly yours, John."

Mary was angry and upset. Why did he have to keep going on about the hearing in York? Why should she go with him when she had done nothing wrong? Why wouldn't he listen to her and just escape quickly away to some place where nobody would know their history? Why wouldn't he return her things? Why did he agree so readily to not seeing her or even writing to her? Why did he ask her to return to Stainmore, a place she now dreaded to visit?

These thoughts churned in her mind on the journey across the Pennines. She arrived at Barras Station where the porter gave her an inquisitive look as she set off down the hill towards the Vicarage. It was a perfect spring morning and all around her the

246

birds were singing, the lambs were skipping in the fields and the trees were covered with the perfect green of new-made leaves. Primroses flowered in pale bouquets among fronds of bracken uncurling their perfection. The familiar sights of this place, where she had spent all her years, touched her heart. All around her she saw innocence and, with sorrow and anger, realised this, her home, was lost to her forever.

When Mary arrived at the Vicarage the door was locked. Why would he ask her to come and then lock the door? She walked around to the back of the house but the kitchen door was locked too and all the windows were closed. Tears sprang to her eyes as she went through the wicket gate into the garden, trampling over the vegetables as she went. A broken fence post was propped against the wall and, without thinking, she took it and started swinging it to break the daffodils and tulips along the side of the path. These flowers, cultivated by John, were treacherous blooms. Here he had picked the flowers which young Thomas brought to the school. Here, she thought, innocence died.

Then she took the post and hurled it at the window, smashing one of the large panes. With her bare hands she pushed the broken shards out of the frame and then climbed through, intent on getting her things and then leaving this place never to return. She was shocked to see old Mrs. Law standing in the doorway.

"Oh, I'm sorry. I thought there was no one here," said Mary.

"What have you done? Why didn't you knock at the door?" asked the old lady. "John had to go out to catch the post with an important letter. He will be back soon. He was expecting you but, but, not to come through the window."

"I did apologise. When I got here and found the doors locked I thought he had done this on purpose to spite me."

"You'd better sit down and wait for him while I go and get a brush and shovel to clear up that glass before anyone gets hurt."

When John arrived home, his mother was waiting for him in the hall, to tell him what had happened. She said: "John, you must get rid of that woman, get her out of this house as soon as

247

possible. She broke in here like a thief. She can only harm you further now."

"Mother, you wait in the kitchen. I will see her. Don't worry." said John.

He went into the sitting room, where glass lay over the floor and settee. He said nothing to Mary but went to the window and looked out at his garden, the daffodils and tulips snapped, lying broken in the soil.

"Why, Mary, did you do this? This is idiotic. How could you?"

"Because you weren't here. You didn't bother to meet me at the station and when I got here the doors were locked. I thought you'd locked me out."

"The doors were locked because I had left my mother on her own. I had to go out."

"You're happy to leave me on my own, week after week..."

"This is foolish, you know I am bearing all the pressure on my own, without your support. You don't even have the courage to prove your innocence. You wallow in self-pity..."

"It's not surprising I feel sorry for myself. You, with your wife, your books, your money, your education. You promised me everything. You made me dream of a better life and then you twisted it and it's you, you who have taken everything away from me. I don't even have a dream left. You, who had everything, you've ruined me, utterly ruined me.....Where are my things?"

"Your things? Why do you want your things? Here are your precious books," the vicar tossed a book across the room at her. It fell at her feet. She stared at him, her face shocked with rage and frustration. She picked up a vase and flung it at him, and continued, picking up every item along the mantlepiece and throwing it. She wrenched the mirror from the wall and would have crashed it down on his head but he grabbed a chair and held it up so the mirror smashed into hundreds of fragments on the floor.

John made to grab her, knocking into a table as he lurched forward. She ran from the room, pushing over a china cabinet as she went. John ran after her. She had wrenched the paintings from the walls of the hall and was now in the kitchen, sweeping her arm across the table so everything fell to the floor. His mother was standing near the door, shocked. John pulled his mother out of the room and said: "Go upstairs, quickly. Go into Ellen's room and lock the door."

Mary had picked up a carving knife and was dancing round the room, smiling at him. "You said you loved me. I stupidly believed you. Your words were empty. I see it now. When I needed you, when at last you could have come to me and we could have run away, what do you do? You ignore me. You spurn me. You leave me to carry the shame."

"Mary, you are wrong. This is absolutely ridiculous. Put that knife down, now, Mary, or I will call the police."

"You wouldn't do that now would you? It's you that's wrong, not me. I can see now, all the way along how you just used me. You are a wicked man and I don't care what you say. All I want is my things. I never wanted you. Look at you."

John took a step closer, holding out his hand, "Give me the knife Mary. Don't do something you will regret..."

"Get back. I won't give you the knife, never, just try and take it from me,"

John turned, slamming the door and went quickly out of the house. He hurried up the fields to the station, running until his lungs ached and his legs were weak. Finally he arrived and asked the station master to wire for the police to come to the Vicarage as quickly as possible. Sweating and red in the face he hurried home again, his sides aching, thinking Mary could have killed herself in the time he had been away, thinking she could be waiting for him still with the knife.

When he got back the house was quiet. He pushed open the door, glass crunching under his feet. Everywhere furniture, books, ornaments lay scattered and broken on the floor. She had obviously continued to destroy things after he had gone. He

249

noticed more windows were broken and bookcases in his library had been pushed over, spilling books and papers everywhere. He could hear Mary crying in the sitting room. He decided to leave her and wait for the police in case the sight of him should anger her again. He went quietly out of the kitchen door and to his garden where he sat on a bench, his head in his hands, exhausted.

Sgt. Storey and Constable Tyson arrived in the late afternoon. They found the vicar sitting, staring at the Vicarage, with its broken windows and smashed flower beds. The vicar explained what had happened and that Mary was still inside. He said she had broken the furniture after they had quarrelled. He did not mention the knife. Sgt. Storey told the vicar that he had wired to Mary's parents to ask them to come.

The police officer and the vicar went indoors. Sgt. Storey went to speak with Mary while the vicar went upstairs to make sure his mother was alright. She came down and, in the wreckage of the kitchen, set about making a pot of tea. After a time Sgt. Storey came into the kitchen and said to the vicar: "Revd. Law, she says she refuses to leave. She does not want to go back to her parents in Darlington. She wants to stay here."

John and his mother looked at each other. "I'm afraid she can't stay here. She must go back to her parents where she will be safe. Should I talk to her?" asked John.

"No, Sir, I think not. It's you she's upset about. She's on the verge of hysteria if you ask me. She needs to be kept quiet as far as possible. Can I take her a cup of sweet tea?"

"Yes, of course," said the vicar. There was a knock at the door and John said: "That will be her parents. I'll go and let them in." John went to the door and found the broad figure of Betty Dennison, Mary's step-mother. Hardly looking at the vicar she pushed past him saying: "Where is she? I've come to take her home."

"She's in there. But where's her father," asked the vicar.

"He's had enough of all this. He's an old man and he can't take much more," she said as she went into the sitting room.

John sat in the kitchen with his mother and the police constable, trying to make out what was being said. He could hear the soothing voices of the police sergeant and Betty. At one point he heard Mary's raised voice saying: "No, no. This is my home. I am staying here. If I go I will lose him forever." John could not bear to hear Mary's desperate voice. The constable cleared his throat and looked out of the window.

After more than an hour the sitting room door opened. Sgt. Storey came into the kitchen and said: "She's going to come quietly now. Mrs. Dennison will take her back to Darlington on the train. I suspect you will not want to press charges against her?"

"No, sergeant, thank you," said John.

"Goodbye, Revd. Law, Mrs. Law." said Sgt. Storey as he and Constable Tyson left. John watched as the two police officers and the two women walked away from the Vicarage, Sgt. Storey holding Mary's arm on one side and her step-mother on the other. At one point Mary stopped and seemed to be struggling to turn back. Tears sprang to John's eyes. He was about to go after her when he felt his mother's hand on his arm. He turned to look down at her face, filled with concern and sorrow for him. His mother put her arms around him and held him as he had not been held since he was a small boy.

Tommy Nixon, who had been having a last look around his sheep to check the few ewes still left to lamb, watched as Mary Dennison, her step-mother and the two police officers walked down the road past the church and on past his home at Upmanhowe. He could hear Mary sobbing and occasionally struggling with the officers. He hurried home after them, just in time to see Mary pull herself away from the officers, climb over the stile into his garden and disappear. The police chased after her and after a few minutes they pulled her out from behind some bushes and carried on down the road.

The following morning Tommy set off early to meet Fred, anxious to tell him what had happened. Fred came slowly down the road, his clogs occasionally clinking on a stone. The two men sat, methodically filling their pipes and, once they were lit, Tommy said: "Well, Fred, ah've got some news. Did you hear the bobbies were at t'Vicarage?"

"Nay, ah nivver heard nowt about it," said Fred. He pushed his cap back and looked keenly at his friend, as if he did not believe him.

"Ay, well, the bobbies came from Kirkby to get Miss Dennison. They took her away but she made a gay carry on afore they got her away. She broke all t'windows in t'Vicarage. She wasn't going to leave but they finally got her away at about nine o'clock last night.

"Ah was in the field yonder, when ah saw them coming along. Mrs. Dennison was there and there was two bobbies and they came along by t'church and along past our house. Our Henry was standing watching them from the door and when she got through Upmanhow field he said she pulled away from the bobbies and popped up aback t'wall and clapped hersel aback of a thorn bush. She wasn't wanting to go you see. They were taking her back to Darlington."

The news of the incident at the Vicarage soon spread. Back at her father's home Mary felt so sick she could eat nothing. Her head was spinning. At about eleven o'clock the following morning, there was a knock at the door and she heard Betty talking to someone on the doorstep. A few minutes later a young man came into the room. He introduced himself as Edward Bell and said he was a reporter from the *Darlington and Stockton Times*. He told Mary he wanted to hear her side of the story about why she had wrecked the Vicarage.

"That's not true," said Mary. "I did not wreck the Vicarage. If you will give an accurate story, without twisting what I say, I will talk to you. Do you promise? If you do not, I shall never trust you again."

The young man in his tweed suit, with a hint of a moustache on his top lip, agreed and sat quietly writing as she spoke. There was something about Mary that impressed him. He wasn't quite sure what it was - she was certainly pretty but it was something more, something about her manner.

"Whatever you have been told is not accurate. I wrote to the vicar to tell him he must not write to me or see me ever again. I asked him to forward some books and things which belong to me to Darlington. He wrote back to me, I could show you the letter, to say he would not return my things and asked me to go to the Vicarage on Tuesday or Wednesday and get them for myself.

"I didn't want to go, but I wanted my books back, so I went yesterday. When I got there I knocked on the door and his mother let me in and said I could wait in the sitting room. When he got back he said he would not give me my books. Consequently there was an argument and it was while we were arguing that the windows got broken. I did not cause a disturbance until he refused to give me my things."

Edward looked up, with an encouraging smile, and said: "But I heard that you had broken the windows with a post and damaged the furniture."

"No, that's quite wrong. The vicar could have broken the windows himself. I didn't wreck the furniture but during the quarrel we threw things at each other and by accident more windows could have been broken. You see, it's not just because he would not return my things, it's also he is angry with me because I will not go with him to the Bishop's inquiry. He has turned against me.

"I am sorry now for what happened but I am determined that these lies about me shall not go uncontradicted. They are doing

253

me a great amount of harm. I can't go out of the house without people pointing and laughing at me. I am frightened about what will happen."

"But, Miss Dennison, what about this Bishop's inquiry? What do you think will happen?" asked Edward.

"I really don't know," said Mary, "and, I think perhaps I have told you enough. Thank you for your interest and I trust that you will remember what I said about telling the truth."

"Of course, Miss Dennison, of course it will be your side of the story. Thank you for talking to me." The reporter left and hurried back to his office, knowing he had gathered a front page story for the next edition. In his office he hammered out the story on his typewriter and then, after speaking to the editor, wired it to some of his national contacts. He knew his copy was worth a few shillings to the dailys.

On Saturday, when Revd. Law picked up his copy of *The Observer*, which he bought once a week to keep abreast of national news, he was shocked to read under the heading "Stainmore Outrage Drama" the following gossip column article:

"Live theatre is happening on Stainmore. If they would only announce the performance the enterprise would be rewarded with a bigger audience. What is known as the Stainmore Outrage is a cumulative drama which is always breaking out in a fresh place.

"It commenced with an outrage on the vicar. It continued with a police trial, an ecclesiastical inquiry and a claim for damages in the Assize courts made by the lady in the case. It has taken on a fresh phase this week and is apparently reaching its closing stages for when, as is alleged, they throw the vicarage furniture at each other we may conclude that we are nearing the end.

"Ossa seems to have been heaped on Pelion throughout and it is a matter for regret that the vicarage furniture should have been finally heaped on both. One expects better things of vicarage furniture. This latest outbreak seems to be a bald conclusion to a particularly interesting narrative.

"If I may be allowed to do so I would express the hope that we are within a reasonable distance of seeing the last of the Stainmore Outrage and that peace may shortly come to a neighbourhood which is badly in need of it."

30
A Baby is Born - June 1910

Jane and Joe moved into their new home just after Christmas. There were only four rooms, two up and two down, with an outside toilet across the garden, but it was home and Jane couldn't have been happier. She set to, to clean out the rooms, white wash the walls, scrub the floorboards and lay rag rugs for carpets. She had made the rugs from hessian sacks, which she had stretched and pegged to a wooden frame. A rough design was drawn onto the hessian and then, using an old sheep's horn, she pushed strips of fabric, cut from old clothes, through the hessian until the sack could no longer be seen for the tufts of fabric.

She had made a patchwork quilt for the iron bedstead and curtains, also made from patches, to cover the windows. They didn't have a washstand, only a metal jug and bowl, which was set on the windowsill. The smaller bedroom had been prepared for the baby. For the time being it would have to make do with a drawer for a crib, but Jane had made a pillow and mattress from goose feathers and she had crocheted blankets to keep the infant warm.

They had little money but Jane was happier than she had ever been. She had helped Joe with the garden and the potatoes, onions and greens they had planted were already well grown. Mrs. Pounder had given her some hens and they had built a hen house in the adjacent field and every day there were fresh eggs. As well as that old Mr. Peacock's rhubarb patch was prolific so Jane made rhubarb and ginger jam, puddings and cakes filled with rhubarb jam.

Every morning Joe would leave the house early because he had set traps for rabbits along beside the railway line. Almost every evening he would bring back a rabbit and after skinning and gutting it, Jane would prepare a rabbit stew for next day's dinner. Her hours were filled with activity with each day dedicated to one main task, whether it be the laundry, baking or cleaning. When she felt tired she would sit for a while and continue to knit clothes for the baby or mend Joe's clothes.

Joe and Jane's baby girl was born in early June. Jane went into labour late one evening and by four o'clock the next morning the baby was born. Daylight was already creeping over the Pennines to the east as Joe held the tiny bundle, wrapped in warm blankets, in his arms and fell asleep with the baby cuddled to his chest. He woke in the morning to the baby's hungry cries and he felt a deep contentment with his life and wondered how he could have ever chased after Mary Dennison.

Every evening, after his supper, Joe worked in his garden or went to lend a hand at the new Mouthlock Chapel which was now, a year after the stone-laying ceremony, almost finished. The joiners were busy now, working into the evenings, to get the woodwork completed in time for the opening service at the end of the month.

Edward Jones was proud of his new chapel with its elegantly arched doors and windows, its solid, dark pews. Whenever he was not working on the railway he was at the chapel helping with whatever work was to be done. The building work had been paid for and there were enough funds in the account to buy new bibles and books for the Sunday School.

The last service in the old chapel, with its plain whitewashed walls, wooden benches and a table for an altar was packed with people and Edward Jones took as his sermon the story of the early Primitive Methodists who had been inspired by John Wesley's visits to Westmorland.

He said: "Brother Hilton, a man like any of you, helped build this chapel with his own hands and, when he died he left money in his will to build the schoolroom and the cottages. Brother Hilton lived at Mouthlock and brought Hugh Bourne, a working man and carpenter by trade, who was one of the founders of

257

Primitive Methodism, to Stainmore. Hugh Bourne preached in this very room.

"Hugh Bourne spoke for the poor, the ignorant, the dispossessed. He suffered persecution from the authorities who said he was stirring emotion among the working classes. He was right to speak for the working man. We are building now on the reputation of these pioneers. It was fitting that Mr. Thomas Hilton from Bishop Auckland, a direct descendant of Brother Hilton, should draw the plans for our new chapel and that his daughter, Amy, should have laid one of the foundation stones a year ago."

He paused for a moment to look around the faces of those before him, and continued: "It is fitting that, as surely as our new Chapel has risen from the ground, South Stainmore Church has fallen into ruin and that the hypocrisy of the vicar has been exposed. I will say no more, only that I trust you will all be here to worship next week in the new Chapel when, after the service and speeches, by several august preachers and by Mr. Irving Mawson we will be holding a tea party.

"After the party there will be a second, equally important service, when we will celebrate God's gift of a daughter to Joe and Jane Stephenson. Their baby will be the first child to be blessed in the new Mouthlock Primitive Methodist Chapel. The Chapel and the child are potent symbols of our hopes for a better future for all who live on Stainmore." The service ended with a hymn. From the general mixture of singing voices two were clear - the lusty, hearty voice of the Slip Inn's landlady Mrs. Pounder and the tenor voice of Henry Bird.

John had stopped holding church services. Now Mary had gone there was no one to play the harmonium and no congregation, even the journalists had long since stopped coming. The church itself had become an unwelcoming place. There was something wrong with the heating system so it was always cold. Some slates had blown off in a winter storm and water was penetrating down one wall, leaving an ugly stain. A window had been cracked and never repaired.

On the altar a vase of flowers had wilted and dried. There were mice in the building and the holy bread had been nibbled so only dust remained. They had even nibbled some of the prayer books to make nesting material for their young. The church door was kept locked so nobody saw the slow but steady progress of decay. Undisturbed, the swallows nested in the porch and jackdaws in the bell tower. The building was slowly being reclaimed by nature.

The churchyard which John had once kept neat and tidy was now knee high with long grass and weeds. John had planted young trees in the churchyard but the gate had been left open allowing sheep in to nibble off all the young shoots until the trees had eventually given up the struggle and died. The flagged path up to the door was thick with weeds.

Occasional sight-seers made their way to Stainmore to look at the sad sight of the neglected church and the places associated with the vicar and his mistress. Rarely did anyone get a glimpse of the vicar himself as he spent all his time in his garden replanting and repairing the damage done by Mary, or he was in his study, preparing his arguments for the case to be brought against him by the Bishop of Carlisle.

31

The Hour of Judgement - July 1910

The process of ecclesiastical law had been turning infinitely slowly since the Bishop of Carlisle's commission of inquiry earlier in the year. The Bishop, on having read all the findings, sent a letter to request that the case of Revd. Law should be remitted to a higher authority, the Chancery Court in York.

The letter informing John of the case was so full of antiquated legal terms that he had to read it twice to understand what had been written. The letter said that, as a result of the Bishop of Carlisle's request, judge Sir Lewis Dibdin was to sit to hear the proceedings in the consistory place in York Cathedral at 11am on 16th July 1910. It went on to say: "Sir Lewis Dibdin will hear the promoter's applications for admission of articles against the Revd. J. G. Law and the defendant's objections thereto."

The promoter for the Bishop of Carlisle was Mr. A. N. Bowman, the Diocesan Registrar, assisted by Dr. Barlow. Revd. Law was to defend himself. The "consistory place" in York, John discovered was a small room in the crypt beneath the Minster. The room was completely filled by officials and by press reporters from London and the provincial towns. There was a small public gallery in which sat a few interested clergymen.

John had spent the months since the Bishop's inquiry studying ecclesiastical law and in particular the two Acts of Parliament which were relevant to his case - the Church Discipline Act of 1840 and the Clergy Discipline Act of 1892. He had brought with him voluminous bundles of paper and told Judge Dibdin that he had technical objections to the articles to be admitted against him.

Firstly John said: "Your Lordship, the title of the judge has been wrongly given on the citation. It says I am to appear before the auditor but this paper says I am to appear before the official principal and auditor."

Judge Dibdin, peering over his glasses, his wig very slightly askew, said: "A clerical error. You managed to find your way here. It is simply the same man wrongly described."

His Lordship then turned to Dr. Barlow and asked: "Why, Dr. Barlow, have you submitted the articles on the old Church Discipline Act of 1840 instead of the new Clergy Discipline Act of 1892?"

Blustering Dr. Barlow stood and bowed to the judge and said: "Your Lordship, the Act of 1840 says that in every case of any clerk in holy orders of the united Church of England and Ireland who may be charged with any offence against the laws ecclesiastical, or concerning whom there may exist scandal or evil report as having offended against the said laws, it shall be lawful for the Bishop to issue a commission for inquiry. This is what the Bishop of Carlisle did."

Judge Dibdin, enjoying himself in the dusty, dry, points of the law, said: "But, Dr. Barlow, there is a difference between the mere existence of a scandal and the defendant causing a scandal by his wrong doing."

John watched as the two men, well rehearsed adversaries, tossed the argument like a tennis ball from one to the other. It seemed Judge Dibdin was sympathetic to his case, or at least, had no particular sympathy for Dr. Barlow and the Bishop of Carlisle.

Unsure what the judge was driving at Dr. Barlow said: "The Bishop's commission found in January this year that there was a prima facia case to answer."

Judge Dibdin queried: "What, for having offended against the ecclesiastical law?"

Dr. Barlow, slightly ruffled that things were not going his way: "Your Lordship, I meant a prima facia case of scandal for having offended against the ecclesiastical law."

Judge Dibdin, slowly removed his spectacles: "Show me an Act of Parliament which enables you to issue a citation on that." There was something about the judge that reminded John of a heron. He sat very still, his glasses half-way down his long nose. At times it seemed he had fallen asleep and then suddenly he would stab at something that had been said, proving he was very much awake.

Dr. Barlow put his hands on one of the books in front of him on the table, as if about to start leafing through in the hope of finding the Act he had been questioned about. He then said: "Your Lordship, there is only section three of the Act of 1840 which says you must allege scandal in connection with an offence."

Judge Dibdin said: "Ah, Dr. Barlow, but you must go a little further. You must charge him with having caused scandal by his wrong doing."

The arguments flew backwards and forwards, droning through the air, until it seemed some of the clergy in the public gallery had nodded off and the reporters had stopped trying to write everything down. John listened carefully to the argument and decided it was simply about semantics. He thought how strange it was that, with each appearance in a court, the arguments had become more and more refined, less and less real, yet the final outcome of this battle of words would affect his life for ever.

Dr. Barlow was saying: "Although the words 'immoral act, conduct or habit' mentioned in the Act of 1840 were repealed by the Act of 1892, we are still entitled to treat the alleged offences as triable offences without offering evidence which suggested these words." One of the reporters, ideally chewing his pencil, wondered if the man knew the meaning of what he had said, or even where his argument was going.

But Dr. Barlow now he had got into the meat of his argument and knowing that Judge Dibdin would soon want to call a break for lunch, continued: "The 75th Canon forbids general impropriety in clergymen. For instance, if a married man met a girl and kissed her, that is impropriety of conduct. If he was an unmarried man there would be nothing improper and certainly nothing immoral." At the words "married", "girl" and "kiss" the journalists had woken up and started scribbling.

At this point Revd. Law was asked to continue with his objections to the citation against him. John said: "I do object to the fact that these proceedings have been taken under the Church Discipline Act when it is obvious they should have been taken, if at all, under the more recent Clergy Discipline Act of 1892.

He continued: "Nor do I understand, your Lordship, why sometimes I am referred to as a defendant and sometimes as a respondent."

Judge Dibdin smiled: "It is like official principal or auditor. It will do either way. If I were you I would not take up purely technical things like that. I suggest there may be points of substance you could bring up."

Fishing for which "points of substance" his lordship might be thinking of, John mentioned the Bishop's inquiry in January. His Lordship said: "I am not interested in that."

Continuing to look for a clue as to what his lordship could mean, John said: "These proceedings should have been taken under the 109th canon and not the 75th canon."

Judge Dibdin asked: "Are you suggesting that the offences relate to uncleaness and wickedness of life?"

John replied: "Your Lordship, all I know is that I am charged with an ecclesiastical offence called scandal."

Judge Dibdin corrected him: "Revd. Law, you are charged with causing scandal by your acts. The question is whether they were immoral acts."

Going back to a point where he seemed to be getting somewhere John said: "Your Lordship, my objection to the articles brought before you by Dr. Barlow, is that if the prosecutor can substantiate his articles and there has been some definite offence against morality as defined by the 75th canon, then these proceedings should not have been taken under the old Act of 1840 but the new Act of 1892."

Judge Dibdin nodded: "I perfectly follow that."

John then said: "Your Lordship, I also object to a paragraph which says I kissed Mary Dennison near a house called Calva and that she was my pupil."

Judge Dibdin frowned: "The time to discuss the details of evidence will come at the trial. This is simply a pleading so that you may know what you are charged with."

"I object, Your Lordship, to the articles mentioning the assault conviction, because I was not convicted of assault." said John.

Judge Dibdin agreed: "Yes, that is immaterial. I will strike that out."

"In addition, Your Lordship, I object to the statement that on or about 10 October 1909 the wife of the respondent left the Vicarage and refused any longer to live with the respondent. That, Your Lordship, does not sound to me to have any relation whatever to the charge now made against me."

Judge Dibdin, continued to look inscrutable: "You object then on the grounds of irrelevance?"

"Yes, Your Lordship."

Dr. Barlow had been sitting quietly considering where to lob the next ball of his argument. He now stood and said: "Your Lordship, if you object to the article alleging the 75th canon then you are perfectly entitled to treat this as an offence against the ordination vow. Perhaps, Your Lordship, the article could be amended?"

Having understood enough of the law to grasp that this was not allowed, John quickly rallied: "If Dr. Barlow is suggesting an amendment then that would make the articles go beyond the citation. If such additions are allowed I may as well retire from this case now."

Judge Dibdin, his wig having taken a serious slide down the left side of his face, pushed it back into place and, looking sternly at Dr. Barlow, said: "Revd. Law has a valid point. There would be a variation between the citation and the articles. Is that not rather serious Dr. Barlow?"

Frustrated Dr. Barlow puffed out his chest and put his fingers in his waistcoat pocket, "Your Lordship, Revd. Law has blatantly aggravated the charges since the assault. Anyone in his position should have been extremely careful that his future conduct should be of the highest kind of propriety. However this man continued his meetings with Mary Dennison thereby adding to the scandal."

Judge Dibdin said: "I agree with you on that point Dr. Barlow. However I do not think there is any need to mention Revd. Law's wife leaving him. That should not be in the articles and could be prejudicial. I therefore strike out that paragraph. I also insist that specific dates and times should be given in the articles and not vague ones so that the defendant knows to what he is answering."

Dr. Barlow, looking at the vicar, said: "If my friend asks for further dates I can happily give them."

Judge Dibdin reprimanded: "If you have further dates they should have appeared in the articles. It places the defendant in a very difficult position if you do not give specific details.

"In addition, Dr. Barlow, the paragraph about Miss Dennison breaking the windows is also prejudicial."

Dr. Barlow retorted: "But, Your Lordship, that was part of the scandal!"

Coolly looking over his spectacles Judge Dibdin replied: "But how can the defendant be responsible for the scandal created by the woman? It is the woman's scandal, not his."

"Your Lordship, I beg to differ. Miss Dennison's breaking of the windows was the result of a whole episode relating to the conduct of the defendant."

Judge Dibdin said: "I disagree. How can it be an item to charge against him? It will be struck out. I will now retire to consider my verdict on these pleadings. I will give judgement at five o'clock." With that he scraped his chair back and left the room.

265

John sighed. He was pleasantly relieved at the way things had worked. Judge Dibdin, despite his frosty air, seemed to be on his side. Certainly he didn't like Dr. Barlow who he had made to look ineffective, implying by default that the Bishop of Carlisle was behind the times, still working on ecclesiastical laws written nearly seventy years before. John decided to go out to find something to eat and drink before the hour of judgement.

When the court resumed in the small, now rather stuffy room, Judge Dibdin entered like an actor to the stage. His wig was now reasonably straight but there was a hint of a stain down the front of his robe where some part of his lunch had escaped.

He sat and then said: "The question is whether these articles ought to be admitted so that this case might proceed to trial. In the first place I over-rule Revd. Law's objection to the title of the judge. The title should have said "or" and not "and" but that is immaterial." The judge then launched into a long explanation of the significance of the Acts of 1840 and 1892 and in particular the 75th and the 100th canons. The journalists were obviously soon lost to the intricacies of his explanation, or if not lost, wondered how they could possibly explain them to the lay person in a newspaper article.

Judge Dibdin continued: "Certain sections of the 1840 Act, including the one referring to immoral acts, immoral conduct and immoral habits has been repealed. The 1892 Act now includes the 75th and the 100th canons which date from 1603 and denounce adultery, whoredom, incest, drunkenness, swearing, ribaldry, usury and any uncleanness and wickedness of life. It is clear that clergymen are supposed to be a living example to people under pain of ecclesiastical censure.

"The articles in this case appear to have been framed with the intention of charging the defendant with having brought scandal on the church by his conduct towards Mary Dennison. As a married man it is alleged he consorted with her for hours at a time. The question is, should these charges lawfully have been brought under the 1840 Act? Before 1892 they certainly should have been.

"If Dr. Barlow is saying that the defendant has committed certain blameworthy acts and that a scandal resulted then this would be a breach of the 75th canon. That being so, the proceedings should have been brought under the Clergy Discipline Act of 1892. It is quite clear that immoral conduct is covered by the 1892 Act and causing a scandal by the 1840 Act. I have no jurisdiction to deal with this matter in its present shape.

"I must remind you, gentlemen, that nothing I have said today, ought to prejudice the case. These are only allegations until proven by evidence. Given what I have said, the order I must make is to refuse to admit the articles against Revd. John George Law on the grounds that the proceedings do not lie under the Act of 1840. This is not, however, to say that the promoter cannot take further steps in this case."

Judge Dibdin then turned to Revd. Law and asked: "Do you have any costs to claim, Revd. Law?"

"Yes, Your Lordship, the costs of the Bishop's inquiry were very heavy as I employed solicitors to represent me."

Judge Dibdin looked at him: "But today you appeared in person so you would have no costs except travelling expenses. These will be reimbursed."

As John left York Minster he felt elated that he had won this hearing and that this might be the end of the matter. But, as the days followed he realised that Judge Dibdin had granted him a hollow victory. His objections had been accepted, but not necessarily because they were right, rather that the opposition had put forward a flawed argument.

If Judge Dibdin had allowed the articles to be admitted, flawed as they were, then he would have stood a chance. He could have then appealed to the High Court and then the case would have been thrown out altogether. John realised that Judge Dibdin had actually played the case into the hands of the Bishop of Carlisle. The Bishop had been shown which cards to play and would now bring the trial against him under the correct Act and the hearing would be held in a local court where the odds would be stacked against him.

32

The Bonfire - February 1911

On Stainmore the summer of 1910 slipped quietly by in the pattern of the centuries. The grass grew tall and fragrant with flowers; the lambs grew fat and lazy; the round of farm work continued day by day. Nobody quite knew what the proceedings in York meant, though it seemed that the vicar had somehow won the case. Mr. Irving Mawson privately assured Mrs. Alston-Dewbanke that this was far from the end of the matter.

Maggie Towers told Happy Teasdale when he came in for his tea that Mr. Irving Mawson had called and there was something going on and that, even though the papers said the Bishop's case had been lost in York, they would still be taking the matter further, and they would get rid of the vicar in the end. Happy sat chewing on a piece of bread and jam in the kitchen, as if ruminating on the news. His face was weathered by wind and sun, but above the cap line, was as pink as a small child's face. He had a permanent smile on his face, hence his nickname, and even when old Dr. Alston-Dewbanke died, it was impossible for him to look sorrowful.

"Ay, well, Maggie. It's a funny old business," said Happy, "Ah's glad in a way ah wasn't there that night. But ah'll be glad when he's gone."

When he had finished his tea Happy pulled on his cap, smiled at Maggie, and went out into the yard behind Borrenthwaite Hall. He decided he would have a walk up the pasture to see Tommy Nixon who was busy building a wall for Mrs. Alston-Dewbanke. Happy thought the wall was an amazing thing - it went almost vertically up the side of the fell and was straight as a ruler. He could see Tommy toiling away, leading stone to where he was

269

working with a wooden sled - the hillside was so steep there was no other way to carry the stone.

Glad of an excuse for a rest, Tommy sat down on the springy grass to talk to Happy, who told him what had been said in Borrenthwaite Hall about the vicar. They sat for half an hour considering the view. Down below they could see Happy's wife out in the garden at Rampson Cottage checking to see if her washing was dry. They could see Henry Bird coming along the bumpy lane with his horse and cart on the round of monthly grocery deliveries. A train whistled and steamed, on a level with them across the valley, as it made its way laboriously up to Stainmore Summit.

"That'll be the 4.20 from Kirkby," said Tommy, "Ah'd better get on an' get this last load walled."

"Ay," said Happy, "You're doing a grand job. Ah can't understand how ye've made it so straight."

"String, Happy, string and pegs," said Tommy, putting the rope over his shoulder to haul.

"It must've been a big ball of string, to go all that way up an' down a fellside."

In his heart, John knew he was defeated, but in his head he was determined to continue to fight to prove his innocence to the end, whatever that might be. He spent many hours in his garden or reading in his library. He wrestled with moral philosophy, with theology and with his own deeply held spiritual beliefs. Although he stayed physically within the same small area of his garden or the Vicarage, he felt as though he had embarked upon a journey.

He travelled across the steppes of Russia with Tolstoy, following the massive scale of war and peace and, with Dostoevsky he explored the torments of the mind. He explored the foundations of philosophy in Ancient Greece and Rome. He strode through the logic of John Stuart Mill and along the streets of human nature with Dickens. He shunned spicy melodrama but felt comfortable exploring middle England with George Eliot. The poetry of Blake left him feeling afraid while Wordsworth calmed his soul.

With each page he read, he felt as though his journey of self-discovery opened a new scene. With each step he took he examined his old beliefs in a new light. Some stood the test, others he felt he could disregard. Many of the books he had read as a young man, now touched him in different ways. The eternal truths of Shakespeare held a power like music to move his mind from the mundane to the sublime.

Books staved off a loneliness which ached in his heart. His garden too was a solace and John gradually grew calmer. He felt close to the early Christians, persecuted by the mob, who kept faith through conviction in their beliefs yet, at the same time, he was deeply moved by Hardy's characters who seemed to epitomise the spiritual questions facing modern man.

When the letter finally came to say that he was to appear before an ecclesiastical commission at Appleby Assizes Court on 22 February 1911 to answer charges of "immoral conduct" he accepted this information as he would have accepted that one of his dahlias had not flowered. It was simply a fact and did not stir in him the emotion and turmoil of the previous court cases.

John travelled by train to Appleby and walked down to the fine old court house on The Sands. Though it was early and cold, a small crowd had already gathered on the pink sandstone steps of the building. Towering behind the court, and built into the face of a sandstone cliff was the Westmorland County Gaol, a place which still had the power to strike fear into the heart as the tortures which had been permitted in the name of punishment remained in living memory.

Making his way calmly through the crowd, John nodded to those he knew, and went into the large court room where his solicitor, Mr. Yelverton, was waiting for him. Mr. Yelverton was a young solicitor, with only a few years' experience of court. He felt like David going to meet Goliath without even a sling and some stones.

The court room was again full of reporters, plus a few police officers and about half a dozen members of the public, including Mary Dennison and her father. John was taken aback to see her but had no idea whether she had at last come to support him, whether she planned to give evidence against him or whether she was merely curious. She sat at the other side of the courtroom, looking elegant and fragile at the same time, in a tailored green coat with a hat trimmed with feathers. She did not look at him.

The clerk called: "All stand" as the five assessors of Revd. Law's fate were led to their seats by the splendidly gowned and wigged figure of Chancellor Prescott. The assessors were introduced as Revd. Canon Menington, vicar of Broughton-in-Furness; Revd. A. J. W. Cross, vicar of St. Cuthbert's, Carlisle; Revd. J. G. Leonard, vicar of Dalton-in-Furness; Mr. Charles Walker and Col. Baldwin, also from Dalton-in-Furness.

The prosecution case brought a total of thirty witnesses to testify against Revd. John Law. Mr. Yelverton gamely tried to cross-examine each one and gained small victories such as when signalman Anthony Boldron admitted that he did not think anything immoral had gone on in the church between John Law and Mary Dennison.

The notebook compiled by his nephew Jim Boldron, which listed 35 separate occasions when the couple met, was submitted as evidence in court. Mrs. Anderson from Rampson gave evidence of the couple continuing to meet after the assault and how she had not thought it right that the vicar should spend two hours or more in the school mistress' private room. Each of the eight young men who had been found guilty of assault, now found themselves on the other side of the fence, giving evidence against the man they had attacked, thereby vindicating their actions.

John showed no emotion throughout the two day hearing. He was polite to anyone who spoke to him but, inside his head, he was so far away from this place that it seemed they were talking about someone else. The words no longer touched him. He knew the six men would find him guilty. He was a thorn in the side of the church establishment which had to be plucked out and disposed of. This was a trial conducted by men as fallible as himself. The truth could only be judged by God and John was strong, unbreakable, in the knowledge of God's forgiveness.

Towards the end of the second day of the trial, Chancellor Prescott gave his judgement that John Law was guilty of improper and immoral conduct under ecclesiastical law. It was now a matter of course that the Bishop of Carlisle would deprive him of his living. However Mr. Yelverton lodged an appeal on behalf of Revd. Law so that the final sentence could not be given but would be delayed until an appeal could be heard.

A few people who had not been able to get into the court room were waiting expectantly on the steps. A press photographer mingled and joked with them. They were all cold standing outside on a February day and continually shuffled to try to keep warm. The door of the Assize court opened and a policeman came out, his face inscrutable. Behind him came Joe, with a broad smile on his face: "We won! It's over!" He was quickly followed by the other witnesses in the case, all happy and excited.

Engulfed in the crowd the press photographer was looking for John Law or Mary Dennison. Finally he caught sight of Mary slipping around the side of the crowd with her father. He managed to push his way through the people, lugging his heavy camera to get an awkward, sideways, shot of them as they headed off up towards the station to catch the train home to Darlington.

There was no sign of the vicar.

The excited crowd listened to accounts of what had been said and how the vicar had looked when he was finally found guilty. The mood was jubilant. Joe then said he was going to the Post Office before it closed to send some telegrams ahead so that people at home would know what had happened. He sent telegrams to Stainmore, Brough, Kirkby Stephen and Musgrave. The messages were all the same: "Victory. Coming from Musgrave. Get Ready."

Joe hurried to catch up with the crowd who were by now heading up to the station. They half expected to see the vicar on the station platform but he was not there. They boarded the train, elated in the knowledge that they had finally been proved right in court, the attack on the vicar had been more or less justified and the good names of Stainmore's sons were cleared.

At Musgrave, the Stainmore party left the train to find Brough Brass Band standing on the station, playing a victory march. Laughing and shouting the group climbed into three horse-drawn brakes and made their way to Brough with the brass band playing and a crowd of villagers parading along behind. A hot dinner was waiting at the George Inn for the witnesses and those closely involved with the case. The meal was followed by speeches by Mr. Irving Mawson, Edward Jones and Joe Stephenson, followed by much applause and laughter.

The three carts returned to collect the party and then, proceeded by the brass band they paraded up and down Brough's main street three times to cheers and clapping from the villagers who lined the street. By now it was getting late and people started to head back to Stainmore. Some of the younger members of Brough Brass band, walked with them, the beat of the drum keeping their pace. Hilarity broke out again when the trumpet player said he couldn't play the uphill sections as he hadn't enough wind.

The happy, chaotic, crowd, arrived at the Slip Inn where Mrs. Pounder was ready to serve refreshments on the house. The tables and benches had been pulled back against the walls to allow for the crowd and, with the band having slaked their thirst with beer, music and dancing started, while outside old Isaac Wilson had set up some fireworks and struggled with matches and fuses until finally he got them to light.

It was about ten o'clock at night by now but lanterns were burning outside all the scattered houses of the parish, to show support for the eight young men. The question had been asked many times since leaving Appleby, where was the vicar? The mystery was now solved when three men arrived late to say they had seen the vicar walking on the road between Brough and Stainmore. He had been wearing a grey cap and a light overcoat and had avoided the crowds by walking on past Brough and up to North Stainmore, before crossing the fields and heading for the Vicarage.

The close community of Stainmore, where families and neighbours had always cared for each other, was now united again. Their consciences were cleared and there would be action at last against the vicar. They had been proved right in a court of law. They had every right to celebrate. Tommy Nixon and Fred Douthwaite sat on a bench together, watching the younger ones dance, and talking of all that had happened that day. Normally teetollars both, except perhaps for a little ginger wine at Christmas, they were both self-consciously holding pint glasses of bitter.

The beer worked quickly to inspire ideas of how to keep the happy celebrations going. They both felt there should be something more. Their feelings were shared by all those in the Slip Inn that night. They wanted something more tangible from their triumph. They would have liked to go along to the Vicarage and shout and jeer at the vicar hiding inside but something held them back. The man was down now, there was no need to kick him.

Fred said: "Ah'd have liked a good bonfire or summat, to finish the night off."

Tommy said: "Well, we can soon hev a good bonfire. There's

been a lot of whin in Upmanhow pasture this year and the hay-time man wanted some work so ah got him to scrub them out. They're just lying where they've been scrubbed out but we could soon hev them gathered up."

"Ay," said Fred, the unaccustomed glow of the beer making him talkative, "we could soon do that. An', best of all, the vicar will be able to see yon pasture from his windows so he'll hev a grand view of the bonfire. There's a barrel of tar at Gillses. If we picked that up on t'way past that would help get them sticks burning."

The plan was explained and, finishing their drinks, pulling on their coats and hats, they set off again, across the fields for Upmanhowe. Fred got some of the men to help him with the barrel of tar while others went to gather the whin bushes into four bonfires. Along the way more people came out to join the crowd once they'd heard what was happening.

It was a bitterly cold night but children, wrapped in their blankets, were pulled out of bed and carried on strong shoulders to see the surreal sight of the bonfires blazing in the dark night. Across the field the outline of the church could just be seen, dark against the starry sky. A field further away was the Vicarage, hiding behind tall, leafless trees.

Branches from the whin bushes were dipped in the tar to make torches and the band started up again, this time with traditional dancing songs, passed from father to son, for generations. Jane's brother Thomas had brought his fiddle and he joined in with the band. The young men started to dance, holding the flaring torches as they danced. The men became a wild primeval swirl of figures in the firelight, dancing faster and faster to the fiddle. It was nearly midnight before the music finally stopped and the dancers walked home, blissfully exhausted.

33

An Offence against Morality - May 1911

John did not have to wait long for his final appearance in court. The appeal against the decision of the Appleby Commission held three months earlier was again to be heard in York before Sir Lewis Dibdin, judge of the consistory court of York.

The Bishop of Carlisle, who brought the prosecution against Revd. Law, was represented by the same legal team - barrister Mr. J. D. Crawford instructed by Mr. J. Irving Mawson, solicitor, from Barnard Castle.

This was to be the fifth time John had appeared in a court of law in relation to the affair. On each occasion he had been represented by a different solicitor and once had represented himself. For his second appearance in front of the higher diocesan power of York, John was represented by Mr. Gawan Taylor, barrister, instructed by Messrs. Wilkes and Wilkes, solicitors from Darlington.

John had travelled to York the day before the hearing was to take place. He had spent some time wandering through the city, enjoying the anonymity the busy streets held. It was warm and sunny weather, full of the optimism of spring. The crowds were going about their business and, as he walked he looked at people and felt he recognised them. He could feel their thoughts whispering around him as he walked through the crowds. The joys, the sorrows, ambitions and worries filled the air like a fog wisping through the sunny streets.

The thought of the appeal case filled him with dread while at the same time seeming unreal. He thought the legal process was like a game of chess - it depended where you put the pieces of the argument and on out-manoeuvring the opponent, but there was also an element of luck which was impossible to predict. The odds were stacked against him yet he still held on to a strand of hope that somehow he would be forgiven by the establishment which was to sit in final judgement of his actions.

On the morning of the appeal Mr. Taylor began the proceedings on behalf of John Law with arguments relating to points of law. He said: "Your Lordship, these proceedings relate to the Clergy Discipline Act. The charges against the defendant relate to immoral acts as defined by the Act of 1892. I submit, your honour, that immoral acts in this context are popularly accepted as sexual acts. However, it is common ground that there is no charge against Revd. Law of a sexual nature. The prosecution's charge is simply that as a married man he consorted with an unmarried young woman as her lover."

Judge Dibdin, peering over his spectacles, at Mr. Taylor said: "The charge is of being guilty of improper and immoral conduct towards Mary Dennison."

Mr. Taylor added: "Sir, the only acts he has been charged with are of kissing the girl."

Clearing his throat Judge Dibdin looked again at the young solicitor, as a school teacher might look at a pedantic pupil, and said: "It is quite conceivable that, on the evidence of the two parties being lovers and having had opportunities to commit misconduct, it may have been considered as a fact that they did in fact commit misconduct. To put it more plainly Mr. Taylor, the assumption is that there is no smoke without fire."

Mr. Taylor looked down at his papers and decided it was time to show that he had done his homework: "Your honour, I would argue that the defendant should have been charged not with immoral habits but rather with offences against the law ecclesiastical, being offences against morality."

He went on to quote several legal opinions in support of his argument and said that Lord Halsbury had recently held that morality amongst clergy must be higher than what is called morality amongst ordinary people.

Mr. Taylor went on: "Your Lordship, I would also rest that much of the evidence brought to court in the case against the eight men found guilty of assault, was prejudicial to the fair hearing of the defendant's case. The presiding judge at the Appleby Commission earlier this year failed to tell the jury to disregard this evidence."

Judge Dibdin, examined the top of his fountain pen, and said: "But, Mr. Taylor, this evidence was first brought out in court in cross examination by Mr. Law's own counsel. You are in a very difficult position."

Mr. Taylor, determined to fight on, said: "It was, your Lordship, prejudicial to admit in court that Mrs. Law had left the vicarage."

The Judge said: "There again, that information was introduced, and I think unfortunately, by Mr. Yelverton, Mr. Law's counsel."

Judge Dibdin and Mr. Taylor looked at each other, understanding the intricacies of the rules of the game they were involved in. Mr. Taylor said: "My point is that these items of evidence prejudiced the trial at Appleby. He was judged and found guilty outside the court and a fair decision could not be reached within the court. I do not doubt that the trial of Mr. Law was not a fair trial."

Mr. Crawford, feeling confident that the defence had found themselves backed into a corner, began his argument. Sitting impassive next to him, Mr. Irving Mawson looked immaculate in his black suit, his thick bushy beard trimmed square under his chin. Mr. Crawford said: "Your Lordship, my first point is there was no need to prove that actual sexual misconduct took place. It was sufficient to bring the case if the defendant was guilty of conduct which was dangerous to the reputation or unworthy of the character of a minister of religion.

"It was proved in court that Mr. Law was seen walking out with Miss Dennison at nights, with his arm around her waist. It was proved that he was seen kissing her, coming out of woods
279

and pastures with her, and talking near a garden wall.

"Your Lordship, do you consider there is a shadow of a doubt that the tribunal at Appleby was not entitled to draw the inference that he was guilty of misconduct? I would argue that the acts were not to be taken alone. It was the cumulative effect of these acts of familiarity that should be considered."

After the lunch break Mr. Taylor continued with his appeal, this time bringing to Judge Dibdin's attention questions of fact. He began by saying: "As you know, your Lordship, Mr. Law was Mary Dennison's tutor, a relationship which quite obviously meant they saw each other regularly.

"In this case the prosecution lodged 25 particulars. Of these only eight could be called acts of familiarity. However, your Lordship, five of the witnesses against Mr. Law had previously been found guilty of assault against him. This was an equally sensational and equally disgraceful act for which these men were convicted and the maximum penalty was imposed.

"I would add that many of the witnesses were related to each other and all came from a close-knit community. In addition many of the witnesses do not belong to the Church of England but are Nonconformists. It is plain, your Lordship, that between April and September 1909 there was an organised system of espionage by the local people. The circumstances being as I describe them here today, the evidence brought against the vicar is open to criticism and should have been treated with anxious care.

"It is equally plain that some of the charges referred to are in fact quite innocent. Two of the charges, for instance, refer to the defendant being seen out on the road with his student. This is not an offence against any law."

Judge Dibdin said: "But, Mr. Taylor, this was not a case where the defendant was seeing Mary Dennison home. They were out on the road between eight and nine o'clock at night for the sake of a walk."

Mr. Taylor said: "I would like to query another piece of the prosecution evidence. On one Sunday in April 1909, Mr. Law was accused of going back into church after the service with Miss Dennison and remaining there for over an hour with no light in the building. That Sunday was in fact 11 April and Mr. Law proved that he was with his sister on that night."

Judge Dibdin replied: "Mr. Taylor, this is one of the difficulties of the case. When his sister was in the box the question was not put to her and I cannot go beyond the evidence given."

Undaunted Mr. Taylor said: "Your Lordship, one of the witnesses, Harold Boldron, said that the vicar stooped as if to kiss Mary Dennison. This is manifestly ridiculous. Stooping can be explained in a thousand ways apart from osculatory intention."

Judge Dibdin smiled and the court room filled with laughter.

Mr. Taylor blushed and continued: "Your Lordship, I would like you to bear in mind Mr. Law's blameless life before this incident and grant permission to appeal against this judgement."

At this point the court adjourned. Judge Dibdin bowed slightly to the room, his wig slipping forwards over his forehead. Pushing it back onto his head he left the room. The room filled with quiet talk as people speculated on what had been said. Mr. Taylor spoke quietly to John and both men looked serious. Mr. Crawford and Mr. Mawson, with nothing to lose and the strong possibility of a case to be won, looked relaxed and joked about the young solicitor's use of the word "osculatory."

When Judge Dibdin returned, John felt empty and sick. He listened but did not hear the words as Judge Dibdin, reading from a sheet of paper before him and occasionally looking over his gold rimmed spectacles, said: "Gentlemen, this appeal has been before several tribunals and, as the judge of the consistory court of York, I have now arrived at a final decision. I must dismiss the appeal against the findings of Chancellor Prescott both on questions of law and of fact.

"On the question of law this appeal must fail because the misconduct of the defendant was found guilty of would have always constituted an ecclesiastical offence. As to the evidence brought

281

to trial being prejudicial, this evidence was brought up by Mr. Yelverton, Law's counsel, and both sides were entitled to pursue it.

"I can see no prima facie evidence for trying this prosecution again. The court has had ample and adequate evidence to find the defendant guilty. What I must impress upon you all is that, though some of the details of evidence might not have been proven, unless it was established that there was a conspiracy amongst something like thirty witnesses then this appeal must fail. Criticisms of the details of the evidence do not affect the result. This appeal is dismissed with costs."

John appeared unmoved by Judge Dibdin's words but inside his world was falling apart. This decision meant he was no longer the vicar of Stainmore. It meant he was deprived of his living. It meant he was no longer a clergyman and all he had worked for was ruined. The people of Stainmore had finally won.

34

The Silver Teaspoon

A week after John lost his appeal he received a letter from the Bishop of Carlisle serving notice on him to leave the parish. Seven more days and John walked up to Barras Station to meet the half past five train. On the train was Rev. R. W. Harvey vicar of Long Marton and rural dean of Carlisle who had been appointed caretaker of the church. Rev. Harvey took over the care of South Stainmore Church on 9 June 1911 and would stay until a new vicar was appointed.

John walked through the fields where it seemed his personal history was laid bare. The drama of the afternoon sky provided the backdrop for Calva where he and Mary had spent so many happy hours and for the stile where they had been attacked. John Law and Rev. Harvey crossed the stile and followed the path he and Mary had taken so many times. These were the fields of John's dreams and his nightmares. The soil itself seemed part of what had happened.

John led Rev. Harvey to the Vicarage where the keys to the church were handed over - the final symbol of what had been and what had now gone. Rev. Harvey said he wanted to visit the church immediately so he headed off down the road. He was keen to survey the church property and said he would later check the condition of the Vicarage. He was also anxious to hold a service as soon as possible in the church which had been locked and neglected for nearly two years. Members of the former congregation had been informed of Rev. Harvey's plan to hold a service on the day of his arrival.

When Rev. Harvey arrived he found the path to the door of the plain little church had disappeared under the summer grass and everything was over grown with weeds. A considerable crowd of people had gathered to meet him. The crowd included Dr. and Mrs. Abercrombie from Augill Castle; Mr. Henderson from Oxenthwaite; Mrs. and Miss Alston-Dewbanke from Borrenthwaite Hall; Mr. and Mrs. J. Parker, a party of people from Kirkby Stephen, Mr. Boldron, Mr. Hill and several of the witnesses against John Law.

Some introduced themselves to Rev. Harvey and there were warm handshakes and welcomes before he finally turned to open the doors of the church. The curious crowd watched as he first fixed a statutory notice to the church door, signed by the diocesan registrar Mr. A. N. Bowman. Then Rev. Harvey turned the big black key and the door creaked slowly open.

The congregation followed Rev. Harvey into the gloom of the church where spiders had spun undisturbed for two years. Spider webs hung like lace from the ceiling and on the windowsill were the corpses of bluebottles and remains of tortoiseshell butterflies which had found themselves trapped in the building. Everything was covered with dust and the air was thick with the smell of damp.

The atmosphere of the building contrasted with the spirit of the congregation who were robustly jovial to cover whatever doubts they may have secretly felt. Mr. Abercrombie volunteered to act as organist and, after brushing the dust off the harmonium, and finding some hymn sheet music, he sat down to play. The congregation waited for the music to take them into the service but the little harmonium was so out of repair it proved impossible to get any music out of it. The only sound it would make was a cranking, wheezing noise, so Mr. Abercrombie returned to his seat beside his wife.

Rev. Harvey then took the evening service followed by a sermon from Isaiah "And they shall build up the old wastes." After dealing with the general meaning of the biblical text, the vicar turned to the local significance of his words. He said: "The parish of Stainmore, your parish, has recently been passing through great unhappiness with the abrupt termination of the pastorate. Misfortune is a common experience for us all. Yet there is God's great promise which never fails: 'They shall build. They shall raise up.'

"I have come here today to help everyone in this parish to make a new start and to face this situation bravely. The Bishop has asked me to fill in as caretaker here on Stainmore but hopefully it will not be long before Lord Hothfield will appoint a new priest. I hope you will give him a hearty welcome when he comes to this beautiful place. The next service will be evensong next Sunday evening at 7pm. I hope to see you all here again then." After a final prayer the first service in South Stainmore Church for two years was completed.

The congregation were emotional, moved by Rev. Harvey's words and Mrs. Alston-Dewbanke had to resist a strong impulse to clap when the vicar had finished and the service was over. Rev. Harvey had made his way to the door and, outside among the weeds of the churchyard, people gathered to talk about how they would organise getting the church cleaned out and the broken windows repaired.

None of the crowd of people who attended the church noticed that a young man, a stranger to Stainmore, did not enter the building with them but, as soon as the doors were closed headed off up the hill towards the Vicarage. The man was Edward Bell from the *North Eastern Daily Gazette* who had previously worked for the *Darlington and Stockton Times*. He had interviewed Mary Dennison after the Vicarage had been vandalised and the story of the love affair had haunted him ever since. He could still recall the pain in Mary Dennison's eyes as she told him her story. He had sensed behind the melodrama a tragedy as old as time.

The only other journalist at the church that day was Mr.

Braithwaite from the Kirkby Stephen paper but he had gone into the church to hear the service and the words of Rev. Harvey.

Uncertain what he would find at the Vicarage and what sort of welcome he might get from this man Mary Dennison had so obviously loved, he walked slowly, taking in the scene of the mature trees around the house and the walled garden to the front. He could see two figures walking in the garden - a tall man and an old woman.

Edward went to speak to the man he assumed must be John Law. He introduced himself and explained that he would like to talk. John asked him to walk with him, away from the Vicarage and up a small hill into a field from where they could sit and view the church where Rev. Harvey's service was now well underway. Behind the church the fields and trees rolled in waves, lush and green in the summer warmth. Further down the valley the heat hazed the view but they could see the ruins of Brough Castle standing guard over the head of the Eden Valley.

The vicar talked easily to the young man, as if they were trusted friends. It was as though they were destined to meet at this moment and Edward was moved by the conversation so that he stopped writing notes. He studied the face of the man who stood in front of him, with his church and his parish all around him. It was a timeless moment when events before and after seemed connected as if by a fourth dimension.

Edward later wrote: "I thought it only right to give him a chance of a final word to that world which has ruled against him and against whose verdict he has put up so game a fight. I felt a pity for the ex-vicar and his aged mother, whom I could see walking in the Vicarage grounds close by and determined that in the common fairness of things it was only right that by the courtesy of that press which has so largely reported the trials of the last two years in this extraordinary case, he should have one final word ere he retires from the limelight of publicity.

"I sat down on the hill side as he stood over me, a clean shaved typical country parson. He said the story of one of the witnesses who said he went back on one occasion with Miss Dennison was absolutely false. He told me it was impossible to have a fair trial after the assault because all the people involved in that were bound to do their utmost to get a conviction against him.

"'Then again,' continued Mr. Law 'I considered some of the papers missed a grand opportunity of attacking the ecclesiastical courts by which I have been found guilty. Here was I, a poor chap, with no or very little money. I hadn't £400 a year but they had the best of legal advice and the Bishop presided in his own courts, the trial was conducted by his own officials and he has it practically all his own way.'

"I asked Mr. Law as to his future and he said he didn't know anything. He had made no plans but in leaving Stainmore he had the satisfaction of knowing that the place had benefited by his being there. He told me that one Stainmore man had suggested a petition to the King and if this were done the case would be re-opened by the Home Secretary and under the circumstance of the approaching coronation might result in the restoration of the living to him. The value of the living was augmented by £20 a year, money out of his own pocket.

"Turning back to the incidents of the trial Mr. Law pointed out how impossible it was for the witnesses to swear with any accuracy to his being seen with Miss Dennison but intimated that there was a great revulsion of feeling against him in the parish.

"'I have,' concluded Mr. Law 'sufficient confidence in human nature to think that all will come right but it has been a terrible thing for me.' At this point he was moved to tears and I did not prolong an interview which was becoming very painful.

"So ends this extraordinary case if indeed there be not yet to follow a libel action against one of the papers for announcing after the appeal at York that he had been "unfrocked" a statement not legally correct although the deprivation of the living may as Mr. Law admitted, morally have that effect."

After the interview John walked slowly back to the Vicarage where his mother still walked in the garden. They would stay

287

that night in the Vicarage for the last time. The following morning it had been arranged that his furniture and personal possessions would be taken down to Kirkby Stephen where they were to be auctioned at the Odd Fellow's Hall. John did not attend the auction but many people, still deeply curious about him and what had happened, turned out and the auctioneer had an easy task.

At the sale, sitting on a hard wooden bench beside his mother, was a small boy with bright blue eyes and dark hair. He did not know that he was the first child the notorious vicar had christened when he came to Stainmore. James Davidson, the gamekeeper's son, now eight-years-old, watched the proceedings with interest. He had never been to an auction before and it was certainly better than school.

He tried not to fidget as his mother had said if he put his hand up, or even just a finger, the auctioneer might think he was bidding. Eleanor Davidson did, however, put her neat gloved hand up when a silver teaspoon came up for sale. She paid 6d for the spoon and, as soon as it was bought, she and James struggled out of the main room to pay for the spoon and collect it, wrapped in a piece of brown paper

Eleanor said to her son as they left: "You know James, I am quite unsympathetic to what those men did. They were completely out of order. But the spoon... we will always keep the Law teaspoon."

After the carts had been loaded with the furniture, John had taken his mother up to Barras Station where she was catching the train to Tebay where his sister would meet her and take her back to Manchester. John marvelled at his mother's strength of mind, unbowed by her physical age. Not for one moment had she doubted him or questioned him. Throughout she had never, to his knowledge, broken down or shown that she was troubled.

She had listened patiently to his self-torture, his grief, his anger, his doubts. She had distracted him from his troubles with talk of books or about his garden. Her faith in him was unshakeable.

Once on the train, she stood by the open window and held John's hand, her old eyes filled with tears at last. They rolled quietly down the creases and folds of her face and John felt his throat tighten. He wanted to sob like a child but, though his chest heaved, the release would not come. He just held his mother's hand, knowing this would be the last time they would ever see each other, until finally, somewhere among the steam at the front of the train a whistle blew and their hands were jolted apart. John walked and then ran alongside the train, his face now suddenly wet with tears, until the platform was no more and the train curved away over the Belah Viaduct.

Gathering what was left of himself, now just one man, he walked back past Mary's childhood home, down the paths of innocence they had shared, across the blessed fields and back, once more to the Vicarage. John went into every room for one last time. He stood by each window and looked out as if to remember forever what he saw. Finally he went into the library to collect his bags, all that remained of his life, before and after Stainmore.

Quietly he left the room, closing the door as if he had left Mary to study a text while he went out on some errand. He closed the door of the Vicarage and walked away, not looking back, his head full of disconnected thoughts and feelings, his eyes stinging, his throat choking. He walked though, as a man trained not to show fear or pain in his bearing. From the outside, to the curious eyes which watched from farmhouse windows, he looked strong and full of purpose, unchanged from when he had first walked these paths eight years before.

When he passed men working in the hayfields, they raised their hands, as he raised his in greeting, as if this were any day of his living here. He walked down the hill to the church and school where he stood for a moment looking at the stones which formed the buildings in which so much had happened. To his eyes it seemed these places could never be the same. There would always be the echo of Mary's laughter in the school and of her music and singing in the church. It could not be that these cold stones had not soaked up some of her joy.

John walked on, feeling he was leaving his whole life behind him and the journey he was setting out on was the passage to heaven or hell, but had no relevance whatsoever to human life. Down past Upmanhowe, where the victory bonfires had blazed, past Gillses and Swinstonewath, over the little beck, now just a trickle in the summer heat.

The afternoon was drawing on and the sun was beginning to dip towards the horizon in the summer sky as he walked towards the new Mouthlock Chapel its gable end filled with two windows and a door, like a face watching him as he approached. Each step took him away, slowly further away from this place on the fells. John had decided this was the only way he could leave, measuring each step, forcing his feet to carry him away from what held his heart.

A cart full of coal was slowly making its way down the hill from Barras Station. Old Isaac Wilson was whistling a tune to himself and to his horse, which occasionally laid its ears back to listen. The Slip Inn came into view and instinctively the horse knew it was time to take off the careful downhill brakes and to make a determined pull to the place where its nose bag would be waiting. Isaac could also see the smoke rising lazily from the Slip Inn's chimney and felt his mouth begin to prepare itself for refreshment.

Then he noticed a figure walking along the road towards the

chapel. A tall man, dressed in black, with a long coat and what must be a bag on his back. He walked like a country man but Isaac's old eyes could not focus clearly enough in the hazy summer light to decide exactly who it could be. His interest was sparked and he wondered if it could be the vicar. The man walked as if he was carrying a heavy load.

When he reached the chapel Isaac said: "Wooa, Bessy," and the horse stopped, puzzled to have been pulled to a halt before reaching the Slip Inn. Isaac waited until the man he could now see was the former vicar, came up to the cart.

"Mr. Law," said Isaac, "Where are you off to, with that heavy bag?"

"I'm going, Isaac," replied John.

"Ay," said Isaac, "Ah thowt you would be some day soon."

"Goodbye," said John, as he turned to carry on walking down the road.

"Wait, Mr. Law, are you off down to Brough?" asked Isaac.

"Yes, that's the first road I'll take," said John

"Well, I'll give thee a lift. There's plenty of room up here and Bessy won't mind. Come on, ah'll dust the coal off this seat. Throw that bag in the back."

"That's very kind of you, Isaac. A ride down to Brough will be much appreciated. I have a long way to go."

Postscript:

In 1911 Rev. Thomas Westgarth was appointed by Lord Hothfield as the new vicar of Stainmore. He took over from Rev. Harvey who returned to his parish at Long Marton. Rev. Westgarth started the restoration of the church which was paid for by Mrs. Alston-Dewbanke who had a new stained glass window installed above the altar in memory of her late husband, Dr. Alston-Dewbanke.

The church was fitted with new oak pews and Harold Boldron from Seats volunteered to put up new oak beams across the ceiling. Paraffin lights were installed so that evening services could be held. The total cost of repairs was £300 and the Bishop of Carlisle came personally to re-open the cleansed church in October 1913.

Rev. Westgarth's priesthood on Stainmore lasted for many years. He loved his parish and served it well.

John Law never saw Ellen or Mary again. He emigrated to Australia where he worked as a teacher at All Saints College, in the country town of Bathurst, New South Wales. He died from pneumonia on 15th June 1927 at the age of 60. He was buried in the Church of England cemetery at Bathurst.

Ellen Law is understood to have continued to live in Ambleside but she returned to Stainmore in 1927, the year of her husband's death, to visit Rev. Westgarth and to see the Vicarage, where her marriage had ended in such dramatic circumstances.

What happened to Mary Dennison nobody knows. After returning to Darlington she seems to have disappeared from the records and so far no trace of what happened to her has been discovered.